COTTONMOUTH Club

Lance Marcum

Farrar, Straus and Giroux

New York

Text copyright © 2005 by Lance Marcum
Front matter art copyright © 2005 by Marc Tauss
All rights reserved
Distributed in Canada by Douglas & McIntyre Publishing Group
Printed in the United States of America
Designed by Jay Colvin
First edition, 2005
3 5 7 9 10 8 6 4 2

www.fsgkidsbooks.com

Library of Congress Cataloging-in-Publication Data
Marcum, Lance.
    The cottonmouth club / Lance Marcum.— 1st ed.
        p. cm.
    Summary: Forced to spend his summer vacation with relatives in Louisiana,
twelve-year-old Mitch Valentine finds himself a candidate for the Cottonmouth
Club when he and a group of local boys become involved in secretive outdoor
activities.
    ISBN-13: 978-0-374-31562-7
    ISBN-10: 0-374-31562-0
    [1. Vacations—Fiction. 2. Friendship—Fiction. 3. Outdoor life—Fiction.
4. Courage—Fiction. 5. Family life—Louisiana—Fiction. 6. Louisiana—
Fiction.] I. Title.

PZ7.M3287Co 2005
[Fic]—dc22
                                                                    2004047187

To Brooks Day,
who started it all,
and Chloe Levin,
who refused to take no for an answer

1

Countdown

Einstein was right—time does stand still under certain conditions. Such as approaching the speed of light, or trying to endure the last hour of the last day of school.

The clock high on the wall behind the Barker's desk showed two o'clock, exactly sixty minutes from dismissal. She glanced up at it, tapped our report cards into a neat stack for the umpteenth time that day, then slowly stood and cleared her throat.

The books had been collected and the desks emptied, so we all knew what was coming: it was her last chance to praise the girls and put down the guys.

"Boys and girls," she began, "you know I've done my best to teach you all of the skills you'll need to be successful in seventh grade." Several girls nodded in support, determined to play the role of teacher's pet until the very end.

The Barker paused to remove and polish her thick bifocals, her watery gaze settling in my general direction. "But frankly, I don't think I've gotten through to all of you in that regard."

I sat up a little straighter as my defensive radar went into Yellow Alert.

"Many of us *have* tried our best this year, and for that I'm grateful," she continued, smiling at the girls in front, "but some of us *still* haven't applied ourselves." She looked directly at me. "Have we, Mr. Valentine?"

Please, God, I thought. *Not again, not now.*

I slumped back down into my seat and stared past her at the clock; it still showed two.

"I know some of you are much brighter than your work has shown this year," she persisted, waddling toward the back of the room, "and I want you to know that I'm personally disappointed by your lack of effort." She sniffed. "Quite disappointed."

She stopped right next to me. I tried not to stare at the lumpy outline of the heavyweight girdle under her old-lady floral dress. I couldn't avoid her old-lady smell.

"We call this phenomenon the Underachiever Syndrome." She paused again, this time for dramatic effect. "Don't we, Mr. Valentine?"

I resisted the impulse to smart off and mumbled instead, "I guess so, Mrs. Barker." No point in spending my last hour of elementary school in the principal's office. I really wasn't in the mood to count the holes in his ceiling tiles again.

But like the bulldog she resembled, she just wouldn't let go. "You *guess* so. I see. Guessing is not knowing, is it, Mr. Valentine?"

I couldn't help myself. "I guess not, Mrs. Barker."

A chorus of snickers and giggles broke out behind her. She whirled around with amazing speed for a woman her size and fixed the perpetrators with a textbook glare.

I looked back at the clock.

Why isn't it moving?

A solitary fly droned around my head, somehow shielded from the time-dilation effect surrounding Room 12. I tracked it for a second, then snatched it out of the air; I had great reflexes.

The Barker had great peripheral vision. "Is there something else you'd care to add to this discussion, Mr. Valentine?"

Every head in the room swiveled back in my direction.

My hand was still up, the fly buzzing furiously in my fist. I said the first thing that came to mind. "I think there's something wrong with the clock."

At that precise moment the minute hand moved with a loud *tick*.

"I think not, Mr. Valentine," she said, flashing a smug grin, "and apparently, neither do you."

I didn't need the *oohs* from the peanut gallery to know that this was getting way too personal.

Be cool, don't blow it now. Fifty-nine more minutes and this horror show is over, I'll be rid of the evil Dr. Barkenstein forever. Hang in there, less than an hour until summer vacation.

Summer and *vacation*, my two favorite words, especially when they're used together. And the summer of 1963 was going to be the best ever. I had big plans for this one. Major-league plans.

My thoughts must have taken on a telepathic quality, because the Barker suddenly shifted gears. "And what are our plans for the summer? Would anyone like to share?"

A dozen hands immediately shot up.

Morons, all of them. Like she really cares.

Jake leaned over and whispered, "A quarter says she calls on Beth Ann."

I shook my head. *Dumb bet. She always calls on her first.*

"Let's start with you, Beth Ann."

Jake and I traded smirks.

"Well, the first thing we're going to do is . . ."

I tuned Beth out and turned my attention back to the fly still trapped in my hand. I knew how it felt, so I let it go. It strafed my face twice in revenge before banking sharply out the doorway to freedom.

Through the windows of Mr. Delaney's room in the next wing I could see his third-graders celebrating the end of the year with punch and cookies.

Great, they get a party, we get a Barkathon.

Mr. D. noticed me watching and raised his Dixie cup in a silent toast. I nodded and smiled halfheartedly.

He was pretty cool, for an adult. I'd gotten to know him a little during the year, since my brother Charley was in his class. He was always cracking corny jokes, and I heard he never lost his temper, not even on Fiesta Day three years back when Carl "the Gas Man" Newell nearly killed the class hamster after eating six bean burritos for lunch. I would have loved to have been there for that.

Word was that he'd occupied the seat closest to the door since kindergarten, his digestive problems guaranteeing him a permanent position near the room's largest source of fresh air. Unfortunately, that meant he sat right next to me.

In fact, the whole back row was made up of boys. The Barker had started out the year with everyone except for the Gas Man seated alphabetically, but that hadn't lasted long. Every time a boy did something she didn't like, he got moved to the back. The front half of the room was mostly girls by Thanksgiving.

To my left was Jake Lister. He'd been moved to the middle of the back row on the first day of school, when we'd all been asked what we wanted to be when we grew up. "Anything but a sixth-grade teacher," he'd said, obviously trying for a laugh. The Barker didn't share his sense of humor.

Next to Jake was Arnold K. None of us could pronounce his last name, which sounded Transylvanian and had fourteen letters in it, all consonants. We weren't sure why he was in the back; probably because Barkula couldn't pronounce his name either.

Booger McDonald sat at the end of the last row next to the trash can, the farthest possible distance from the Barker's desk. I leaned back just in time to catch him dropping his index finger from nostril to mouth again. Apparently he needed constant snacks to tide him over between meals.

I became vaguely aware of Charlotte rambling on about her summer plans, which more than likely involved horses. We'd sort of been friends for a while, until I'd started calling her Mrs. Ed, after the talking horse on TV. Some people just can't take a joke.

I checked the time again. 2:28. Half an eternity to go.

To the left of the clock was a puke-green Civil Air Defense poster showing us what to do in case of a nuclear attack. Back in the fall, when everyone had been afraid that the Russians were starting World War III, we'd had to practice getting under our desks for protection. Like that would have done any good against nukes.

On the bulletin board behind the Barker's desk were *Life* magazine photographs of the seven Mercury astronauts, America's first space pilots, along with the names of their capsules and dates of their flights. For the millionth time I studied their clean-cut faces. All of them but Deke Slayton looked like the heroes they were, handsome in an all-American sort of way. Deke wasn't Quasimodo with a flattop or anything, but his nose seemed a little too big for his face and his ears kind of stuck out. He reminded me a little of my father. Dad's curly dark hair made for a lousy crew cut, so he kept it military-short on the sides and long enough on top to comb, but other than that, they looked like they could have been cousins.

My favorite was Gordon Cooper, the last one to go up. A few weeks back he'd had to land his *Faith 7* capsule on manual control when his autopilot went out during reentry. My dad said that Gordo "did one of the best pieces of flying" he'd ever heard of, and Dad should've known; he was an Air Force fighter pilot, which was the reason I'd gotten in trouble with the Barker in the first place. I know it sounds like a lame excuse, but it's true.

Dad took school very seriously when it came to Charley and me. "Boys," he would say, "we all have jobs to do. Mine is to serve the United States of America. Your job is to go to school and do good work." He was constantly telling us the same thing Gus Grissom told the people who were building his space capsule at McDonnell Douglas: "Do good work."

And the thing is, up until sixth grade I had. School had always been easy for me, so even though I was starting all over again at a new one, I'd begun the year with a reasonably good attitude.

The Barker took care of that the first day. Like teachers everywhere, she made us write an essay about how we'd spent our summer vacation. When it was my turn to read, I told the class about our move from the Air Force Academy in Colorado Springs, about stopping off at Edwards Air Force Base in the Mojave Desert to watch them test the latest jets, and about hanging around the flight line at Norton Air Force Base south of town, watching Dad train young pilots in the art of touch-and-go landings in T-33s. Most of the kids, especially the guys, were fairly impressed.

But not the Barker. "So you're an Army brat," she said.

I thought at first that she was trying to be funny—then I noticed she wasn't smiling. "Air Force," I corrected. I wasn't smiling either. If there was one thing I really hated, it was the term "Army brat."

I sat there doing a slow burn, debating whether or not to defend myself. Then Mom's voice echoed in my brain: "If you can't say anything nice, don't say anything at all." I didn't say a word.

At dinner that night I told Dad what the Barker had said. He scowled for a second, then said, "Son, she's a civilian. You'll just have to deal with it. Do good work and I'm sure you'll win her over."

So I did what Dad said, but she never did come round. I guess that's why I just quit trying and started working only hard enough to keep her off my back. Besides, I'd already learned half the stuff she taught, and the stories in the literature anthology were boring, so I ended up spending most of my time in class drawing or daydreaming.

I'd been absent for a few days after Halloween and had come back to school on crutches to find out I'd been moved to the back, too. That was okay with me; the farther away, the better.

I never did figure out what the Barker had against military kids. My dad said that maybe when she was younger, she'd been dumped by some guy in uniform. A Civil War uniform, no doubt.

Mary Lynn Strickland's shrill voice penetrated my consciousness. "—and then we're going to Disneyland, and then we're going to Knott's Berry Farm, and then we're going to visit my cousins in Idaho for two weeks, and then—"

The clock ticked. I looked up at it.

So did the Barker. It was 2:59.

"Thank you, Mary Lynn, I'm sure you're going to have a wonderful summer." She picked up the stack of envelopes. "My, my, how time flies. I'm sorry, boys and girls, but it appears there won't be time to pass out report cards."

Most of the girls went pale. The boys all cheered.

"So you'll all have to stay after school."

Every chin in the room dropped but mine.

I raised my hand into the stunned silence.

"Yes, Mr. Valentine?"

I stood up.

Thirty seconds and counting.

"Wouldn't you like to know what *my* plans are for the summer, Mrs. Barker?"

She hesitated. We made eye contact for what I hoped was the last time.

"All right. What will *you* be doing this summer, Mr. Valentine?"

Ten seconds. Commence countdown.

"I'll be building a portable atomic bomb."

This time *I* paused for dramatic effect.

"I'll be testing it in your neighborhood."

Five.

"And by the way, *Edna,* my *name* is Mitch."

I was out the door before the bell even stopped ringing.

. . .

I was opening the combination lock to my ten-speed when I heard Tick shout my name behind me.

I finished setting the numbers to my birthday and looked up. Weaving his way toward me through a wave of noisy parolees was a skinny redhead wearing horn-rim glasses and a mile-wide smile. Thomas Kelly Murphy to his parents, T.K. to his friends, and Tick to his best friend, me.

Tick and I had hit it off the first time we'd met, which had been late the past summer at the Officers' Club pool. I'd been waiting in line at the diving board when a high-pitched voice behind me said, "Betcha an ice cream sandwich I can do any dive you can."

I turned around and saw a scrawny, freckle-faced kid with a carrot-orange crew cut and matching swim trunks at least two sizes too big. He didn't look like he could even *jump* off the board, much less dive. "You're on," I said. I was a pretty good diver. I could do front flips, backflips, twists, even gainers when I could work up the nerve. I did my best dive, a flip with a half twist, ending up in a can opener. I quickly swam to the side and held on to the ladder.

"Nice dive," he said, stepping up to the end of the board, his toes just over the edge. "I give it a nine point five." He paced off three precise steps back, then paused and took a few slow, deep breaths, his eyes closed in concentration while he shook his arms and fingers to loosen up. He looked like he knew what he was doing.

Great, I've been hustled by Opie Taylor.

He stood perfectly still for a few more seconds, then began his approach. He pressed down hard on the end of the board and launched himself with an amazing spring for someone so light, absolutely soaring into the air. Then suddenly he became a flurry of arms and legs gyrating wildly in what seemed like every direction at once. Flips, twists, you name it, he did them all at the same time, then landed face-first with a tremendous splash. It was just about the funniest thing I'd ever seen.

He broke the surface grinning. "Well, whadya think? Pretty good, huh?"

"I think you better pay up. My name's Mitch, what's yours?"

T. K. Murphy and I quickly discovered that we had more things in common than Siamese twins. He liked everything I liked; I hated the same things he did. We were best friends before we even finished our ice creams.

His dad was a cargo pilot, and had just been transferred to Norton from MacDill Air Force Base in Florida, so T.K. had a million questions about San Bernardino. It turned out that he'd just moved into my neighborhood, only three streets away, so we'd both be going to the same school, though he was a year behind me.

When my mom arrived to pick me up, the first thing I said was, "Mom, this is T.K. Can he spend the night?"

"Sure. Where's Charley?"

I had completely forgotten about Charley.

Fortunately I quickly spotted him in the shallow end with a bunch of other little kids. We gathered him up and went to find T.K.'s mom.

Mrs. Murphy said it was okay for him to stay over,

and after Mom gave her directions so she could bring his stuff by later, we all piled into the car and headed home.

T.K. became Tick that night at dinner. I'd asked Mom to fix Southern fried chicken with mashed potatoes and gravy, my favorite meal. T.K. practically inhaled his first two helpings, and quit eating only when we finally ran out of food.

He was sopping up the last molecules of gravy off his plate with a pinch of roll when Mom said, "T.K., for someone no bigger than a tick, you sure do have an appetite."

"T.K., Tick. Perfect," I said, more to myself than anyone else.

Charley piped up. "Would you be ticked if we called you that?" He didn't miss much.

T.K. broke into a stupid little grin, so to me and my family he was Tick from then on.

"Mitch! Check it out!" Tick announced in his deejay voice as soon as he reached the bike racks. "It's over! It's three-oh-one in the sunny p.m. and it's summertime, summertime, sum-sum-summertime!"

"And the livin' is easy," I sang back.

He quickly unlocked the bike next to mine and said in a terrible John Wayne drawl, "C'mon, Pilgrim, time t' be moseyin' on along."

"Just a sec, we gotta wait for Charley."

To tell the truth, I would just as soon not have had to wait for my kid brother. I'd been keeping a wary eye on the Barker's door, half expecting to see her come flying out on her broom after me, and the longer I hung around the more nervous I was getting.

Tick noticed. "What's the matter? You miss Woof-woman already?"

"Like I miss polio." I explained what had happened.

"Holy underwear, Batman, that's great! I wish I could've seen the look on her face."

"You'll get your chance next year."

"Thanks for reminding me."

Just then Charley rounded the corner of the primary wing, clutching his lunch box in one hand and a fistful of papers in the other. I was actually glad to see him.

"Mitch, look!" he said when he got within earshot. "All A's! I'm rich!" We got a dollar for each A.

"Good for you, Charley boy. Now let's get a move on."

"What'd you get?"

"Same as you, shrimp. Let's go."

I helped Charley take his bike out of the rack and then looked at Del Rosa Elementary School one last time. I raised my fist high into the air and shook it. "So long, suckers!" I yelled in my best gangster voice.

"Hi-yo, Silver, and away!" Tick shouted.

We mounted up and rode off into the summer.

2

Tick Talk

My dad's oldest brother once told me that the thing he missed most about being a kid was summer vacation. "Oh, sure," he'd said in his slow West Virginia twang, "we grownups git a vacation ev'ry year, but it ain't the same. A body needs the whole summer, not jus' a few measly weeks." He'd gotten kind of a faraway look in his eyes and squeezed my shoulder hard. "You enjoy ev'ry durn minute of it, you hear?"

Tick and I had spent months planning out ev'ry durn minute of the summer. We'd decided that the only way to not waste one second of vacation was to be organized; our schedule had been set by Easter. It wasn't a "schedule" schedule like adults had to follow, but we knew everything we wanted to cram in and sort of in what order.

The first order of business was to celebrate the end of school in his tree house fort, so we rode by my house to escort Charley home and then hightailed it over to Tick's.

Mrs. Murphy already had a platter of assorted cookies and a pitcher of cold lemonade waiting for us on the kitchen counter. We said a quick "hi" to her and scarfed all of it down in about eight seconds. Then Tick grabbed a box of Wheat Thins and a jar of Skippy, I snagged a couple of Dr Peppers out of the fridge, and we headed out back.

The Murphys' back yard was like most of the others in the ranch-style neighborhood, nice but not too big, with flowers and bushes next to the redwood fence that surrounded the lawn. But it had one thing in it that hardly any of the others did, and that was a big tree, an oak of some kind, near the back fence. About ten feet up, perched securely on two big branches, was the coolest tree house in the world.

According to the Murphys, the previous owner had been a carpenter who'd built it for his four kids; he must have been a master. To start with, all of the wood was store-bought lumber, not random pieces of scrap that kids usually have to scrounge up. It was all the same color, a weathered grayish brown, and was fitted together perfectly, with no gaps and no rusty nails sticking out to give you lockjaw if you accidentally got punctured.

The ladder was bolted to the end of the fort farthest

from the trunk, its base hidden in the grass. I climbed up first and unlatched the door. It was a real door that had been cut in half, with hinges and everything. Wood-burned into the front of it were the words "No Girls Allowed." That had been my idea.

I crawled onto the floor, carpeted with a dirty brown-and-gold remnant. That was Tick's idea. It hardly ever rained in Southern California, so we didn't have to worry much about it getting all mildewy.

The walls were tongue-and-groove planks that came up to my chest and had a ledge. I leaned over it to catch the emergency rations, since we only used the rope pulley for big loads. Tick tossed them up and joined me in the hideout.

The whole James gang could have hidden out in that fort. It was eight feet square and even had a roof, a shallow A-frame supported by tall four-by-fours and covered with redwood lattice. We could stand up and still not touch the center beam. It was just about my all-time favorite place.

Tick and I had spent a million hours in there listening to the radio, reading comics and magazines, or just hanging out and shooting the breeze. We planned on practically living there during the summer.

I was still starved, so I scooped up a wad of peanut butter out of the jar with a bunch of Wheat Thins, crammed it all into my mouth, and reached for my Dr Pepper. "Eefergawdabawloper."

"What?"

My mouth was glued shut, so I pointed to the bottle cap and pantomimed.

"Oh, right. I'll go get it."

"Gittarayo do."

He was back in no time with not only the opener and his new transistor radio but also a couple of throw pillows and a handful of comics. He even had two more sodas. He put it all in the picnic basket, and I roped it up. We were set for the rest of the afternoon.

"You're a good man, Gunga Din," I said after a couple of swigs.

"Yeah. You got the list?"

I reached into the back pocket of my Levi's and pulled out a grimy square of binder paper. I carefully opened it and set it on the carpet between us. It had been folded and unfolded so many times that it was nearly in four pieces and was covered with pencil-gray smudges, but to Tick and me it was the most beautiful piece of paper we'd ever seen. Printed on it in two different styles was three months' worth of kid heaven.

Monster movies was the first thing on the list. We'd both seen just about all the horror and science-fiction movies ever made. Between us we had every issue of *Famous Monsters of Filmland*, and had started collecting plastic monster model kits but hadn't built any yet. That was on the list, too.

"I can't wait for tomorrow," Tick said.

"Me neither." Tomorrow at the Crest Theater downtown was the summer's first Shock Saturday Matinee, and they were showing all three of the Creature from the Black Lagoon movies. Tick had missed *The Creature Walks Among Us*. I'd seen them all, but never in a row.

"It's gonna really be great."

"Yeah," I agreed, "six hours of buttered popcorn and Junior Mints with the Gill Man. We'll probably have to get our stomachs pumped."

Next on the list was **10-S 2 RRC**. That stood for "ten-speeds to Redlands, Riverside, and Crestline." Tick and I had identical imported racing bikes, $270 worth of precision European engineering. I'd hustled up some mowing and watering jobs the past summer and had saved most of my allowance for what seemed like forever. Finally I'd been able to walk into Bob's Bikes, plunk down $135 in cash, and say to Bob himself, "I want *that* one." It was one of the best days of my life.

Actually, our bikes weren't identical. Mine was British racing green; Tick's was gold. When he first saw mine, his mouth fell open and he said, "I've *got* to have one of those." A few days later he was leaving thin skid marks on my driveway. "Check it out, Mitch! Now we can go *any*where!"

It was terrific that now we'd be able to take long trips together, and it was impossible not to be happy for Tick, as excited as he was. But later that night I'd started feeling kind of lousy about it. It just didn't seem fair that I'd had to mow a bunch of crummy lawns in a heat wave and hadn't been able to spend any of my measly buck-and-a-half-a-week allowance, and then he got one just like that. I mean, it wasn't a huge deal or anything, but it did bug me for a while.

Mom's good at picking up on things, so when she asked me what was wrong, I told her about it. "Tick's an only child," she said after a moment, "and there's just plain more money to go around. What would you rather have, a free bike or your brother Charley?" I had to think about it.

So bike trips were high on the list. We gradually bought accessories like water bottles, tool kits, and speedometers, and to Tick's credit, he only bought his when I'd saved enough for mine. He was pretty good at picking up on stuff, too.

We'd ridden to Redlands once the past summer, just before school started. It was about ten miles away, so we'd really had to sell our parents on the idea. They finally okayed the trip after we pointed out that we could have just lied about it and gone anyway. "And besides," I'd said, "haven't you always told us that honesty is the best policy?" They didn't have a leg to stand on. Tick's bike at the time was only a three-speed, so he'd had a hard time keeping up. That wouldn't be a problem this summer.

Riverside was twice as far away as Redlands. There were some tough hills along the way, so those low gears were going to be lifesavers. But the big trip, with any luck, was going to be up to Crestline.

Crestline is a touristy, weekend-cabiny kind of place a half hour away in the San Bernardino Mountains north of town. The first time I'd been up there had been in January. It was my parents' anniversary, so they'd gone out of town for the weekend. Charley stayed with a friend, and I spent the weekend with the Murphys.

Mrs. Murphy had read about some "cute little antique shop" in the Sunday paper and decided it would be fun to drive up there to take a look. Fun for her, maybe, but not for the rest of us.

Major Murphy was in a foul mood and drove like a maniac the whole way. The highway had been newly paved and expanded to four lanes, and I think he used all of them. I was sure we were going to die.

Crestline turned out to be a few blocks of dumb shops and a couple of gas stations. Tick and I were bored after about five seconds, so his folks let us wander around on our own while she shopped and he sulked.

We quickly located all the food sources and spent what money we had. We'd just finished our caramel apples when I stumbled into the world's greatest comic book store. Literally.

"Thanks for dropping in," cracked the old man behind the counter.

"We should sue," Tick said, helping me up.

"Tick, look." I pointed. "Back issues!"

Thumbtacked to every square inch of wall space were bagged covers of *Tarzan, Turok, Superman, Mystery in Space, Tales from the Crypt*, everything. It was unbelievable.

We were still salivating when the Murphys found us. Tick conned his mom into springing for an old *Uncle Scrooge*. She lent me fifty cents for a new *Tarzan's Jungle Annual* and the latest issue of *Mad* magazine.

"See you next fall," the old man cackled as we were leaving.

So we already knew we needed to come back for more comics, but the real kicker happened on the way home. Major Murphy had calmed down by then and was driving fairly sanely. We'd just gone around a curve when I happened to look up from the "Spy Vs. Spy" comic in my *Mad*.

Stretched out in front of us was a wide ribbon of downhill straightaway, an infinity of smooth black pavement that nearly faded into a vanishing point before curving off to the right. It was a ten-speed magnet, and I was ninety pounds of iron filings.

I nudged Tick with my knee. He was off somewhere with Uncle Scrooge and the Beagle Boys. I tried it again, this time with my elbow.

He looked up with a this-better-be-good expression.

I nodded toward the front.

He stared out the windshield for a few seconds, then

turned to me and whispered, "You thinking what I'm thinking you're thinking?"

I nodded twice.

"You're nuts," he said, but never took his eyes off the road the rest of the way down. By the time we got back to his house, we both knew we were going to do it sooner or later.

"Paul still gonna take us up next week?" Tick asked, digging for the last of the Wheat Thins.

"Last I heard. I'll remind him again tomorrow."

Paul Sonnenberg was the son of one of my dad's crazy pilot buddies. Actually, he was kind of a hood, with Elvis hair and veiny forearms, but he was friendly to us. He was also sixteen and had a pickup truck big enough to put two bikes in the back. We'd been bugging him about it for months, and he'd finally agreed to take us up next Wednesday. We had to pay for the gas.

We'd already bought extra brake shoes in case we burned ours up trying to keep our speed down, and had told our parents we were going on a long bike trip that day. We just hadn't told them exactly where yet.

We knew they'd never let us ride down twenty miles of mountain highway at forty or fifty miles an hour, so we were going to have to be "cagey" about it, as my dad would put it. Basically, that meant we were going to have to lie. We figured we'd cross that bridge when we came to it.

Paul also figured a little into the third item on our list, **skateboarding**. A lot of kids called it "sidewalk surfing," but that sounded really dumb to Tick and me. Don't get me wrong; I loved surf music and had even started letting my hair grow longer in front like the Beach Boys, but a skateboard wasn't a surfboard by any stretch of the imagination. What it was was a two-foot length of two-by-four with the front and back halves of a skate nailed into each end. Big hairy deal. And we didn't ride them on sidewalks since there weren't any in our neighborhood.

But we did have the Hill. A five-minute walk up Palomar and across Foothill past the curve took us to the base of Hemlock Drive, known to every kid in the area as the Hill. It was worthy of the capital letter. It seemed to go straight up, past widely spaced driveways leading to expensive hillside lots. Cars had a hard time climbing it, even in low gear.

The view from the top was phenomenal, like an asphalt Olympic ski jump. Of course we had to skate it.

Our first attempt was right before Halloween last year. Tick stayed at the bottom to stop any cars that might be coming around the curve. Paul took me up on the back of his motorcycle and dropped me off at the third driveway, just to be safe. Even from there it was pretty intimidating.

It took me a minute or two to work up my courage. *No guts, no glory*, I thought, and pushed off. I was going too fast to stop before I even passed the next driveway. There was no way I was going to make the turn.

But we never found out because I suddenly hit a hardened glob of concrete that someone hadn't bothered to scrape up. The front wheels ripped off the board in a flash, sparks flying. The end of the board splintered and stopped.

I didn't. I went flying into the air and landed with a perfect hook slide about ten yards downhill.

Tick signaled "Safe!" Then he noticed that I'd left most of the skin of my right leg on the pavement. I already knew that.

By the time Paul hustled me home, the outside of my whole leg was an oozing slab of raw hamburger. I thought my mom was going to pass out.

It was a couple of months before my skin grew back and I felt like trying it again, but I insisted on some strategic changes. From then on we never started any farther up than the *second* driveway, we used screws instead of nails, and I never rode in shorts again. I may have been dumb but I wasn't stupid.

Swimming was next on the list; that was a given. Right after school started last year Dad surprised us all by having a pool put in. It was some pool, too: forty feet long, twenty feet wide, and nine feet deep, with chrome ladders and a top-of-the-line diving board. Dad really outdid himself.

It had been a coolish spring, so the pool hadn't gotten

a lot of use. We planned on completely breaking it in this summer.

Printed sideways along the rattiest edge of the paper was **sleepovers / stay up late / sleep in / TV / cartoons / Stooges**.

Tick and I were both huge Three Stooges fans, so getting to watch Moe, Larry, and Curly commit mayhem on each other for an hour every weekday afternoon was a major bonus.

"So when we gonna climb Mount Lugosi?" he asked, thumbing through a *Strange Tales*.

It was the only item on the list that we didn't exactly agree on. "I dunno," I said nonchalantly. "No hurry." It wasn't that I didn't want to climb it; I'd thought about it almost every time I looked at it through my bedroom window. Its outline looked amazingly like Bela Lugosi in *Dracula*.

The ridge we'd inspected through the binoculars looked like it went all the way up. We didn't know how high it was, but it would probably take a whole day to climb up and get back before dark, even in the summer. No problem.

The problem was rattlesnakes. On our weekend hikes in the foothills we'd already seen two and heard one. They didn't seem to bother Tick too much. They bothered me a lot. Take five or six feet of camouflaged evil, add coronary fangs and lethal venom, and you've got a

Western diamondback rattlesnake. It was my sincerest wish to never see one again.

I deftly changed the subject. "Turn on the radio, man. Maybe we can catch 'Pipeline.' " It had come out in the spring and was still my favorite song.

Tick's transistor was permanently set to 1290 KMEN, our favorite station. He thumbed it on. A few minutes later the deejay answered my request. "Now here are the Chantays with 'Pipeline.' " The opening bass run swelled from the speaker and washed over us.

"There *is* a God," I said.

"Amen," Tick agreed.

I put a throw pillow behind my head and leaned back against the wall. The oak's leaves rustled softly in the slight breeze; the warm afternoon sun cast hypnotic patterns of light and shadow that seemed to keep time with the pulsating rhythms of the tom-toms and guitars.

I closed my eyes and smiled. Life was very good.

· · ·

"Mitch! Your mom just called!" Mrs. Murphy yelled from the house.

"Whuh?"

"She says for you to get home right now."

" 'Kay," I yelled back. "Timezit?" I asked Tick. We must have dozed off.

He yawned and checked his watch. "Five after six."

I was late. When Dad wasn't gone, we always ate dinner exactly at six, right after the national news on TV.

I refolded the list and put it back in my pocket.

"Call me after you eat."

"Quick as I can," I said from the top rung. I dropped
to the ground and ran to my bike.

"Gentlemen, start your engines!" Tick announced to
the whole neighborhood.

I opened the gate and got ready.

"And they're off!" he yelled.

I almost laid rubber tearing out of their driveway.
Three and a half blocks and twenty-eight "Mississippis"
later I bounced into mine, cut between our cars, and
skidded to a stop with a stylish squeal in the middle of
the garage.

I toed the kickstand, pulled the garage door down,
and hustled into the house. The kitchen lights were on
and the table was set, but no one was there.

"I'm home! Sorry I'm late!"

I heard Mom giggle in the living room.

"In here," said Dad.

I stopped at the half wall. Mom and Dad were sitting
in their chairs, his and hers plaid recliners. Charley was
on the couch facing them. It looked like a family meeting.

"Family meeting," Dad said, tilting his cocktail toward Mom. "Your mother has an announcement to
make."

Mom had a funny smile on her face, like she was

keeping the world's biggest secret and had to tell someone soon or she'd explode.

I suddenly remembered a conversation in their bedroom I'd sort of overheard a while back. They'd been
talking in low voices about maybe having another baby. I
hadn't thought much about it since, but now I knew exactly what she was going to say.

*That's just terrific, one more mouth to feed. No way am
I gonna share* my *room.*

"Guess what, boys?" She was grinning like an idiot.
"We're going away for the summer!"

3

Doomsday

I reached for the wall to steady myself. Mom was still talking, but the surf roaring in my ears drowned her out. "What?"

"I said we're going to PawPaw's for the summer. Isn't that great?"

Giant breakers pounded the inside of my head. "Who's *we*?" I managed to ask.

"All of us. Even Rebel."

A tsunami thundered through my brain. I fought for breath. "What?"

"We're leaving Tuesday for two months. The plans have all been made."

So have mine, not that anyone cares.

Mom must have read my mind. "I know you and Tick

had plans of your own, honey, but they'll just have to wait. There'll be other summers."

My stomach started to ache.

"How long does it take to get to Louisiana?" asked Charley.

"It's a three-day drive," Mom answered. "It'll be fun!"

Charley burst out with a "Hooray!" and clapped his hands. He wasn't old enough to know any better.

I looked at Dad. He was taking a sip of his highball. Our eyes locked. My face said, "Isn't there anything you can do about this?"

He swallowed and said, "It's a done deal, sport. I'll be on temporary duty at the Pentagon most of the summer. Just got the orders this morning." He paused to light a cigarette with his Zippo. "Besides, your mother needs to be with PawPaw. He may not have many summers left."

I wondered why our collie was panting so loudly— then I realized he wasn't in the room. It was me.

"Haftagotoda bathroom," I mumbled.

"You wash up, too, Charley," said Mom. "We'll discuss it more at dinner." She got up and walked past me into the kitchen, a goofy smile still plastered on her face. I don't think she even saw me.

But Dad did. I flew out of the room before he could see my tears.

. . .

Like most guys, I don't like to cry, especially not in front of my dad. But I was alone in a locked bathroom and my life was over, so it didn't matter. My vision blurred as hot tears began streaming down my cheeks. Then the inside of my nose liquefied, adding to the mess. Sobs forced themselves out of my throat like the whimpers of a dying animal.

I turned the tap on full blast to drown out the sounds and splashed cold water on my face until I finally got a grip on myself. I toweled off, blew my nose a few times, and then inspected the damage.

Staring back at me from the mirror was a preteenage vampire with a pale complexion and glassy blue eyes. A damp lock of black hair had fallen from a cowlick onto my forehead; I wetted it down some more and shaped it into a widow's peak.

My upper lip curled back in a menacing sneer to reveal gleaming, even teeth. My fangs weren't very pronounced yet, but they were already deadly. I was of average height for an undead of my age, and was thin but not bony.

Suddenly I hissed and spun around, swirling my cape up and across my face to shield my eyes. "I . . . dislike . . . mirrors," I said in my best Lugosi. "Van Helsing . . . will explain."

I'd seen the original *Dracula* so many times that I had most of the dialogue memorized; it was my favorite horror movie. In fact, Tick and I were going to watch it again on TV at midnight, when *Friday Fright Night* came on.

How am I going to break the news to Tick?

I'd been feeling so sorry for myself that I hadn't even thought about his summer being just as ruined as mine. Mom had said there'd be other summers, and that was true. But maybe not with Tick, not in the military. We could be transferred at any time, so we knew not to plan too far ahead.

My stomach started aching all over again.

"Boys! Dinner!" Dad ordered.

"Be right there!" I called back in my deepest voice. I flushed the toilet to buy a little more time.

Think! I can't just let them wreck everything for me and Tick. That's it! I could stay with the Murphys! I could take care of the dog and the house during the day, and Mom and Dad wouldn't have to pay anyone to mow the yard or clean the pool. It would save them a ton of money. They'll have to agree with my logic.

I blotted my eyes one last time, took a deep breath, and stepped into the hallway. I immediately tripped over Charley, who was crouched down just outside the door. Only my supernatural vampire reflexes kept me from being seriously injured.

"Were you crying, Mitch?" he asked, wide-eyed.

"No, I was practicing my acting, you ignoramus. You almost killed me! Don't *do* stuff like that, okay?"

"I'm sorry," he said softly. I could tell he was kind of shook up. After all, he'd evidently just overheard his big brother totally losing it in the bathroom.

I pulled him to his feet. "Sorry I called you an ignoramus."

"That's all right." He grinned up at me. "What's an ignoramus?"

"Like you don't know," I said, marching him toward the kitchen. "C'mon, let's eat." I shifted my face into neutral, as if the last few minutes hadn't happened. Talk about acting.

. . .

Friday midnight arrived, and for the first time in nearly a year I wasn't sitting in front of a TV set with Tick. Instead I was stretched out on my bed staring at the ceiling, my arms folded in an X across my chest like a mummy. The faint glow of my rocket night-light seemed lost in the gloominess of my darkened room. I felt the same way.

I'd convinced myself that once I explained my plan to Mom and Dad, they'd agree to it immediately, complimenting me on my initiative and ingenuity in the process.

I must have been temporarily insane.

Tick called after dinner, wondering what was taking me so long. My bombshell was followed by a long silence on his end of the line.

"I can't believe this," he finally said. "This isn't happening."

"Believe it, Ripley. We leave Tuesday morning. At the crack of dawn."

"Don't they execute people at dawn?"

"Tell me about it."

Our conversation quickly petered out. Neither one of us really felt like watching *Dracula* anymore, so we canceled out on the rest of the evening, too.

"We'll pick you up at eleven for the movies tomorrow," he reminded me.

"If I don't kill myself first."

"Yeah. Seeya."

I hung up and retreated to my room.

Six hours later I was stretched out on my bed, wide awake and still angry.

I reached behind me on the headboard to turn my clock radio on.

"—you would cry too if it happened to y—"

I slammed the radio back into silence and buried my head in the pillow.

. . .

All day Saturday I was a zombie. The triple feature I'd looked forward to seemed hokey, and the blaring soundtrack and cheesy dialogue quickly got on my nerves. The cola tasted funny, and the popcorn was like buttered cardboard. I didn't even finish my Junior Mints.

The ride home was a blur. As Mrs. Murphy turned the corner to my house, I came out of my fog just enough to notice that the street was jammed with parked cars.

"Your dad's having a barbecue," she explained as she dropped me off. "We'll be over shortly." Dad had apparently decided to throw an impromptu bash for everyone in the Air Force.

Mom saw me before I could sneak off to my room. "Come on," she said, escorting me out back, "join the fun."

The party was already in full swing. The patio buzzed with dozens of conversations that competed with the corny big-band sounds blasting from the hi-fi in the living room. The pool was a choppy sea, heads bobbing everywhere. The shallow end was standing room only. Kids I didn't even know were lined up at the diving board.

Dad waved from the corner of the yard, where he was busy burning hamburgers and hot dogs on the grill. A knot of crew-cut pilots in dumb Ban-Lon shirts and plaid shorts surrounded him, cocktails or beers in hand. Smoke from cigarettes and stogies drifted into the mushroom cloud rising over the scorched meat.

I smiled and started edging back into the house. I wasn't fast enough. Our next-door neighbor Mrs. Scales collared me and dragged me off toward the deep end. "My nephews are visiting from back East," she said, too loudly, "and I just *know* you'll hit it off!"

I knew I was in for a long night.

. . .

Sunday morning was spent pre-packing with Mom. Since she was a maniac for planning and organizing, Charley and I had a summer's worth of stuff laid out and ready to go before lunch.

We cleaned the pool and did yard work all afternoon, so by dinnertime I was starved. The day's chores had given me an appetite again; I even had seconds on the Spam.

As soon as I helped clear the table, I gathered up my overnight stuff, said my good nights, and headed off to Tick's on foot. It was going to be our last sleepover for a long time.

I had decided to quit moping and make the most of the little time we had left, and so had Tick. We listened to the radio all evening while we worked on models, read comics, and ate constantly, practically wiping out the Murphys' kitchen.

When his folks finally went to bed a little after midnight, he and I headed to the tree house. We spread out our sleeping bags and pillows, then watched for their bedroom light to go off. It soon did, and after waiting a while longer just to be on the safe side, we grabbed our flashlights and sneaked over the fence.

Tick and I wandered around all night, talking about everything in general and nothing in particular. We had no destination and were in no hurry to get there. We ended up in the big orange grove next to the reservoir, admiring the purple predawn sky from the catwalk of a thirty-foot-high water tower.

The spell was suddenly broken by the sound of dogs barking in the distance.

"Listen to them . . . the children of the night," I began.

"What music they make," Tick joined in.

We looked at each other and grinned.

Just then the first sliver of daylight edged over the horizon. Both of us hissed and shielded our eyes. We fled to the safety of our caskets before we were incinerated by the rays of the rising sun. Or by Major Murphy.

· · ·

"You're not gonna believe what my dad just did," I said to Tick as I climbed back into the tree house later that afternoon.

"I suppose canceling the trip is too much to hope for," he muttered into his *Superboy* comic.

I whisked it out of his hands and set it down without losing his place.

"Pay attention, knucklehead," I ordered.

"Nice haircut," he said, staring at the top of my head.

Dad had picked me up at the Murphys' at noon and hauled me off to the base barbershop, informing me that no son of his was going to visit relatives "looking like that." I'd had no say in the matter.

"Bowl number one or bowl number two?" Tick asked.

I nodded. "Both." Military barbers only know two styles—short and uneven, and shorter and uneven.

"So check this out. We're heading home up Sterling as usual when suddenly he takes a hard left just before Highland. I ask where we're going, and he says we have one more stop to make, it won't take very long. A few blocks down he turns right, into this strange neighborhood. I'm still trying to figure out what we're doing when he pulls over to the curb and stops the car in front of this old pink house. He turns the engine off, leans back against the door, and says, 'By the way, Mrs. Barker called Friday after school. She said something about a report card you left behind.' "

Tick's mouth dropped open.

"That's what I did, too," I said. "So then he tells me I not only have to go in there and get it but I also have to apologize to her. He made me practice it right there in the car."

"You're kidding!"

"No, but he was. I have my hand on the door handle when he takes the report card from his shirt pocket, hands it to me, and says, 'I picked it up for you.' Then he says, 'I also told her I didn't much appreciate the way she treated you this year.' "

"Way to go, Major Valentine!"

"Yeah, but get this. He starts the car, and we're driving off when I say something about how sad and dumpy her house is."

"Just like her."

"No, it really was. I was even feeling kinda sorry for her. So then he turns to me and says, 'Oh, that's not her house. I haven't the foggiest idea where she lives.' Is that a riot or what?"

. . .

Our last hour together we joked around as usual, even though we didn't really feel like laughing. Eventually the moment of truth arrived.

"Thomas Kelly!" his mom called from the patio door. "Time to change. We have to leave soon." They were going out of town for the evening and wouldn't be home until late. This was it.

I said it first. "Well, I guess I should get going."

"Yeah, guess so." He wouldn't make eye contact.

"Have fun this summer," I said, my voice threatening to break.

"You, too." He held out his hand. I shook it.

We both knew what each of us was thinking.

But not too much fun. Especially not with a new best friend.

4

Automatic Pilot

Tuesday morning I was awakened by what sounded like a giant woodpecker drilling into my door at jackhammer speed. It wasn't. It was Dad, rapping his Army Air Corps ring against the door faster than seemed humanly possible.

I forced myself out of the warmth of my bed and stumbled to the bathroom, knuckling sleep out of my eyes. By the time I was done, Charley was waiting in the hall, leaning his head against the doorjamb. His eyes were screwed shut, his hair a firecrackered bird's nest.

Fifteen minutes later we were in the car, a red-and-white '57 De Soto Fireflite, waiting for Mom to make one last run through the house. Opening one eye, I saw her slide onto the front seat and close her door, mission accomplished.

Dad punched the De Soto's push-button transmission into reverse and backed out of the driveway; the instant the car started moving, Rebel shook himself. In seconds we were enveloped in a zero-visibility collie storm, saliva and fur flying everywhere.

As we slowed for the stop sign around the corner, Mom leaned over and asked Dad in a little-girl voice, "Are we there yet?" then looked at Charley and me and started giggling.

I pounded my pillow into position and closed my eyes.

. . .

I was having a weird dream about being surrounded by a mob of crazed *Daily Planet* reporters, their flashbulbs popping in my face while squadrons of B-52s thundered overhead, when a sonic boom jolted me awake. I opened my eyes just in time to be blinded by the nearby strike of a brilliant lightning bolt, followed immediately by another tremendous thunderclap.

We were in the middle of a colossal thunderstorm. Jagged lightning strobed all around us, revealing a flat, tree-lined landscape. Apparently we were also in the middle of nowhere. "Where are we?" I practically had to shout over the downpour.

"About fifty miles from the farm," said Dad. The torrential rain and near pitch-darkness had obviously made driving impossible, so he'd pulled off onto the shoulder to wait it out. "An hour's drive, once this storm lets up," he added.

Rebel trembled next to me, terrified by the storm. I put my arm around his neck to try to calm him down. Rebel was a great dog, but he made a lousy traveling companion. Collies are a little high-strung to start with, and he was no exception, so for three days we'd had to force tranquilizers down his throat to keep him from going berserk in the car. Fortunately for him, they worked.

But unfortunately for us they also turned his breath, not the most pleasant of aromas at best, into a lethal weapon. A near miss brought tears to your eyes, while a direct hit could blister your face and singe your eyelashes. Our clothes could be fumigated, but I was sure we'd never get the stench out of the upholstery.

Collies are also noted for their long snouts. Rebel's measured exactly six inches, from his eyes to the tip of his constantly wet nose, and was responsible for the condition of the backseat windows, which were smeared with dried nose tracks and covered with a thick layer of long, gold-and-white collie hair.

They were useless as view ports, having been completely smudged up by the time we stopped for breakfast on the first day at a Sambo's coffee shop near the Arizona border. Charley and I had to wait to use the bathroom stall, so by the time we joined Mom and Dad in the corner booth, Dad already had his quarters laid out.

Dining out with my dad was an experience. After the previous tip had been cleared off, he would carefully line up ten or twelve quarters in a precise row along the edge of the table. Then every time our waitress forgot something or fell short of his expectations of prompt, courteous service, he would wordlessly remove one quarter. Even the most dim-witted ones eventually caught on to his system, and since two or three bucks was a substantial tip, we rarely got poor service, at least not for very long.

Driving cross-country with Dad was quite an experience, too. I'd once watched him fly an F-100 Super Sabre, one of the hottest jets in the world, putting it through high-speed climbs, dives, loops, and barrel rolls with supreme skill. But put Dad or any other fighter pilot behind the wheel of a powerful car, and you've got a demolition derby. They're either overconfident and reckless, driving as fast as possible at all times, or they're overconfident and inattentive, constantly drifting onto the shoulder or into oncoming traffic. Either way, it's Mr. Toad's Wild Ride.

Dad was overconfident, reckless, *and* inattentive, especially on long, boring stretches of straight desert highway. If Mom hadn't been such a good copilot, we'd have never made it. She was also the navigator, since Dad had an amazingly poor sense of direction, and there were unfortunately no avionic instruments in the cockpit of a De Soto.

As often as not, he'd pull back onto the road after gassing up or eating and head back the way we'd just come. Mom would usually wait a few seconds for him to realize his mistake and then say something like "Sweetie, you sure we're going the right way?"

He'd scowl and say, "Of *course* I'm sure. I'm a *pi*lot, for cryin' out loud!" About ten seconds later he'd see a road sign showing the mileage to the last town we'd driven through, then slam on the brakes and pull off to turn around, swearing the whole time. No one would say a word for the next few miles.

. . .

On our first day, we made it as far as Lordsburg, New Mexico, and checked into a reasonably nice Best Western motel around sunset. While Mom and Dad unpacked, Charley and I walked Rebel, which took a while since he'd been holding it for hours. He probably killed every bush on the premises.

After locking him in the room with his dinner bowl, we all walked across the road to a Mexican restaurant that had been highly recommended by the manager. Even though the place was half empty, we had to wait for a table. The service and the food were both lousy, so Dad walked out with a pocketful of quarters.

Charley and I had a hard time getting to sleep that night. It wasn't the constant highway noise that kept us up, though that didn't help, and it wasn't that we'd slept most of the day and were still wide awake.

It was the refried beans.

Dad had already warned us to settle down when Charley let the first one. It wasn't very loud, a soft *poot* that was barely audible over the hum of the window-mounted cooler next to our double bed, but it was loud enough, so the giggling started all over again.

A minute or so later I answered with a more substantial effort, and the competition was on. We both got off a few more as the beans worked their way through our systems, each one followed by a "Sorry" and muffled snickers. It was a good thing the room was air-conditioned.

Dad's third and final "Knock it off" quieted us down, and after a couple more SBDs, we finally ran out of gas.

I was almost asleep when Dad sneezed and cut a huge one at the same time. It sounded like a wet sheet being ripped apart, and sent Charley and me into hysterics. I was amazed it didn't blast Mom right out of their bed.

It did get her up, however, sending her shuffling off to the bathroom muttering, "You're *all* disgusting."

Rebel started whimpering, then a few seconds later the smell reached our side of the room. Suddenly it wasn't so funny. My eyes started to burn, and I had to breathe through the pillow. I wished I'd packed Grandpa Jake's World War I gas mask.

The next day I'm sure we all wished we had gas masks. Dad was still having trouble with the Mexican dinner and had compounded the problem by having a sausage-and-eggs blue plate special for breakfast; every time he cracked his window we all knew we were in big trouble.

That afternoon we'd driven by a paper mill somewhere in Texas, its smokestack pouring choking, noxious fumes into the air. Even with the windows up and the air conditioner on full blast, the smell was overpowering. It was also an improvement.

But other than the occasional gaseous interludes provided by industry and my dad, the long hours on the road were mainly just boring. Our family car games of Ford versus Chevy and Billboard Alphabet quickly got old, Mom's preference for country-western music nauseated me, and the scenery never seemed to change. When I was awake to see it, that is.

I could sleep anytime and anywhere. No position was too uncomfortable, no surroundings too noisy. I'd learned early on that it was a great way to avoid reality.

So I spent most of the three days unconscious, awakening only when it was time to get out of the car for food or pit stops. All I remembered about Wednesday were the gas attacks and swimming in a plastic-domed motel pool that reeked of chlorine.

Thursday was more of the same, with one exception—Rudy's Reptorama. Charley read the green roadside signs for hours, getting more and more excited as the distance decreased.

**2-Headed Rattlesnake—Rudy's Reptorama—
180 miles**

Exotic Iguanas—Rudy's Reptorama—100 miles

Giant Scorpions—Rudy's Reptorama—1 mile

Charley had always been fascinated by things that crawled or slithered and was constantly trapping them to add to the miniature zoo in his room. By the time he'd read a dozen or so signs promising "reptilian delights galore," he was practically jumping out of his skin.

Rudy turned out to be a wild-haired old lady, the Reptorama a handful of mesh cages with half-dead horned toads and lizards baking in the sun.

"What a gyp!" Charley said disgustedly. "*I've* got a better collection than that."

Charley wasn't suckered by the signs because he was dumb—far from it. In fact, he was probably the smartest person I knew. He'd been born with what's called an eidetic memory, which means that he never forgot anything. He could quote any page from any book he'd ever read, word for word, and since he could read almost before he could walk, he was also a talking encyclopedia.

"Did you know that Louisiana is the crayfish capital of the world?" he asked during a lull in the thunder.

"We Southernahs say *craw*fish," Mom drawled.

He nodded. "Or that it's home to three of the largest egret colonies in the United States?"

"Really?" Mom said. "Tell us more." She loved playing the memory game with Charley.

Believe it or not, the first thing he'd done after finding out that we'd be spending the summer in Louisiana was to look the state up in our encyclopedia. He had to be the only kid in the world who actually did research before going on vacation.

"Louisiana became the eighteenth state on April 30, 1812," he said. "It was officially nicknamed the Pelican State, but is also called the Bayou State, despite the fact that it is nearly half covered with forests."

"What's a bayou?" I asked, trying to trip him up.

"Bayous are the state's chief natural drains of overflow river water. Louisiana covers 48,523 square miles, including 3,417 square miles of inland water. Farmland covers one-third of the state, with an average farm size of 270 acres." He paused just long enough to take a breath. "Crops account for nearly two-thirds of Louisiana's farm income, with soybeans, cotton, rice, sugarcane, and corn being of the most importance. Beef cattle, dairy cattle, milk, and hay are also key sources of revenue."

"Thanks, Professor Knowledge," I said, "but could we talk about something more interesting now? Like the history of the combine harvester?"

"Sure. It began in 1831 when Cyrus Hall McCormick inven—"

"Just kidding, brainiac," I said, a little too sharply. "Enough with facts and figures, okay? Nobody cares."

"Watch it, sport," Dad warned me. "Just because you're ticked off about everything, don't take it out on your brother."

Tick. I haven't thought about him since we left.

"Or the rest of us, for that matter," Mom chimed in. "You're going to be here for two months whether you like it or not, so you may as well make the best of it."

I didn't respond, so Mom and Dad probably thought I was thinking about what they'd just said. But I was really wondering why I hadn't given Tick a single thought for three whole days.

"Look, son," Dad continued, "things aren't always going to go your way, you know. Part of growing up is learning to accept what you can't change."

"Yeah, I know."

"Looks like it's letting up," Dad said. "Let's press on."

The thunderstorm's trailing edge passed overhead, bringing with it a cobalt sky and a clean smell to the air.

Dad pulled back onto the two-lane state highway, checked his aviator's watch, and announced, "Tower, this is Tango Two-niner requesting clearance for takeoff on runway one. ETA Pitkin, Louisiana, twenty-thirty hours." That meant 8:30 p.m. in civilian time.

I rolled my window down and stuck my hand out into the wind stream. As I experimented with different aerodynamic shapes, I studied the landscape whizzing by in the twilight.

Silhouetted in the distance stood forests of tall pines, creepy in their stillness. Between them and the crude fencing that lined the road, fields of strange-looking crops alternated with pastures randomly dotted by clumps of motionless cows. Occasionally a tractor or something would drift into view, blurry in the gathering darkness. I couldn't tell whether the equipment had been abandoned or was just waiting patiently for the next day's work.

Every mile or so a lonely mailbox whipped by, seeming to stand guard over an isolated farmhouse set far back from the road. Despite their dimly lit windows, the houses seemed uninhabited.

Mom draped her arm across the back of her seat and turned to face me. "Let's go over everybody one last time, okay? Do you remember Aunt Grace's husband's name?"

"Who's Aunt Grace?" I asked.

"Very funny. You know perfectly well who . . ."

I tuned Mom out since I really did know the whole Miller family tree. Not that there'd been much choice. She'd hauled out all her old photo albums and made Charley and me match faces, names, and relationships until we got every single one right. He'd only needed to be told once. I'd had to work a little harder, but that was only because I didn't really care. I already knew the only thing I needed to know, which was that I had to spend eight weeks living with total strangers.

Just because I knew their names didn't mean I knew who they were. Technically I'd met them all once before, but since I had been barely four at the time, I only had a few vague memories of them and the farm. Mom had flown back for funerals twice after that, but the rest of us hadn't been there since Charley was a baby.

Mom was mainly going to see her dad, PawPaw Bill, who was in his late sixties and evidently not in great health. Her older sister Nelda had taken care of him and the house since MawMaw Inez died, moving back to the farm with her husband, Mack, and their three kids.

Uncle Mack died a few years back, and both girls had since moved out on their own. I figured I wouldn't be spending much time with PawPaw and Aunt Nelda, so that only left my cousin Woody. He was the one I was worried about.

All I knew about him was that he was a year older than I was and had really short hair, or at least he did a few years ago, when our most recent snapshot had been taken. Judging only by his lame haircut and the gap between his front teeth, he didn't look too promising.

Mom was the first one to see the "Pitkin—9 miles" sign. "Almost there, boys," she announced, "almost home."

She'd spent the first seventeen years of her life in the same house. Until she left Pitkin to go to Louisiana State, she'd only moved once, and that was from one bedroom to another. Marrying an Air Force officer had definitely made up for that.

"Where are we going to sleep?" I asked.

"Don't worry," she said, "we'll all have beds. This is the country, not the wilderness."

Usually when you're getting near civilization, you start seeing things that indicate a population increase ahead, like billboards or lights, maybe even an outlying business or two. Not in Louisiana. The next sign of life was the "Pitkin" sign, which stood all by itself on the shoulder of the road. Pitkin was nowhere to be found.

A few seconds after we passed the sign, Dad suddenly slammed on the brakes, sending Rebel tumbling into the front seat. "Almost pranged an armadillo, boys," he explained as Rebel unleashed another hairstorm. "Look at the size of that thing."

Slowly making its way across the road was a living dinosaur the size of a beach ball, its prehistoric armor shimmering in the twin cones of our high beams. About a hundred yards beyond the armadillo and on the other side of the blacktop I could just make out a dozen or so unlit buildings, boxy monsters lurking in the dusk among shadowy oil drums and abandoned cars.

"So where's Pitkin?" Charley asked.

"Right over there, honey," Mom said, pointing across the road past the armadillo.

Ohmigod.

"And how far away is the farm?"

Not far enough.

"Just a mile or so up the next road," she answered.

The armadillo finally made it to the center line, so Dad started forward again. A few seconds later he swerved left onto a narrow unmarked road. The cricket concert we'd been listening to for the past hour was immediately drowned out by the deafening roar of tires on gravel.

The farther from California we'd gotten, the worse the roads had become; we'd gone from smooth, modern interstates to rough state highways to potholed county roads, and now to gravel.

What farmhouses I could see were built closer together than those outside of town, but were still nowhere near shouting distance of each other.

"Slow down," Mom cautioned, straining to see in the near darkness, "we should see the wagon wheels any second now."

Sure enough, twin wagon wheels suddenly flashed by on our left, one embedded into each side of the dirt driveway Dad had just overshot. As usual, he hit the brakes too hard, sending the car fishtailing in the loose gravel. Then he overcorrected with the steering wheel, so by the time we skidded to a stop we were facing back the other way.

The farmhouse was now on our right, set about thirty

yards back among a few large trees. By the time we cleared the wagon wheels, the brightly lit front porch was alive with people getting up from rocking chairs and others throwing open the screen door.

"Look! There's PawPaw! And Nelda! Hi! Hi!" Mom screeched out the window, waving like a lunatic.

As we neared the house, a tree-mounted floodlight came on, illuminating a half dozen old cars parked willy-nilly out front. Dad pulled up onto the grass next to a battered dark-green pickup and shut down the engine.

A trio of ugly short-haired dogs approached our car to investigate, sniffing the air between fits of barking. Rebel started barking back and, before I could stop him, made the mistake of scrambling over me and out the window. He bounded up to the pack and stopped, tail wagging.

The largest one took a step forward and started growling, teeth bared in a hideously scarred face. He was about half Rebel's size but looked twice as strong, whipcord muscles rippling beneath a mangy coat. They froze nose to nose for a few heartbeats, then Rebel moved to sniff the leader's hindquarters. That was his second mistake.

Mutant Dog attacked. Suddenly the air was filled with vicious snarls and snaps as they all swarmed around him. I was sure he was going to be turned into Alpo.

Dad was halfway out of the car when a bib-overalled

adult waded into the pack, yelling and kicking. Every blow of his work boots was immediately followed by a yelp or a squeal, and in seconds it was all over.

Rebel just stood there panting rapidly, dazed but apparently unhurt. Saliva flecked his muzzle and matted his coat. He shook himself violently, then cocked his head and stared straight at me.

Sorry, pal. Welcome to Lousy-ana.

5

The First Supper

By the time Charley and I got out of the car, Mom had already been swallowed by the noisy mob on the front porch. Dad and whoever had broken up the fight were kneeling on the ground next to Rebel, giving him the once-over just to make sure he was okay. Charley and I joined them as they were getting to their feet.

"Mitch, Charley," said Dad, "say hello to your uncle Robert."

"Howdy, boys," Uncle Robert said, extending a hand the size of a fielder's mitt. "Sorry 'bout them cussed dogs. They ain't the friendliest ones around." He shook hard enough to pop my knuckles, then put his arm around Dad's shoulder. "Cold beer sound good, Marc?"

"Talked me into it," Dad said as they turned and headed toward the house.

Dad and Uncle Robert joined the rest of the Millers on the porch, prompting another round of loud greetings and hugs. Charley and I exchanged here-we-go glances and brought up the rear.

The entrance to the porch was jammed, so we hung back at the foot of the steps and waited for the crowd to thin out. After a few moments, a large woman wearing a red-and-white checked apron over a washed-out cotton dress detached herself from the group and held her fleshy arms out toward us. "Mitch! Charley! Come give your aunt Nelda a big old hug right now." Or at least I was pretty sure that's what she said.

A recording of Aunt Nelda's greeting would have sounded something like "Miyutch! Chahhrrlee! Cuhum giyuve yoah Eyeunt Nailda uh biigg ole huuug rat nahyow," like a 45-rpm single played at 33 and a third.

Charley and I hesitantly stepped up onto the porch and were both instantly enfolded by Aunt Nelda's smothering embrace. Not only did she squeeze us hard enough to make breathing difficult, I nearly gagged on her aroma, a suffocating mixture of sickening-sweet perfume, kitchen smells, and sweat.

Just when I thought I'd pass out, she let go and stepped back until she had us at arm's length, a strong hand gripping each of us by the shoulder. "Ah do declare, Mitch, you've shot up like a weed! An' Charley, as Ah live an' breathe, you're the spittin' image of your mama!" Then she turned to Mom and said, "God's truth, Laverne, he looks jus' like you did when you were his age."

There really was a strong resemblance between Charley and Mom. They both had fine-textured, sandy-brown hair, small noses, and thinnish lips that all looked "like they'd been ordered from the same catalog," as Mom liked to say. Both of them smiled at Aunt Nelda, their grayish-green eyes crinkling the same way at the corners.

"Boys," Mom said, putting her arm around the shoulders of a frail-looking old man wearing faded denim overalls over a sweat-stained blue work shirt, "say hello to your PawPaw."

PawPaw slowly extended a liver-spotted hand and gently mussed my hair, then cupped the back of Charley's neck. Squinting in concentration, he examined each of us for a few seconds, then smiled and said to Mom, "Sugah, ya done good." Even through his thick, old-fashioned glasses I could see where Mom and Charley got their eyes and laugh lines.

Aunt Nelda introduced us to the rest of our aunts and uncles, and the next thing I knew, Charley and I were being spun around and steered firmly toward the end of the porch, where four skinny boys stood fidgeting in front of a large hanging swing.

"Let's meet your cousins, boys."

I'd already sneaked a couple of glances at them through the crowd of adults and hadn't exactly been encouraged by what I'd seen. Like PawPaw and Uncle Robert, each one of them was wearing bib overalls. But that was all they had on—no shirts, no socks, and no shoes.

Extra! Extra! Read all about it! Scientists invent shoes!

As Aunt Nelda marched us up to them, the tallest one cupped his hand around his mouth and said something to the others. I couldn't make out what it was, but it must have been funny since they all started snickering.

"Mitch, Charley," said Aunt Nelda, "say hidey t' your cousins. This is Larry, that's Barry, this tall drinka water's Gary, they're all Robert's boys, and that last one there's m' Woody. Y'all'll be sharin' his room. You boys get acquainted now, heah?" Then she turned back to the adults and said, "Y'all jus' visit a spell, we're fixin' t' eat soon," and disappeared into the house.

We'd all mumbled hellos of one kind or another during her introductions; now it seemed that none of us knew what to say.

I decided to break the ice. "So what is this, Overalls Headquarters?"

Charley started to laugh, but cut it short when none of them joined in.

I tried another tack. "So what was so funny?" I asked Tall Drink Gary. "I could use a good laugh about now."

Gary smiled and said, "Nothin', jus' a little joke. Y'all have a good trip?"

"It was okay. So really, what's the joke?"

"It wasn't really that funny," he insisted, then glared at Barry.

Barry glared back at him, then looked at me and grinned. "He said you boys sure do dress funny."

Charley and I glanced at each other. I knew he was thinking the same thing I was.

We *dress funny?*

It was like Moe calling Larry and Curly imbeciles.

Charley had on a brown-and-gold striped T-shirt over tan shorts, white crew socks, and slip-on white tennies. My T-shirt was a cool combination of blue, yellow, and green stripes, which looked great with my Levi's. I was wearing my favorite shoes, black cross-country racers with three diagonal white stripes on the sides. Anybody who was anybody in San Bernardino had a pair.

"That *is* pretty funny," I said. "Thanks."

Woody leaned back against the railing and spoke for the first time. "Ain't y'all hot in all them clothes?"

Actually, I was dying, but there was no way I was going to admit it. The heat had steadily gotten worse the last couple of days, as had the humidity, but the De Soto's arctic air-conditioning had pretty well let me ignore that fact.

The porch, however, definitely wasn't air-conditioned,

and the hot, heavy air was squeezing sweat out of every single pore in my body. My T-shirt felt permanently glued to my skin, and my socks were soaked. Even my jockey shorts were wet.

"Yeah, it's a little warm," I acknowledged. "Let's go inside and cool off, okay?"

"House ain't got air," Woody said, a trace of a smile tugging at the corners of his mouth.

"You're kidding, right?"

"Nope, but we got us a coupla fans."

"Nobody in town 'cept the Finnertys an' the McKeans has air," Gary said as he fiddled with one of the chains that held up the swing.

"Jus' wait'll it gits *really* hot, 'long 'bout July," said Barry. He looked at Woody and smiled. "Might even git so bad he'll hafta git himself some overalls, too."

Barry hooked his thumbs under the straps of his overalls. "Shoot, I'll bet you boys a sodey pop y'ain't even wearin' skivvies by the Fourth. *We* don't."

Charley's eyes widened. "You aren't wearing any underwear?"

"He's just kidding, Charley boy," I assured him. "You *are* kidding this time, right?"

Barry broke into another grin. "Had ya goin' there, didn't I?"

I decided to change the subject. Actually, that's not exactly true; it was my bladder that made the decision. "Where's the bathroom?" I asked Woody.

"Ain't got one of them neithah," he said, without smiling. "We'se jus' hicks in da sticks, 'membah?"

Gary quickly said, "Enda the hall."

I nodded and started toward the screen door. Just then Aunt Nelda opened it and stepped onto the porch, a triangular dinner bell in one hand and a ladle in the other. "C'mon, y'all, wash up," she said, clanging the triangle like she was rushing to a four-alarm fire. "It's suppahtime!"

. . .

Everyone else in the United States has agreed to call the day's major meals breakfast, lunch, and dinner. For no reason I could think of other than to confuse everyone else, Southerners insist on having breakfast, dinner, and supper.

But what a supper it was.

I smelled it long before I saw it: it was fried chicken, Southern-style. The aroma hit me full force as soon as I stepped into the kitchen. Silently beckoning from the center of a massive, round wood table was a huge silver platter piled high with mounds of crispy, golden-brown chicken parts, steaming stacks of breasts surrounded by jumbled heaps of thighs and legs.

On each side of the platter was a big serving bowl overflowing with mashed potatoes. Next to them were smaller bowls of greasy, mouthwatering milk gravy. Beans, peas, and corn on the cob competed for table space with sliced tomatoes, cornbread, and butter. Somehow Aunt Nelda had even managed to find room for two big pitchers, one filled with iced tea and the other with watery-looking milk.

"Don't be shy, boys," she said to Charley and me, "hep yourselves."

I didn't have to be told twice. In the blink of an eye my plate was a plain of chicken legs, a sea of string beans and black-eyed peas, and a volcanic mountain of mashed potatoes, complete with a gravy crater lake.

Things are definitely looking up, I thought as I sat down to feed. *I might even gain some weight this summer.*

I had just reached for the saltshaker when Mom put her hand on my shoulder and said, "Hold on, honey, let's wait for grace."

"Where *is* she?" I asked, unable to tear my eyes away from my plate. "I can't wait much longer."

"Not *Aunt* Grace. We need to give the blessing first."

"Oh, let 'em go ahead, Laverne," said Aunt Nelda. "It's late. Besides, the Lord won't mind. He knows they're thankful, huh, boys?"

I cast a quick glance Heavenward and vigorously nodded my head.

"Go on now, dig in," Aunt Nelda ordered.

I grabbed my shovel and started digging. About three minutes later I set it down and resumed breathing. Except for the chicken bones, my plate was empty.

I knew it wasn't polite to have seconds until everyone else had filled their plates, so there wasn't much else to do for the next few minutes but sip my iced tea and Observe the Natives.

One of my favorite games was Alien Anthropologist, where I was an advance scout from another planet, sent to Earth to secretly study humans in their natural habitat. I tuned out the background clatter of silverware on dishes and prepared myself to enter Observer Mode. I silently repeated the Mission Directive, "See everything, miss nothing," then brought my concentration into sharp focus and initiated Scan Phase.

To my left, Dad was telling Mom's older brother Robert about the accident investigation school he'd be going to the week after next. Uncle Robert was too busy eating to say much in return, but he was a World War II veteran himself, and his periodic grunts were obvious signs of interest.

Uncle Robert's wife, Dorothy, sat next to him, listening to Aunt Marjorie chatter away about a new dress shop in Leesville. Aunt Dorothy was doing her best to seem interested, but her frequent darting glances around the table indicated otherwise.

Aunt Marjorie appeared to be the only fashionable one in the family, her stylish red-and-white polka-dot dress obviously store-bought. With her bright red lipstick and black crayon eyebrows, she looked remarkably like a portrait of Mom I'd finger-painted in kindergarten.

The pleasant-looking man to Aunt Marjorie's left was Uncle Cecil, the younger of Mom's two brothers. His wife's fashion sense must have rubbed off on him, since he was the only Miller male who wasn't wearing bib overalls. His ugly brown-and-tan plaid shirt wasn't much of an improvement, however.

Uncle Cecil flashed me a knowing smile, and I suddenly realized that he'd been watching me Observing them. A split-second later I knew that he knew that I knew I'd been caught. A diversionary tactic was in order.

"Uncle Cecil, could you please pass the cornbread?"

Mom looked at me in surprise. "Since when do you like cornbread?"

"Just thought I'd try it. Maybe I'll like it now."

I was the only one in my family who hated cornbread; it was just more bad luck that it was the only thing in front of Uncle Cecil.

"Thank you," I said, taking the smallest piece on the plate.

Everyone else had started eating by then, so it was the perfect time to ask for seconds. When my plate was loaded up again, I casually took a bite out of another leg and continued Scanning, but more carefully this time.

The oldest Miller sister, Grace, was seated next to Uncle Cecil, at the one-o'clock position. With her bigger nose, fuller lips, and dour expression, Aunt Grace didn't much resemble Mom or Aunt Nelda. She and Uncle Nolan hadn't been "blessed with children of their own," as Mom put it.

Uncle Nolan leaned slightly to his right and said

something I couldn't catch to Aunt Grace. She shook her head, the corners of her mouth turning down even more. He shrugged and then leaned back and took another sip of what looked like whiskey.

Aunt Nelda sat next to Uncle Nolan, or at least she did when she wasn't bouncing up to fuss over something or other. Between refilling serving bowls and checking pots on the stove, she couldn't have eaten much. Not that she needed it.

PawPaw didn't seem to be eating much, either, but that was probably because he ate so slowly. Every forkful seemed to take forever to get to his mouth, and eons for him to chew. He even swallowed in slow motion, making it look like a snail was inching its way down his throat.

Mom turned to him and asked, "Can I get you anything, Daddy?"

He patted her forearm. "No, sugah, doin' fine. Nice t' have ya home." I wasn't sure, but his eyes seemed to tear up a little. Maybe it was just the lighting.

Then he yawned and said, "Think I'll turn in now. Been a long day."

He pushed himself stiffly out of his chair and slowly left the kitchen to a chorus of 'Night, Daddys or 'Night, PawPaws.

"Don't let the bedbugs bite," Mom said softly.

The momentary hush brought on by PawPaw's departure was suddenly shattered by the sound of glass breaking. "Dang it, Gary, look what ya made me do!" Woody snarled from the small square table next to the Frigidaire.

"I didn't make ya do nothin'!" Gary said. "It was your fault for startin' it."

Woody shook his head and scowled. "You lie like a rug."

Aunt Dorothy came to the rescue. "Quit fussin', you two," she said, rising from her chair. "Just sit still now while I get this mess picked up." The drab linoleum floor next to their table was spattered with pale milk and jagged shards of glass.

I couldn't resist. "That's right, boys," I said with a smirk, "no use lyin' over spilt milk." Everyone laughed but Woody.

Mom stood and said, "We'll take care of the kitchen. Why don't y'all go on out t' the porch an' visit."

By "y'all" she must have meant the menfolk, because they were the only ones who moved. Dad and all three uncles put their napkins down almost simultaneously, said their thank-yous, then got up and paraded out of the kitchen.

Charley and I weren't far behind.

6

Bug Off!

Eavesdropping, or as Observers call it, Listening, wasn't always interesting when the subjects were adults. As I Listened to Dad and my uncles on our way out to the porch, I knew right away that their conversation was going to be no different from hundreds of others I'd Heard, about the weather and the economy and people I didn't know.

But even if they'd been talking about local UFO sightings and little green men, I wouldn't have been able to concentrate for long on what they were saying. That was because of the bugs.

It wasn't that I hadn't seen any earlier. I'd noticed all the moths flitting around the floodlight when I'd gotten out of the car, and had definitely been aware of the fact that there were a lot of other things buzzing around my head, but they hadn't seemed threatening.

Evidently though, they were just the reconnaissance drones, sent ahead to scout out suitable targets, because the instant Charley and I stepped out onto the porch, the main force surrounded us. They swarmed in a vibrating cloud over our heads, millions of tiny wings flickering in and out of the harsh yellow light of the bare bulb above the screen door.

They followed us over to the swing, maintaining formation while we made futile attempts to swat them away with our hands. They must have interpreted our gestures as hostile, because that's when they began their attack.

Suddenly squadrons of minuscule mosquitoes peeled away from the swarm and started strafing our faces. Then the larger ones began dive-bombing us from all sides, wave after wave of them bombarding our position on the porch swing. I slapped at my neck and arms as one after another bit me, the red smears on my palms and fingers evidence of their successful kamikaze missions.

It was obvious that defensive countermeasures were called for, so I began swinging my legs faster, on the theory that a rapidly moving target would be more difficult to hit. My strategy had no effect on the aerial blitzkrieg; all it did was send the swing shimmying out of control, nearly throwing us off.

"Let's get out of here!" I said, bailing out. We both hit the deck running.

As I yanked the screen door open I heard Uncle Cecil say, "Skeeters ain't too bad tonight."

Charley and I burst into the sitting room just as our cousins entered it from the kitchen, where they'd had to wait for Aunt Dorothy to clean up the broken glass. They took the sofa, and my brother and I plopped onto mismatched old armchairs.

A few moments of awkward silence followed before Gary said, "Hey, y'all wanna listen t' the radio?"

"I'd rather watch television," I said and then, remembering my manners, added, "if that's okay with you guys."

"Fine by us," said Woody. He waited for a couple of beats while I scanned the room for its location. "Too bad for you we ain't got one."

I was speechless.

Charley wasn't. "So what do you guys do for entertainment around here?"

"We make do," said Woody.

"Listen t' the radio," Barry said, moving toward the corner next to the window. "I'll turn it on." He crouched down in front of a large antique cabinet, pulled open its doors, and twisted a dial.

Nothing happened for a few seconds, and then a faint hum came out of it, gradually increasing in volume until it was replaced by loud hissing and crackling. Barry adjusted the tuner, and the interstellar static was suddenly drowned out by the twang of steel guitars and an obnoxious nasal voice singing something about hillbilly heaven.

"Turn it down," ordered Woody. "PawPaw's tryin' t' sleep."

I was trying to think of a polite way to ask them to turn it *all* the way down when Mom called out from the kitchen, "Is that Conway Twitty I hear?"

A second later she was standing in the doorway, a dish towel in her hand and a smile on her face. "Mitch doesn't much care for country-western," she said, "but y'all know what good music is, don'tcha, boys?"

"Yes, ma'am," Gary agreed.

"Only music worth lis'nin' to, Aunt Laverne," said Barry.

Mom flipped the towel onto her shoulder, then stepped between Woody and me. "Nice to see all you boys together," she said, a catch in her voice. "There's nothin' like family."

"Amen t' that, Li'l Sis," Aunt Nelda said, joining us from the kitchen. She stopped next to Mom, looked back and forth between Woody and me, then crossed her arms and said, "Laverne, I swan if the two a them don't look alike.

"Look," she pointed out, "same strong chin an' high cheekbones, like Daddy's, same nose, straight as an arrow. Ears a little diff'rent, Mitch's lobes is biggah, but them cowlicks is like two peas in a pod."

I had to admit that Aunt Nelda was right about the cowlicks. Woody's hair was more brown than black, but the only difference other than that was the source of the bad haircuts.

Aunt Nelda still wasn't through. "In fact, I reckon if Woody's eyes wasn't brown, folks'd think they was brothahs."

Mom got into the act next. "I see what you mean, Nelda; about the only other thing different is their mouths." Then she grinned. "Mitch's is bigger."

It was a perfect setup. "That's for sure," Charley said, getting a laugh all around.

I was sure they would have gone on like that all night, but Dad saved me. "Let's get the car unloaded, boys," he said through the screen door. "If you'll all grab something, we can do it in one trip."

I was the first one out.

. . .

As I stood in the tall, wet grass next to the De Soto, watching Dad lift suitcases out of the trunk, I assessed my situation. I'd known from the beginning that the summer wasn't going to be a trip to paradise, but the reality was even worse than I'd imagined. Like Jiminy Cricket, Mom had always told me to accentuate the positive, so that's what I decided to try.

In the minus column were hick cousins, no television, intolerable weather, and bugs. On the plus side was food.

Four to one. Sorry, Mom.

As Dad slammed the trunk lid shut, Charley asked, "Where's Rebel?"

He was nowhere in sight. Dad whistled for him, and Charley and I called out his name, but he didn't come.

"Probably just exploring," Dad assured us. "Mitch, you empty out the car while the rest of us take this stuff in, okay?"

I opened my car door and climbed in back. I stepped right on Rebel, who was lying on the floor, his head on the transmission hump, ears tucked back.

"I don't blame you, boy," I said, patting his head. "I'd do the same thing if I could."

Rebel refused to come out, so I left him there, with the door open in case he changed his mind, grabbed the pillows and everything else I could carry, and followed the line of luggage into the house and down the hall. That's when I saw Woody's room.

Make that five to one.

I took two steps into it and stopped, my head directly beneath a bare lightbulb socketed into the ceiling. Two more steps and I would have crashed into the opposite wall. In Woody's room that could have been fatal.

"Watch out for the horns," Gary said as he set my suitcase down next to Charley's on the hardwood floor.

"Count on it." I stared at the paneled wall across from me. Staring back were a dozen or so sun-bleached animal skulls, knotty yellowish pine showing through their empty eye sockets. Half that many pairs of crudely mounted steer horns stood guard among them, a barrier of protective bone.

Guarding those were the ones Gary was referring to, a giant set of varnished bull horns mounted at eye level and projecting dangerously into the room. I dumped my load on the floor and reached out a thumb to test the sharpness of one of the tips. It was sharp enough.

Barry materialized to my right. "How'd ya like t' be on the wrong enda them babies?"

"I almost was. So what's the story with Bullzilla here?"

He grinned and said, "That was Big Buck, the meanest Brahma bull ya ever saw. Fin'lly died a coupla years ago."

"From what?"

"Orn'riness, prob'ly."

"Don't miss him one bit," said Gary. "He like t' killed me a coupla times."

I heard a toilet flush.

"Holy moly," Charley said from the corner next to the window. "Is this a cat skull?"

"Hey, careful with that," Woody said from the doorway behind me. "I ain't shellacked it yet."

Charley gently set the skull back down on the antique dresser. "Where'd you get all this great stuff?"

Woody smiled for the first time. "Found most of it. Glad ya like it."

I scratched a bug bite on my neck and said, "Charley collects weird stuff, too."

"I'm going to be a scientist when I grow up," Charley said.

"A *mad* scientist," I cracked, throwing Woody a grin.

Woody didn't throw it back. He just pointed to the dresser and said, "Y'all git the bottom two drawers. Mama made me empty 'em out for ya. Cots're yours, too."

I looked at the two olive-drab rectangles of drooping canvas, then glanced past them at the comfortable-looking twin bed in the corner.

"Bed's mine," he said.

Just then Mom barged into the room. "You boys gettin' settled, Mitch?"

"Like the pioneers," I said.

"Good. It's been a long trip; we could all use a good night's sleep."

"No such thing as a bad night's sleep, Mom."

. . .

One Saturday morning a couple of years back, Charley and I had had a discussion about roosters. We'd been watching a Merry Melodies cartoon where Bugs Bunny fools Elmer Fudd's barnyard rooster into crowing at night. The instant he cried "Cockle-doodle-doo," I started in.

"That's so phony," I said. "Roosters don't go 'Cockle-doodle-doo,' they go 'Er-erer-erer.' Any nitwit knows that."

"No they don't," he said defensively. "If they went 'Er-erer-erer,' he would've done it that way in the cartoon."

At the time Charley was still at the age where cartoons and real life were pretty much the same thing, and since we didn't know anyone with a rooster, the matter never had been properly resolved.

Until our first morning on the farm, that is.

I was sitting up in my cot, my back against the wall, numbly gazing at the dawn sky through the screen of Woody's open window. Pearly gray and pale pink streamers had gradually streaked the eastern horizon, washing out all but the brightest stars.

The instant the sun rose the resident rooster announced it, apparently using a powerful public address system located just outside the window and set to maximum volume.

"COCKLE-DOODLE-DOO!"

Charley opened his eyes and grinned at me from his cot. "See?" he whispered triumphantly, "I *told* you it wasn't 'Er-erer-erer'!"

"All right," I whispered back, "so it sounded *sorta* like 'Cockle-doodle-doo.' "

Mighty Mouth's second crow settled the issue for good. It was even louder than the first, a bone-jarring, filling-rattling, ear-shattering, all-out sonic attack: *"COCKLE-DOODLE-DOO!"*

It sounded just like the cartoon.

"Okay, wise guy," I conceded, "so this rooster watches Merry Melodies. The rest of 'em *still* go 'Er-erer-erer.'"

"You just hate being wrong, that's all."

Charley was right; in fact, I hated being even a little wrong. And I had been completely wrong about there being no such thing as a bad night's sleep.

It started with the bug bites. By the time everyone had gone home and Charley and I had stripped down to our jockeys for bed, he'd been bitten, by my count, twenty-nine times, mostly on his legs. I had more bites than that on my arms alone.

". . . thirty-eight, thirty-nine," Charley finished, his left index finger aimed at a burning, itching welt in the middle of my forehead.

"Forty," I said, pointing to my underwear and grimacing.

"Y'all need anything?" Aunt Nelda asked from the doorway.

I automatically reached for my jeans.

Aunt Nelda took a step toward me and said, "Lordy, boy, you been eaten alive! You, too, Charley." She turned and called down the hall, "Laverne, let's get the calamine."

About ten minutes later Charley and I were dotted all over with ugly pink splotches, like atomic mutants. "Well, that should help the itching," Mom said as she gathered up the used cotton balls. "Try to get some rest now."

Hours later I was still trying, but so were the heat and humidity. The fans Woody had mentioned hadn't helped, since neither one was in our room.

Woody didn't appear to be affected by it. He'd said a quick " 'Night," turned his back to us, and immediately fallen asleep. Or done a great job of faking it.

Charley and I weren't so lucky. We twisted and thrashed for hours, sweltering in the stifling heat. He'd finally passed out after midnight, from dehydration I guessed, judging by the pool of sweat I was floating in. I probably wouldn't have been too far behind. But then the calamine wore off.

On one of our sleepovers Tick and I had somehow ended up talking about Heaven and Hell. At the time I hadn't been convinced of the existence of either one.

But by the end of that first night on the farm, after a sleepless eternity of tossing and turning on a saggy cot and sticking to soggy sheets, after countless eons of breathing superheated liquid air and trying to scratch everywhere at once, I arrived at a slightly different conclusion. I decided then and there that while I still wasn't sure about Heaven, I knew for a fact there was a Hell. And that it couldn't be any worse than Pitkin, Louisiana.

. . .

Dad and PawPaw both nodded greetings over their steaming mugs as I shuffled past them at the dining table and slumped down onto the straight-backed chair next to Mom.

"Mornin', Mitch," Aunt Nelda said from the stove, where she was turning thick strips of sizzling bacon. "Sleep well?"

"Okay."

"Calamine help?" Mom asked as she poured cream into her coffee.

"For a while."

Mom looked me over while she stirred it. "Looks like it's worn off. Let's put some more on you."

I offered no complaint, so she abandoned her cup after one sip and walked me back to Woody's room. He hadn't budged.

Charley had. The *kerchug* of the toilet flushing was quickly followed by the sound of his bare feet softly padding down the hall and back to bed. He plopped down onto his cot, flopped the back of his hand onto his forehead, and let out a dramatic sigh.

Mom rolled her eyes at him. "Guess I'd better put some more of this on you, too." He didn't complain either.

I got my second wind after breakfast, or, rather, because of it. The bacon and coffee smells in the kitchen were soon joined by the aromas of homemade biscuits, milk gravy, and fried eggs, and eventually the dining table was almost as crammed as it had been the night before. And like the night before, I ate everything in sight. Except for one thing.

"Don't care for grits neithah?" PawPaw asked me,

then dabbed his cloth napkin at the corners of his mouth.

"Nosir, not really," I said, jabbing another forkful of egg into mine.

"Never would eat 'em, Daddy," said Mom.

"Cain't be a Southanah if ya don't like cornbread or grits," Aunt Nelda teased. "Woody, soon's ya finish up, why don't ya show the boys around?" It wasn't really a question.

Woody had joined us at the table just as his eggs were coming out of the skillet, then had quickly filled the rest of his plate and gotten down to business. He hadn't said a word the entire time. " 'Kay, Mama," he muttered obediently.

"Go on, now," Mom said to Charley and me. "Y'all take a good look at where your mama grew up."

· · ·

The back porch steps led to a small yard of hard-packed red dirt broken by patches of sparse grass. Past the yard and to our left a low chicken-wire fence enclosed a large vegetable garden. A half dozen cows loitered in the pasture beyond the garden, framed by a wide field of tall corn that seemed to stretch all the way to the pines on the horizon.

As I Scanned to the right, I saw three pigs in a pen and a corral with no horse, but since there was a haystack under the massive oak, I figured they probably had one.

"So *this* is what a farm looks like," I said to Charley.

Woody came up behind me a split second before the kitchen screen door banged shut. "It's what *this* farm looks like."

"Is that the barn over there?" Charley asked as he pointed to the right toward a large, dilapidated wood-and-tin structure about thirty yards off.

"No, you idiot!" I snapped. "It's a top-secret nuclear research facility!" It was an instant reflex, since Charley's enthusiasm had exceeded the level a person in my condition could reasonably be expected to tolerate at that hour.

"He always like this?" Woody asked him.

"Not always," he said in a small voice.

Oops.

But before I could apologize, a loud commotion erupted, followed immediately by a huge red rooster that streaked around the corner of the house, high-stepping and squawking as if his life depended on it.

I guess it did, because Rebel came snarling around the same corner a second later, hot on its tail. Hot on Rebel's heels came the rest of the canine attack pack, all three of them yapping maniacally and snapping at empty air. I didn't know if they'd worked out their differences with Rebel or had only called a temporary truce in pursuit of the rooster.

Either way, they all tore across the yard in front of us, a blur of blood-red feathers and flying fur, then skidded around the other corner of the house and disappeared. Slowly settling dust and rapidly fading barks and clucks were the only reminders of their passing.

"If that's the loudmouth that broke my eardrums," I said, "I hope they get him."

"It is," said Woody, "and they won't."

"How do *you* know? Rebel's pretty fast."

He gave me a blank stare and said, "Dog ain't done it yet." Then he skipped down the porch steps and headed in the direction of the barn.

I turned to Charley, intending to give him my what's-with-him? look, but he'd already jumped the two steps down to the yard and hustled off to catch up with Woody.

. . .

I dragged myself back into the kitchen about fifteen minutes later. Mom and Aunt Nelda were the only ones there, still working on the breakfast dishes. "That didn't take very long," Aunt Nelda said, raising what looked to me like a suspicious eyebrow.

"Well, Mitch, what do you think?" Mom asked with a grin. "Can't you just see your ol' mama pitchin' hay and sloppin' hogs? I did, you know."

"That she did," Aunt Nelda said as she wiped a kettle, "and as good as her brothahs, too."

"Well, Ma," I said, trying to wipe the sweat off my brow with the bottom of my damp T-shirt, "now I know what a farm looks like."

Now I know what it smells *like, too.*

Until then I'd been under the impression that I'd already experienced all of life's foulest odors. After all, I'd endured years of classrooms that reeked of B.O., halitosis, and stale flatulence, had smelled a dead cat, and had even survived driving cross-country with Dad. But none of those experiences prepared me for the stench of a working farm.

I lost my second wind the second I got my first wind of it. It smelled like crap. Not figurative crap, like "junk" or "garbage," but literal crap. As in "feces."

There was crap everywhere. Horse crap, cow crap, pig crap, dog crap, chicken crap, it seemed to cover every square inch of ground. And it came in all shapes and sizes, from crap pellets and crap logs to crap patties and crap pancakes. There were piles of corn-laced crap, straw-filled crap, old dried-up crap, and fresh fly-covered crap. I even saw crap on top of crap.

It was enough to make anyone throw up.

"Where's Charley and Woody?" Aunt Nelda asked.

"I dunno," I said, leaning up against the refrigerator for support, "probably still in the barn. Could I have a glass of orange juice, Aunt Nelda? I don't feel very well."

As Aunt Nelda got a glass from the cupboard, Mom walked over to me and felt my forehead. "Could be runnin' a slight fever," she pronounced. "Hard t' tell in this heat. I'll get the Bayer just in case."

I soon had a glass of cold, fresh-squeezed orange

juice in one hand and two orange aspirin tablets in the other. I looked at Mom and joked halfheartedly, "Take these and call you tomorrow?"

"Exactly. Then go lie down on our bed. You look like you could use some sleep."

Truer words had never been spoken.

7

Hamburger Heaven

It took me a while to wake up, about eleven hours, as close as I could figure. I vaguely remembered Mom trying to rouse me a couple of times, but I'd ignored her and she'd eventually gone away. Dad's ring finally did the trick.

I found him and Mom on the front porch with Paw-Paw and Aunt Nelda, sitting in rocking chairs and chatting in the early evening heat. Dad took a big swig from a sweaty can of Hamm's beer and said, "Gonna live, sport?"

"Huh?" I said, still only half conscious.

"I asked if you were still among the living."

"Yeah, more or less. Where's Charley?" I asked.

Aunt Nelda pointed in my direction with her glass of iced tea. "Out in the north forty with Woody."

"They went exploring with Rebel after lunch," Mom

said as she fanned herself with a magazine. "Should've been back by now," she added, a hint of worry in her voice.

"When's supper, Aunt Nelda?" I tried not to stare at the tiny beads of sweat that dotted her upper lip.

"Soon, it's fixin' now. Pull up a chair and set a spell."

Luckily, just then Charley yelled out my name from a distance. I turned in the direction of his voice and saw him and Woody emerge from the pinewoods that edged the field about a hundred yards off. Rebel wasn't with them.

When I still hadn't seen him after a few more seconds, I started to hit the panic button, but he finally showed up, padding slowly along, his head down and tail dragging.

Aunt Nelda sighed and hoisted herself out of her rocking chair. "Well, guess I'll see t' suppah."

Mom got up, too, and followed her to the screen door. "Tell Charley he'll need a bath first thing, okay?"

"Okay," Dad and I answered at the same time.

I eased into Mom's rocking chair without interrupting its motion and watched the expedition return. Charley's lips were flapping a mile a minute, his hands gesturing wildly in obvious excitement. I didn't see Woody say anything, but I did notice him put his arm around Charley's shoulders.

"Well, if it isn't Lewis and Clark," I said as they clambered up the steps.

"Have fun, buddy?" asked Dad.

"Yeah, Dad, this place is great!" Charley gushed. "To-morrow we're gonna go to the *south* forty, aren't we, Woody?"

Before Woody could answer, Dad said, "Afraid that'll have to wait, son, we're going into town tomorrow."

"What for?" I asked.

"I have to service the car, and your mother needs to get a few things." Then he grinned. "Why, you have a date?"

Normally I would have grinned back. "Just wanted to know, that's all."

"We'll also visit Robert and Dorothy and the boys," he said, pausing to glance at Charley and Woody empty-ing their pockets on the porch swing, "and by the looks of things, you could use the company."

PawPaw chuckled from the rocker next to Dad's. "Dog looks plum tuckered out."

Rebel had finally reached the bottom of the steps and stopped, his ID tags clinking softly in time with his rapid panting. He tentatively lifted a paw onto the first step and held it there, staring at the top one as if it were Mount Everest.

Dad whistled softly and patted his thigh. "Come on, boy."

Rebel looked at Dad, hesitated again, then slowly started up the steps. After an agonizingly slow ascent, he finally made it to the top and then collapsed in a heap at my feet, too tired to stand any longer. I was exhausted just from watching him.

He rested there for a few seconds, trying vainly to get his tongue back into his mouth, then started crawling on his belly toward Dad, like Lassie crossing Death Valley to get help for little Timmy.

Rebel got just close enough for Dad to be able to pet him, then rolled over onto his side and lay still, his chest heaving and the tip of his tail softly thumping the porch boards.

"Reckon he's awful hot with all that hair," said Paw-Paw.

Reckon he'd *like to go home now, too.*

"Mitch, look at all the great bugs Woody helped me find," Charley said from the swing.

"A little later, okay, squirt? Mom said for you to take a bath before supper." I got up from the rocker and started inside. "I'll go find you a towel."

I had my fingers on the screen door handle when Charley said, "That's okay, Woody'll get me one, won't you, Woody?"

I'd already committed myself, so I opened the door and went on in. I didn't mean to slam it quite so loudly.

· · ·

Aunt Nelda had another feast waiting for us on the table, pot roast and potatoes with all the trimmings, but even though I hadn't eaten anything since breakfast, for some reason I didn't have much of an appetite.

"No seconds tonight, Mitch?" she asked when I folded my napkin and set it down next to my empty plate.

"No, ma'am, savin' room for dessert."

After the dishes were done, Aunt Nelda served up homemade vanilla ice cream and fresh strawberries, which we ate on the front porch. Although it was getting dark, the porch light hadn't been turned on yet, so when the first fireflies came out we spotted them at once. Charley immediately abandoned his position on the front steps, where he and Woody had been lost in quiet conversation since supper.

"Look, Woody, fireflies!" he said, like he'd never seen one before. "Let's catch some!" He ran out into the yard, flailing his arms like an escaped mental patient.

"I'll get the jars," Woody said as he dashed into the house. He was back a few seconds later, holding a large lidded jar in each hand. He quickly crossed the porch to the steps and then abruptly stopped next to the railing, as if he'd forgotten something. He looked over his shoulder at me and said, "Want one, too?"

"That's okay, I'll just watch."

"Don't like lightnin' bugs neithah?"

"They're all right, I'm just not in the mood."

He shrugged and said, "Suit yourself," then shuffled down the steps to join Charley.

Super Rooster woke Charley and me up again at sunrise, but fortunately we were able to fall back asleep for a couple of hours, until Mom got us up for breakfast.

As I was polishing off my last stack of pancakes, she walked by my chair, wrinkled her nose at me, and said, "Bath time, stinky, we're goin' into town in a bit."

I quickly sniffed my armpit to see if maybe I didn't really need one, but to tell the truth I was getting pretty ripe, even for me.

By the time I got clean clothes, a towel and washcloth, and latched the bathroom door, I'd become so aware of the slime covering my body that I was almost looking forward to the bath. Until I looked inside the tub, that is.

Of course I'd used the bathroom a bunch of times already to brush my teeth and take care of more urgent business, but I'd been in and out so fast that I hadn't really paid much attention to it. I had noticed the ancient, foggy-mirrored medicine cabinet on the mildewy wall above the sink, and couldn't help but see the gross rust stains in the basin directly beneath the faucet. But I'd only glanced at the tub, a freestanding, four-clawed white monster that looked deep enough to give you the bends.

When I leaned over it to turn the taps on, I saw that its bottom was completely covered with rough-looking, brownish-red rust. The instant I touched it, its sandpapery surface sent shivers up and down my spine, worse than fingernails on a blackboard.

No way am I putting my bare bottom on this.

Since the faucet only produced a trickle of brownish water, I had plenty of time to think about it. By the time the tub was finally full enough, I'd already decided my underwear wasn't coming off.

It was probably the quickest bath in history, but I did get clean. Or at least as clean as I could get in a bath in my underwear, since all the junk that I just washed off got right back on me when I got up out of the water. But it did make my bug bites itch a little less.

. . .

"Well, you certainly look better," Mom said as I walked onto the front porch, dressed in clean Levi's and my other favorite shirt, a red-and-white striped boatneck. "Smell better, too," she just had to add.

Dad slid his aviator sunglasses on. "Let's saddle up. Robert's expecting us by ten."

Charley slid off the porch swing to join us. "Isn't Woody coming?" I asked him in what I meant to be a sarcastic tone of voice.

He shook his head. "He's got chores to do."

"He'll be at Robert and Dorothy's for supper," Mom informed me. "But it's nice that y'all are gettin' along."

After Dad fishtailed out onto the road to town, Mom turned to Charley and me and said, "Ready for your first trip to Pitkin, boys?" like it was New York City.

About three minutes later we were pulling into a small, run-down-looking Gulf station at the corner where the gravel intersected the asphalt of the main highway. Uncle Robert stopped stacking oil cans when he saw us, grinned, and waved Dad forward into the service bay. Just when I was sure we were going to crush him against the back wall, he held up a grimy paw and said, "That's good, Marc. Shut 'er down."

As we all piled out of the car, he wiped his hands on his greasy gray coveralls and said, "Mornin', Sis. Hey, boys. Why don't y'all go on inta the cafe while me an' Marc talk 'bout this here De Soto."

Charley and I followed Mom past the two orange gas pumps to the screen door at the other end of the building. I was holding it open for them when Uncle Robert yelled, "Help yourselves t' whatever ya want, boys, it's on me."

The first thing I noticed was that we were the only people in the cafe. All four booths were empty, as were the six stools in front of the counter and the grill area behind it.

"Sure is quiet in here," Charley began, looking at me expectantly.

"*Too* quiet," I finished with a worried nod.

The only sounds were the soft, rhythmic squeaks of a slowly turning ceiling fan and the high hum of a rapidly swiveling one set on a wooden chair next to an unplugged jukebox in the far corner.

"I'm thirsty, Mom," Charley said, eyeing the massive red Coca-Cola machine that sat beneath the backward "Robert's Cafe" lettering on the front window. "Can we have a soda?"

I walked over to the machine and lifted its heavy lid. Inside was soft drink heaven, row after row of bottled sodas suspended by their caps in ice-filled water. Uncle Robert had them all, from Coca-Colas, Dr Peppers, and Hires Root Beers to Nehi grapes and cream sodas.

The instant Mom nodded approval, Charley slid a Nehi grape along the parallel metal strips of one row, then I pinched the top of a Dr Pepper and moved it out of another. We popped the caps in the opener on the front of the machine and greedily took our first gulps. The soda was so cold it burned my throat and made my teeth ache.

We each picked one of the red vinyl stools and bellied up to the counter. That's when I noticed the candy and gum racks next to the stacked-up cigar boxes against the wall.

"Would it be okay to have a Moon Pie, Mom?" I asked hopefully.

"Not at ten in the morning, young man," she said, checking her makeup in the mirror of her compact. "Be thankful I'm lettin' you have a soda this time of day."

"You boys git what ya want?" Uncle Robert asked as he and Dad walked into the cafe.

"Yessir, Uncle Robert, thanks," said Charley.

"Robert says it'll take a couple of hours for the car," Dad told Mom, "so why don't you and the boys go on and do your shopping while I keep him company."

Mom shot Dad her you-owe-me-for-this look. "Come on, boys," she said, snapping the compact shut and dropping it back into her purse. "Finish your drinks and I'll give y'all the Pitkin grand tour."

"An' when ya get back," Uncle Robert said, "your aunt Dorothy'll fix y'all the best hamburgers ya ever ate in your life."

. . .

Mom's so-called grand tour of Pitkin could have been over in about ten minutes, but she managed to drag it out for almost the full two hours. I ended up being glad she did, though, because otherwise I wouldn't have met Finn when I did.

After we walked past Uncle Robert's automobile graveyard, the small lot next to his garage that housed the half dozen wrecks I'd seen the night we arrived, we went into the small market next door. Mom had known the elderly couple that owned it ever since she'd been a little girl, or "knee high to a grasshopper," as Mrs. Whateverhernamewas said, so it took them a while to catch up.

Mr. Whateverhisnamewas wasn't nearly as talkative as his wife, not that he could have gotten a word in anyway, and was hard of hearing as well, but he seemed okay. Maybe that was because he gave Charley and me each a free candy bar, and then, even after seeing that Mom didn't exactly approve, sneaked us a handful of Bazooka bubble gum when she wasn't looking.

The next building was boarded up, so we kept on moving. The surface we'd been walking on, a hard-packed mixture of dirty red clay, pebbles, bottle caps, and oil stains, suddenly turned into a wood-plank sidewalk. Unfortunately I was looking for bottle caps, so I didn't notice that until after I tripped on it.

My catlike reflexes fortunately enabled me to quickly recover, and since there were hardly any people out on the street, I was pretty sure the incident had gone unnoticed. Except, of course, by Mom and Charley. He started to crack wise but thought better of it when he saw my face.

"I think I broke my big toe," I moaned, forcing back tears. There was an old wooden bench in front of the first window of the Mercantile, so I quickly hopped over to it and sat down. "Gimme a coupla minutes, okay, Mom?" I started massaging my throbbing toe through the thin canvas of my cross-countries.

"How old's this building?" asked Mr. Curiosity.

"I think it was built in aught-seven," Mom said.

"Which century?" I muttered.

"Most of the others were up by the twenties," Mom continued, ignoring me.

I decided I preferred a sore toe to Mom's history lesson. "Okay, I think I can walk now."

"We'll do our shopping last," Mom said. "I don't want to have to carry everything all over town."

We continued past the Mercantile to the red-brick building next door, which was also out of business. "This used to be Finkey's Drugstore," Mom said. "I had a vanilla phosphate here first Saturday of every month for years."

"What's a phosphate?" Charley asked.

"It's what we used to call ice cream sodas," she said to him. "Watch your step, Grace," she said to me.

The sidewalk ended at what used to be Finkey's. Pitkin ended a block down, after Polson's Grocery Store, an Esso gas station, a small general store, and another cafe. I figured we'd be back at Uncle Robert's in no time.

I figured wrong. Mom spent twenty more minutes visiting at Polson's, and we wasted about the same amount of time at the service station before we finally got back to the Pitkin Mercantile.

The biggest building in town, the Mercantile looked like a frontier general store from a Hollywood western. It stocked everything from grain and feed to needles and thread. Barrels of nails, screws, and bolts stood next to rakes, pitchforks, and shovels. Shelves jammed with medicines and salves stuck out over bins full of soaps and cleaners, sponges and steel wool. About the only thing it didn't have was magazines and comic books.

Again Mom introduced Charley and me to the owners, a silver-haired couple named Finnerty. Charley stayed with Mom, so I just wandered around by myself, killing time.

I happened to be in the men's and boys' clothing section, feeling the stiff, rough denim of a stack of bib overalls, when someone behind me said, "Needa new paira overalls?"

"Like I need more bug bites," I said, then turned around.

Facing me was a muscular kid who looked to be a year or two older and three or four inches taller than I was. He swept a lock of wavy black hair off his forehead and said with a smile, "Yeah, them skeeters jus' love city blood."

"How'd you know I'm from the city?"

"Shore ain't from round here." His dark, shiny eyes stared at my racers. "So where'd ya git them slick shoes?"

"California. So how come you're not wearing overalls?" He had on faded blue jeans, a white T-shirt, and black high-top Keds. "Everyone else around here does."

"Overalls?" He sneered. "I don't need no stinking overalls."

I couldn't help but smile.

"Them's fer farm boys. I'm a city boy, jus' like you."

He held out his right hand. "Name's Finn."

"Mitch," I said, shaking it. "I'm visiting the Millers for the summer."

"Yeah, I know."

"Oh yeah? You know Woody?"

"Oh yeah, I know Woody," he said in a tone of voice that told me they weren't exactly blood brothers.

I finally made the connection. "Finn, like short for Finnerty? Those are your parents?" I asked, looking past him toward the back of the store, where they were still visiting with Mom.

He slowly nodded. "Purdy old, ain't they?"

"That's not what I meant. Finnerty, as in your house is air-conditioned?"

"Yeah. What of it?"

"Think your folks would adopt me for the summer?"

Finn smiled again. "You'll get used to it. They tell ya 'bout the swimmin' hole yet?"

I shook my head. "First I've heard of it."

"Git Woody an' the boys t' take ya there. Me an' m' boys go there near ev'ry day. I'll innerduce ya to 'em."

"That'd be great."

"Man, I like them shoes," he said, checking out my cross-countries again. "Too bad they're too small for me or I'd buy 'em off ya. Well, gotta go get some money from the ol' man; m' boys're waitin' on me at the cafe."

"Robert's Cafe?"

He paused for a second before answering. "Naw, Dixie's, down the other way. Drop on in sometime."

"Hey, thanks, I will. Really."

Finn turned to leave.

"Seeya around," I said.

"Not if I see ya first," he said over his shoulder as he wove his way through a cluster of clothing racks. He walked right up to the old-fashioned brass cash register on the back counter, punched the No Sale key, and scooped a wad of bills out of the till. "Takin' some money, Daddy," he called across the store, then slammed the register shut and headed toward the door.

He paused by a rack of work gloves near the front, cocked his head toward me, and said, "Careful on that sidewalk, city boy, could trip an' hurt yourself."

And then the door banged shut behind him, cowbells jangling.

. . .

"What do you think of the Finnerty boy?" Mom asked me as she peppered her onion burger.

I held up a finger while I chewed the first bite out of my cheeseburger. "He seems okay," I said after I swallowed. "He's gonna introduce me to his friends." I resalted for my next bite.

Mom just nodded and set her shaker down, having finally achieved total coverage with the pepper. "Don't use so much salt, honey, it's not good for you."

"Look who's talking, Mom."

Uncle Robert called out from the screen door, "Well, boys, did I lie t' ya?"

"Nosir, best burger I ever ate," I called back with a mouthful of it.

I wasn't lying either.

8

Diamond in the Rough

"You sure seem to be in a better mood," Dad said to me later that day while we waited in the car for Mom. "You haven't complained about anything since lunch."

It was true—driving around Pitkin in the midafternoon heat hadn't fazed me one bit. I'd even managed to fake an interest in the sights Mom kept pointing out, like the sagging barn where she'd gone to dances, her old brick schoolhouse, and the small church where she'd been baptized.

"Yeah, I made a new friend today."

"What's her name?" Dad asked, trying to get a rise out of me.

"*His* name is Finn. His folks own the Mercantile."

"He your age?"

"A little older, I think."

"Well, just remember to think for yourself, sport," he reminded me for only about the millionth time.

I know, Dad. Be a leader, not a follower.

"Be a leader, not a follower," he said, right on cue.

"Boy, this place really gives me the creeps," Charley said.

"You guys have been watching too many monster movies," said Dad. "There's nothing scary about cemeteries."

The place really was kind of creepy. We were parked on the side of a dirt road a couple of miles outside of town, completely surrounded by large, mossy Sleepy Hollow trees. It would have been a perfect location for a zombie movie.

Mom was a ways off at the back of the graveyard, kneeling in the gloom in front of her mother's headstone next to the black wrought-iron fence that enclosed the grounds.

"What's taking Mom so long?" Charley asked.

"She's just paying her respects, son. You'll understand when you're older."

I'd always hated it when adults said that, as if getting older automatically made you smarter; frankly, most of the adults I'd ever met didn't seem all that bright. But when it came to weird stuff like death and girls, I suspected that they were actually right for a change; I probably *wouldn't* understand until I was older. Much older, when it came to girls.

Mom finally finished and was slowly heading back to the car, so Dad turned the ignition on, mercifully bringing the air conditioner back to life.

"You all right?" Dad asked as she slid back onto the seat and closed her door. She briefly nodded but didn't answer. The drive back to town seemed much longer than the trip out, the silence broken only by the De Soto's blowers and Mom's occasional sniffles.

Dad sped back through the main drag and turned left at Uncle Robert's station, nearly into the path of an oncoming pickup. The driver honked at us and shook his fist, veins bulging in his forehead. Dad waved back, oblivious to it all.

After we bounced over the railroad tracks, Dad suddenly made another hard left, spraying gravel everywhere. A second later we were sliding onto a rough dirt road that went past some large old houses set in front of a dense pine forest. Dad rocked the car to a stop between an old brown-and-yellow Chrysler and an even older pea-green Hudson.

Charley and I checked ourselves for whiplash injuries while we waited for the dust to settle. By the time it did, Gary, Barry, and Larry were already at the car doors, like overalled vultures on roadkill.

"Y'all're jus' in time for cold watermelon," Gary said. "C'mon!"

"Don't mind if I do," I said as I climbed out of the car. "Don't mind if I do."

. . .

Maybe it was just because things were finally starting to go my way, but I actually enjoyed hanging out with my cousins that afternoon. Of course, the comics may have had something to do with it, too.

We'd hosed ourselves down after the watermelon feed and then gone inside to cool off. These Millers were obviously better off than PawPaw, their house being much larger and more nicely furnished. My favorite pieces of furniture were the fans.

"Y'all like funny books?" Gary asked as we filed down the hall behind him.

"Does Popeye like spinach?" I asked back.

"You mean comic books?" Charley asked.

"Yeah," Gary said, opening his door. "Got a trunkful in my room."

I didn't take him literally until I saw him bend down to open the lid of a huge old steamer trunk at the foot of his bed. "Holy moly," I whispered. The whole thing was filled with comics.

I immediately knelt on the hardwood floor in front of the trunk and breathed deeply, savoring the comics' musty aroma. Then, from the top of the first stack to the left, I picked up an *Archie* and the handful under it.

"Where'd you get these?" I asked, shuffling through

the *Archie*s, *Betty and Veronica*s, and *Jughead*s. "I didn't see any in town."

"Oakdale," said Gary, " 'bout twenny miles up the road."

Charley reached in next to me for a *Chip 'n' Dale*.

"Try t' keep 'em in order," Barry said.

"An' careful with the covers," added Larry.

I nodded, struck dumb by what I was seeing. Two rows of four stacks each totally filled the trunk, eight straight paper skyscrapers that reached to its top, like a view of Gotham City from the Batplane.

They appeared to be organized by category, separate piles for funnies, westerns, war stories, superheroes, horror, and science fiction. Dells, DC's, and Charltons dominated, but there was a fair share of Marvels, EC's, and Gold Keys as well.

As I silently inspected the treasure chest, I soon realized that Gary's collection was also arranged alphabetically within each category, and then by date of issue. "This is a serious collection," I said.

I was trying to estimate how many comics were there when Gary said, "Nine hunnerd an' sevendy-four," and grinned from ear to ear. "Twenny-six more t' go."

"And then what?" I asked.

"Then I start on my second thousand."

I nodded in sincere admiration.

I finally whittled my selection down to a fistful of favorites: a *Strange Adventures*, a *Mystery in Space*, and a *Flash*, and for old times' sake, a *Red Ryder*, a *Lone Ranger*, and a *Roy Rogers* that I remembered reading when I was a little kid.

After Charley picked out a few more Disneys, Gary and his brothers grabbed a bunch of comics each and we all found a place to hunker down for the afternoon.

Until Mom came in a few hours later, the only noises I heard were the steady hum of the fan and the soft rustling of pages being turned, along with an occasional chuckle. "Hey, boys," she said, throwing the door open a second after she knocked, "y'all hungry? Supper's almost ready."

I looked up from a *Tales of the Unexpected*. "Hey, Mom. We gonna be goin' to Oakdale anytime soon?"

. . .

After another huge meal, even by my standards, I waddled out to the front porch, where I eased myself down and slumped against the yellow wall of the house to let my food digest, like a boa constrictor that's just swallowed a pig whole.

Charley, Larry, and Woody followed me out but sat at the homemade picnic table in the yard next to the cars. Woody, PawPaw, and Aunt Nelda had shown up just before supper, arriving in the beat-up green pickup I'd thought was just a junker. Charley and Larry were sitting next to each other on the bench across from Woody, elbows on the table and chins on fists, in rapt attention.

Larry, who was the same size and age as Charley,

eight going on nine, was the youngest of the Miller brothers. He was the quietest one, too, seeming to be content to just listen and observe. He had the same dark brown hair and bad crew cut as his brothers, like a lawn that's been cut by two different mowers. They all had blue eyes, but his were an even lighter shade, like the scary pale blue of a Siberian husky.

I looked over at Gary and Barry, who had been forced to help with the supper dishes and were now sprawled on either end of the barely moving porch swing, their mouths half open and their eyes closed. Even though Barry was only ten, he was already as tall as I was. Gary, the oldest at twelve, was a good head taller than both of us, all arms and legs.

All three of them shared the same small, straight Miller nose, but Gary's was the only one with freckles, a light sprinkling of dots across his bridge that made me want to connect them with a marker.

"So what's with all the cars?" I asked. "That's the third one I've seen go by in the last five minutes."

"Ball game tonight," Barry mumbled without opening his eyes.

"Whadya mean?" I said as I watched another carload of people drive past the house.

"Little League. We're playin' Elizabeth tonight."

"Baseball?" I asked, passing up the joke. "Pitkin has a *baseball* team?" I'd only seen five guys since I'd arrived, and four of them were relatives.

"Two of 'em," Gary said through a yawn. "We played last night, won seven t' one. Pine Knots play tonight."

"Gary threw a two-hitter an' hit a homer an' a triple," Barry said proudly. "He's gonna be a big-leaguer someday."

"Had a good game," Gary acknowledged. He stretched, cracking his knuckles at the same time.

"Where's the field?" I asked.

"Enda the road," said Barry, "next t' the Finnerty place."

"When does it start?" I was in no more hurry to watch a baseball game than I would be to watch snails race, but I was rapidly approaching my boredom threshold.

"Not 'til seven-thirty," Gary said with another yawn. "We got time."

"Well, I'm gonna check it out now. You guys comin'?"

"In a bit. We'll meet ya there."

I hoisted myself off thc porch boards and started down the gravel road. Four more cars rumbled by in the time it took me to walk to the dirt parking area at the end of the road.

Sitting there in the middle of the middle of nowhere was an honest-to-God baseball stadium, with fences and lights, actual dugouts, and a real pitcher's mound. It even had a scoreboard.

I wandered toward the third-base bleachers, long,

green-painted wooden seats that rose above my head, then drifted over to the tall chain-link fence that separated the playing field from the stands, where I just stood for a while and Observed.

A burly man in baggy shorts and a sweaty undershirt was slowly striping the first-base line while a gangly old guy in overalls and a straw hat knelt at second base, securing the bag to the ground with spikes and a hammer.

A handful of players in light-gray uniforms, "Elizabeth" spelled out in blue letters on the front of their shirts, warmed up in the outfield, casually lobbing practice balls back and forth.

A few seconds later the unmistakable aroma of frankfurters wafted into my nostrils from somewhere behind me. Like a bloodhound that's just caught the scent, I immediately spun around to track it down. And that's when I saw that Pitkin Field also had a snack bar.

A concrete-and-wood building painted the same John Deere-green as the bleachers, it was set about twenty feet behind the huge home-plate backstop. The top half of it was a roofed scorer's booth. I saw a middle-aged man with a potbelly and gold wire-rimmed glasses start up the wooden stairs on the side, microphone and score book in hand.

I started moving toward the snack bar like a moth drawn to a flame. Just then Charley and all four cousins rounded its corner, heading my way.

"Will Dad be here soon?" I asked Charley as he walked up to me.

"Pretty soon."

"They said they're all comin' over soon's they clean up," said Barry.

"Good."

Charley questioned me with his eyebrows.

"Dad's got my twenty bucks," I explained, "and I need it for the snack bar." Mom and Dad had promised Charley and me twenty dollars each in spending money for the summer, but Dad hadn't given it to us yet, saying that he'd hang on to it for safekeeping until we needed it.

The snack bar looked like it was getting ready to open. A thin woman wearing a blue gingham shirt and matching bandanna poured kernels into the popcorn machine while a smallish kid in a navy-blue baseball cap and a white "Pitkin" uniform shirt started filling the racks with candy and gum.

"Let's get us a good seat," Barry said, nodding toward the bleachers. "Best view's from the top, just lefta center."

I thought about waiting at the snack bar until Dad showed up with my money, but I was still kind of full from supper, so I decided instead to head for the bleachers along with everyone else. Everyone but Gary, that is.

"Save me a seat, y'all," he said as he walked off toward the snack bar.

It took another ten or fifteen minutes for the rest of the players to get there, and it was another half hour or so after that before the lineups were finally given to the umpire.

Dad and my cash showed up just as the speaker on top of the scorer's booth crackled to life, announcing the start of the game between the visiting Elizabeth Papermakers and the Pitkin Pine Knots. "Let's play ball!"

. . .

Gary still hadn't returned by the top of the third inning, so I decided to mosey on over to the snack bar to see what was keeping him. That, and I couldn't wait any longer to spend some of my cash.

Unlike Charley, who had practically every cent he'd ever earned, found, or been given, along with a savings account to keep it all in, I was not exactly a responsible person when it came to money, which explained why I was usually broke.

Gary was still there, slouched against the counter talking to the kid in the Pitkin uniform that I'd seen filling the racks earlier. Gary's friend was leaning across the other side of the countertop, his elbows resting on the green plywood, his fingers drumming on it. As I walked up to them, the kid blew a tremendous pink bubble, then expertly sucked it back into his mouth.

"Hey, Gary," I said, "what's takin' so long?"

I looked at the kid and said, "Could I get a Dr Pepper

and a Bit-O-Honey?" Then I noticed the "NY" insignia on his cap. "Hey, I've got a Yankees cap just like that." I'd only brought it along for sleeping in the car.

"I know," he said with a twinkle in his cat-green eyes. "Gary stole it off ya an' gave it t' me."

Gary had seen me stash my stuff in Woody's bottom drawer, so I wasn't a hundred percent sure it was a joke until I saw him roll his eyes. "Skeets, this's my cousin Mitch, from California. Mitch, this's Skeeter."

"Pleased t' meetcha, Mitch," he said in a high-pitched voice. He extended a slim right hand to shake mine. "An' here's your cap back," he added, taking it off with his left.

That's when I saw a long blond ponytail fall out the back of the cap. A second later I noticed that the *I*'s on the "PITKIN" shirt stuck out a little more than the other letters did.

"He" was definitely a "she."

"Oh," I said, dropping her hand like a hot potato. Suddenly my face felt like it had a third-degree sunburn.

Skeeter quickly turned to get me my soda. Fortunately she had to fumble around a little bit searching for a Dr Pepper in the ice-filled tub behind her, which gave me enough time to recover.

"Cain't seem t' find one," she said, straightening up with a gold-colored bottle in her hand. "But try a cream soda. It's m' fav'rite, 'specially with a Bit-O-Honey."

"Never had one," I croaked.

"Ain't no charge if ya jus' don't love it," she added. "I kin always finish it m'self." And then she smiled at me.

I never did get back to the game.

9

Out on a Limb

Sunday morning I woke up feeling more like Dr. Jekyll again, instead of his evil alter ego, Mr. Hyde. Even Woody couldn't ruin my good mood.

"Hey, Woody," I said between mouthfuls of biscuits and gravy, "whatcha wanna do today?"

"Whatevah Charley wants t' do," he said, deftly spearing a chunk of sausage.

"Can we go to the south forty today, Woody?" Charley asked, a hopeful look on his face.

Aunt Nelda shook her head. "Y'all stay close today, boys, resta the fam'ly'll be here aftah we get back from church."

Church?

I looked at Dad for help; he didn't offer any. That was because Mom's eye daggers told us both that we'd better not even *think* of arguing, or else. I finished my breakfast in silence, like a condemned man eating his last meal.

A short while later Charley and I were being forced into our car by the warden, who wore a yellow sundress and looked exactly like Mom.

The drive to the execution site didn't take nearly long enough; before I knew it I was being marched up the steps of the gas chamber, a white wood building with a steeple on top and a "First Baptist Church of Pitkin" sign in front.

Most of the pews were already filled, so we ended up in the back row, having to squeeze by two old women wearing huge Sunday hats and floral print dresses, both of whom refused to give up their aisle seats.

The instant we sat down someone said, "Let us stand in prayer," from somewhere up front. Suddenly all I could see was floral dresses. The women even smelled like flowers, their rapidly fluttering paper fans flooding the already suffocating air of the church with their gaggy, sweet perfumes.

The men in the congregation were also in their Sunday best, tugging at too-tight collars and sweat-soaked dress shirts, looking like they'd rather be anywhere else.

After a long opening prayer, we were told to be seated by the minister, a white-haired old man who could have put the makers of Sleep-Eze out of business all by himself. I started getting drowsy about eight seconds into his sermon, but I wasn't alone. Dad and most of the other men were having as hard a time keeping their eyes open as I was. If it hadn't been for the Reverend's frequent shouts of "Pur*raise Jee*suzz!" that startled us awake, I was sure he'd have eventually been drowned out by the sound of mass male snoring.

But I guess God truly is merciful, because just when I thought I couldn't take another second of it, everyone stood and started singing the last hymn, "Bringing in the Sheaves." Or rather the women sang; the men just kind of mumbled or mouthed the words.

Of course, before we could leave we had to shake hands with the minister at the door and tell him how much we'd enjoyed his sermon. Then I escaped to the car, a free man once again.

As we drove away from the church, Mom turned to Charley and me and said, "Well, boys, that wasn't so bad now, was it?"

Not having much choice, I shook my head.

"Did y'all learn anything?" she asked, pressing the issue.

Yeah, Mom, I learned how long Eternity really is.

I did have one question, though. "Mom, tell me. Just what the heck *are* sheaves, anyway?"

. . .

As soon as we changed out of our church clothes, Charley and Woody told Mom and Aunt Nelda that they were "goin' on a short safari."

"Be back in an hour, heah?" Aunt Nelda said. Then she glanced across the dining table at me. "Ain't Mitch goin' too?"

"Can if he wants ta," Woody answered, in a way that said he'd really rather I didn't.

"That's okay, Aunt Nelda," I said. "It's too hot anyway."

The truth was, I really wouldn't have minded going with them, but only because I knew that if I stuck around I was more than likely to get stuck with an unpleasant chore or two, maybe even actual work.

Sure enough, about three minutes after Woody and Charley took off, Mom hollered out from the kitchen, "Mitch, honey, can you come help us a second?"

"Sorry, Mom," I yelled back, already off the porch swing and heading for the wagon wheels, "changed my mind, gotta hurry, seeya later."

I caught up with them a few hundred yards up the road. "So where're we going?" I asked Woody as soon as I caught my breath.

"Jus' up the road t' the Boudreaux place. Somethin' I wanna show Charley."

"What about me?"

"What about you?"

"Don't I get to see it, too?"

"Cain't stop ya. It's a free country."

"So, Wood Man," I said, one step behind him, "what exactly is your problem?"

He stopped in his tracks and turned around to face me, his mouth slightly open. "Beg pardon?"

I decided I'd better try a different approach. "How come you've been acting like I've got leprosy?"

His jaw muscles twitched as he considered my question. "Maybe," he finally said, "it's 'cause ya do." Then he pivoted in the gravel and walked off.

Charley looked at me and then at Woody, confusion on his face. He glanced my way once more and then took off after Woody.

So much for brotherly love.

Suddenly I got an idea. I jogged up next to Woody and said, "Hey, man, that's a lot of bull."

Without breaking stride, he turned his head and glared at me.

"No, that's not what I meant." I grinned and pointed to the pasture that had just come into view. "What I meant was, *that's* a lot of bull."

"Oh," he said, fighting off a smile, "that's the Boudreaux's Brahma. That's what I was fixin' t' show Charley." Then he put his arm around Charley's shoulders and said, "C'mon, son, let's take us a look at a real live Brahma bull."

Even from as far away as we were it was obvious that he was pretty big, but by the time we reached the wood rail fencing that surrounded the pasture, I realized that he wasn't just huge, he was Moby Brahma, the Great Gray Bull.

"What do you think he weighs, Woody?" asked Charley.

"Mister Boudreaux figgers 'im at jus' under a ton."

"A ton as in two thousand pounds?" I said incredulously.

Woody nodded twice.

"This fence strong enough to keep him from bustin' through?" I asked, nervously eyeing the behemoth staring at us from about thirty yards away.

Woody reached out to rattle the top railing. "Prob'ly not, but he's too dumb t' try."

The bull reacted to the sound by snorting and stamping the ground.

"He's Big Buck's son," Woody said. "An' even meanah than his daddy."

"Great," I said. "Two thousand pounds of mean and stupid."

"With horns," Charley added.

Son of Buck snorted again and shook his head, probably to give us a better view of his horns. They stuck out over two feet from the sides of his massive gray head, ending in needle tips that I swear gleamed in the sunlight.

"What's the hump for?" I asked, looking at the huge, lighter-gray mound between the Brahma's shoulders.

"They store fat in it," Woody said. "Like camels."

"Sure is ugly," I said.

"Not to a lady Brahma."

"Actually, it's Brahman, with an *n*," Charley said softly.

Woody and I both looked at him. "They're originally from India," he continued, "and they're named after the highest caste there, called Brahmans. With an *n*."

Woody slowly shook his head and smiled. "Where's he git all this stuff?"

"He reads a lot."

The bull suddenly took a couple of steps toward us. I instinctively backed away from the fence, pulling Charley with me.

"Don't move," Woody said quietly.

We didn't. "I really wish you hadn't worn that red shirt," I muttered to Charley out of the side of my mouth.

"They're color-blind," Woody said. "They only react t' movement, so y'all be still now."

The bull slowly but steadily approached us until he was right next to the fence, pinning us with his beady black eyes. I could have reached out and touched him if I'd wanted to; I had absolutely no desire to do so.

"Well, this certainly has been fun," I whispered. "You guys ready to head on back?"

"Whatsa mattah, Mitch?" Woody said. " 'Fraid of a li'l ol' bull?"

"Not me," I said automatically. "But, you know, if all he's gonna do is stand there and give us the evil eye, what's the pointa stickin' around?"

"Betcha ain't got the nerve t' play Dare the Bull."

"Depends. How do you play?"

"See that big oak yondah?" he said, pointing to a large solitary tree maybe fifty yards off in the middle of the pasture.

"Hard to miss."

"Whatcha do is, ya hafta tag the tree an' get back ovah the fence 'fore he gets ya."

"Is that what Gary was talking about the first night we were here?" Charley asked.

"Shore was. Me an' him used t' do that with Big Buck all the time." Then he looked right at me. "Think ya can do it with them fast racin' shoes of yours?"

"Sure," I said, "if we wait 'til he's at the farthest part of the pasture."

"Of *course* ya hafta wait 'til then," Woody said, like he was talking to the village idiot. "We ain't crazy."

"You guys serious?" Charley asked, glancing first at Woody and then at me.

"Serious as crop failure," said Woody.

"Sure, why not?" I said. "You only live once."

You only die once, too.

"Then count me in," said Charley.

"No way!" Woody and I said, almost at the same time.

A few minutes and one argument later, it was obvious that Charley wasn't going to take no for an answer, so Woody and I huddled privately until we came up with a safe plan.

"Okay, Charley," I said in my most serious tone of voice, "we'll all go together, but you have to do exactly what we say, promise?" He solemnly nodded agreement.

"All right," said Woody. "Now here's what we gotta do . . ."

. . .

We sat without moving for ages until the Brahma lost interest in us and wandered off, finally ending up in the far corner of the pasture, contentedly grazing on tufts of grass.

He was a football field or so past the oak, about twice as far from it as we were. We'd casually edged our way along the fencing until we were directly across from the tree, with a straight shot to the trunk. Then we'd quietly slipped through the timbers and waited for the best moment to make our move.

"Okay, boys," Woody said, " 'membah now, I'll take the lead. Charley, you're in the middle, jus' run right behind me. Mitch, you bring up the rear." Woody and I had figured that the safest place for Charley was between us; that way, if anything happened, either one or both of us would be able to help him. "We oughta be at the tree 'fore he even knows we're there," Woody continued, "then we'll jus' outrun 'im back t' the fence."

We waited, hearts pounding, or at least mine was, until the bull turned away from us at last. Then Woody whispered, "Go!"

The Brahma whirled around almost the instant we took off. We hadn't covered twenty feet when he started moving toward us. By the time we were halfway to the tree I knew we were in trouble. We'd beat him there, no question, but the problem was going to be getting back—there was no way we'd be able to.

And then Charley slipped. He didn't trip or twist his ankle like they do in bad movies, he just slipped. In bull manure.

We'd seen that the pasture was littered with large patties and had picked a path to the tree that avoided most of them. But somehow Charley wasn't able to miss the biggest one, a deep pile of dried dung the size of a manhole cover. The second he stepped on it, his shoe went in up to his ankle and his foot shot forward, leaving a ripe brown gouge in the patty and sending him sprawling. It would have been hilarious if a two-thousand-pound monster hadn't been bearing down on us with murder on his mind.

I got Charley to his feet as fast as I could, but it still took too long. Now we'd be lucky to even get to the tree before the Brahma reached us. Woody was almost to the trunk before he realized something was wrong. When he turned toward us, I saw a look of pure panic take over his face.

As Charley and I neared the tree, Woody scrambled up to the lowest branch, a thick limb seven or eight feet off the ground. "Throw 'im upta me!" he yelled. "Hurry!"

I half shoved, half launched Charley up to Woody, who pulled him onto the branch to safety. I risked a quick glance at the bull before starting up myself. I shouldn't have; he was almost on top of me, hooves thundering and head down, his horns aimed right at my chest.

"C'mon!" Woody screamed. "Jump!"

No more than a couple of seconds after I did, the bull charged like a runaway freight train through the space I'd just vacated. He plowed to a stop ten yards past the tree, sending grass and dirt clods flying. Then he turned back and stamped and snorted beneath our branch, his tail twitching angrily and his eyes blazing with frustration.

None of us said a word for a few minutes, mainly because we couldn't. Charley and Woody looked as pale as I was sure I was. We all knew it could have turned out a whole lot worse than it did.

And when Moby Brahma lowered himself to the ground directly beneath us, we also knew we were going to be late for dinner.

. . .

"Boy, I could sure go for a cream soda right now," I said, breaking about a half hour silence. We'd hoped that if we didn't make any noise, the bull would forget about us and go on about his business. He hadn't.

"Not a Dr Pepper?" questioned Charley.

"I'm a cream soda man now," I said, trying for the hundredth time to find a comfortable position on the branch above him and Woody.

"Since when?"

"Since last night. Skeeter gave me one."

"Is that her real name?"

"It's Helen Louise," Woody told him, "but don't call her that unless ya want her t' pop ya one." Then he looked up at me. "She's Gary's girl," he said, boring holes into me with his eyes.

"Whadya mean?"

"He's sweet on 'er," Woody said. "Whose shirt d'ya think she was wearin'?"

I thought it was a little big for her.

"Don't worry," I assured him, "we're just friends." Even though she hadn't actually done or said anything to make me think that she *really* liked me, I was sure she at least liked me. And I knew that I liked her. Maybe even *really* liked her.

"Mitch has got a cru-ush," Charley sang from the safety of his branch.

"Shut up, squirt, I *said* we're just friends. Besides, you're not old enough to understand anyway."

I can't believe I just said that.

Moby Brahma started getting to his feet. A few seconds later the bull thumped the tree with his shoulder. It felt like about a 6 on the Richter scale. Then he backed up a step and hit the trunk again, this time with a force of at least 7.5.

"Evacuate the area," I said as I tightened my grip on the branch above me. "This is not a drill. I repeat, this is not a drill."

10

A Close Shave

"Surely they'll send out a search party pretty soon," I said a while later.

"I 'spect so," Woody said. "An' don't call me Shirley."

I ignored his wisecrack and eyed the bull for about the thousandth time. He'd given up on trying to knock us out of the tree and was just lying by the trunk again, waiting us out.

"Woody," I said, "this is the first time you've done this with Moby Brahma here, isn't it?"

He didn't answer for a few seconds, then looked at Charley and nodded. "Yeah, last time, too. He's a lot fas-tah than his daddy was."

"That's what I thought."

No one said anything else for a few minutes; we just listened to the bull's patient breathing and waited for help. Then suddenly we heard Gary and the guys calling out our names from the road. All three of us immediately started hollering and waving back, like we were pilots downed behind enemy lines and they were the rescue choppers. We'd have fired off flares if we'd had them.

It took them a few minutes of whistling and arm waving to draw the bull away from the tree, and a few more to get him to go to the end of the pasture. By then we were on the ground, hiding single file behind the trunk, just in case. When the coast was clear, we all did our best Road Runner impressions and then dove through the fence rails into neutral territory.

On the way back to the house, we took turns telling them what had happened. When Woody got to the part about me swinging up onto the branch just in the nick of time, Barry's eyes got wide, and then he grinned at me. "Wow, you were almost a Mitch-ka-bob, huh?"

"That reminds me," I said over the chuckling, "any of you guys know what's for dinner?"

. . .

I knew from Mom that Sunday dinner at PawPaw's was a family ritual; each week after church every relative within driving distance of Pitkin would descend on the farm like swallows returning to Capistrano.

The front yard looked like an antique auto auction, and the porch was packed with people, some of whom I didn't recognize. As we neared the house, Aunt Nelda opened the screen door and stepped out, with her arms crossed and a stern look on her face. She was probably tapping her foot, too, but we couldn't tell because of the two guys sitting on the steps, blocking our view.

"William Woodrow Wilson!" she hollered. "You bettah have a mighty good excuse!"

Woodrow Wilson?

Even though the story we'd decided on was really pretty lame, I must say we put on a great act. "Sorry, Mama, but we jus' plain lost tracka the time, and that's the truth," Woody said, his face a mask of total sincerity. "Won't nevah happen again, promise."

"It's really me an' Charley's fault, Aunt Nelda," I said as planned. "We wanted t' keep exploring and he was jus' being polite." Woody and Charley nodded in agreement.

"Well, y'all wash up," she said, evidently satisfied with our alibi. "These folks must be starvin' half t' death."

I know the feeling, Aunt Nelda.

The boys on the porch steps turned out to be two more of our cousins, Kenneth and Curtis, who, like Charley and me, were almost three years apart, but two years older. They belonged to Mom's other sister, Hazel, and her husband, a pharmacist in DeRidder named Vern Beeson.

Woody's sisters were there, too. Mom called Charley and me over to the end of the porch where everyone was hovering around the rocker occupied by a thin, horsey young woman who had a baby cradled in her lap. A pudgy, dopey-looking guy knelt next to her, beaming at them both.

"Mitch, Charley," Mom said, "this is Woody's big sister Betty and her husband, Eldon, from Oakdale." She pointed to the pink-on-pink infant. "And this little bundle of joy's their first baby, Sarah. Ain't she a sweetheart? She's six months old today."

I leaned over to get a better look at the rosy face peeking out of a mass of blond curls. As soon as I did, her big blue eyes welled up with tears, and suddenly she was wailing like an air-raid siren.

"Mitch," Eldon said, "do ya always have this effect on the ladies?"

Not with Skeeter.

While Betty patted the baby on the back to calm her down, Mom finished up the introductions. "And this is June, Woody's other sister," she said, nodding toward the tall, plain brunette in a white sundress who was standing behind the rocker. "She lives in Oakdale, too. Just got a job at the bank, didn't ya, hon?" June smiled shyly and kind of nodded her head.

Fortunately, about three seconds before I was going to die of boredom, Aunt Nelda called out from the kitchen. "Okay, y'all, let's eat!"

I didn't sit next to Woody's sisters.

· · ·

"Think it's time t' break the boys in?" Barry asked from the back porch railing, where he sat swinging his legs.

"Yep," Woody said from the steps.

"What're ya talkin' about?" I asked as I slumped into my usual post-meal position against the wall.

Woody and Barry looked at each other and grinned. "Corncob fight," they said at the same time.

"I'm one captain!" Curtis claimed.

"Dibs on th' other!" shouted Kenneth.

It ended up being Curtis, Woody, Larry, and Charley against Kenneth, Gary, Barry, and me. Charley and I were the last ones chosen.

"So what're the rules?" I asked as we trooped off to the barn.

Barry and Woody laughed. "Ain't no rules," Gary said.

Free-for-all. Cool.

They didn't know it, but I was what was called a ringer, kind of like in *Shane*, when they find out that behind his peaceful exterior lies the fastest gun around. I was a veteran of years of organized kid warfare. In second grade I'd survived my initiation into dirt-clod battles and could prove it; permanently etched into my left cheek was a faint, inch-long scar that I wore as proudly as if it were the Congressional Medal of Honor. Starting in fourth grade at the Academy, I'd more than held my own in the neighborhood pinecone wars and was considered by the guys in San Bernardino a valuable ally in our running orange grove skirmishes.

Although I had a pretty good arm, my specialty was defense. I was frequently able to catch the enemy's ammunition out of the air and hurl it back immediately, usually with more speed and greater accuracy. Once I practically made an orange explode on the back of a kid's head.

So my cousins were all in for a surprise, and I was in a hurry to get started. I especially couldn't wait to get Curtis for not picking me to be on his side.

I had no idea why, but it seemed that there were almost as many dried-up corncobs lying around as there were crap piles. We all had at least a handful before we even reached the barn, and had stockpiles built up within a minute or so of our arrival.

"Okay," Woody said as we all gathered in the middle of the barn, each of us armed with as many corncobs as we could handle. "*Gunfight at the O.K. Corral.* We're the Earps, y'all're the Clantons. Which door d'ya want?"

Barry nodded toward the large opening behind us. "This'n." His voice dropped to a whisper. "Sun's at our backs."

Without another word, Woody and the rest of the Earps started backing up, fanning out as they went, and then stopped, four silhouettes in the opening about fifty feet away. We did the same.

"Well, if it ain't John Law," Barry began with a sneer.

"Afternoon, gents," Curtis called out. "Nice day for a fun'ral."

Gary spat loudly onto the ground in front of him. "Yeah, yours."

"Draw, ya lily-livered lizards," Woody growled.

"You first, *law*man," I snarled, getting into the act.

Nothing happened for a second or two, and then the next thing I knew, the air was filled with spinning missiles that whistled out of the shadows and became visible only when it was too late, a fact I discovered when the first one I saw hit me right between the eyes a split second later. It stung like crazy.

Rubbing my forehead with the back of my hand and swearing under my breath, I charged forward and let fly. Another corncob hit me, grazing my arm and leaving a nasty friction burn. I made a lightning cut and changed direction, angling toward one of the horse stalls. Before I got there two more corncobs nailed me, one on my neck and the other right at the base of my spine.

I knelt behind a bale of hay at the front of an empty stall, reassessing the situation and waiting for my eyes to adjust to the barn's shadowy interior. Even when they finally did, I still had to watch a few flurries of cobfire before I could figure out where everyone was.

All of us were crouching or hiding behind something: a post, stall fencing, a saddle, anything that would provide some protection. But basically they had the side under the hayloft and we had the other.

Suddenly Curtis made a break for the ladder to the loft. I knew we couldn't let him gain the advantage of high ground or we were dead, so I stood, aimed, and fired, flinging my corncob like Jim Bowie hurling his hunting knife. It hit Curtis hard right on the back of his collar and ricocheted away.

He paused for a second to rub his neck, holding on to the top rung with only one hand. My next shot caught it full on the knuckles, knocking his grip loose and forcing him to jump back down and scramble to safety.

"Cover me!" I yelled, then fired my last two corncobs as I zigzagged to the ladder. I took a couple of harmless body hits crossing over to it, and one elbow stinger on the way up before I rolled into the loft and out of the line of fire.

After that it was just a matter of time. My guys tossed ammo up to me, which I used to cover them. Every time one of the Earps would try to come out from below the loft, I'd drill him from above. It was the most fun I'd had in a long time.

As we all walked back to the house for cold drinks, recapping the highlights and laughing, Gary came up next to me and said, "You can be on my side anytime."

"Yeah," said Woody, "purdy good for someone who puked in there the first time."

Curtis never said a word.

By bedtime Sunday night, even Woody's room didn't seem so bad. After we turned the light out we talked for a while, mostly about Son of Buck and the corncob fight. It wasn't like Woody and I were suddenly best friends, but it wasn't terrible either.

I was starting to nod off when he said, "Maybe it won't be such a bad summah after all."

"Yeah," I agreed, "maybe I'll even get used to the heat."

. . .

Monday the heat wave hit. The three of us were up before dawn, already sticky with sweat. It even got Woody's attention.

"Gonna be a scorcher today," he said as he stretched. "Better lie low."

"No argument here," I said.

Woody climbed into his overalls and headed toward the kitchen before Charley and I even had our shorts on. By the time we got there, he was sitting down at the small table with his orange juice, across from Dad and PawPaw. PawPaw's legs were stretched out, revealing his calf-high work boots.

"Hey, PawPaw," I said, stifling a yawn, "aren't your feet gonna burn up in those boots?"

PawPaw dabbed at his forehead with a red print bandanna, then started tying it around his neck. "Yeah, but it shore beats gettin' bit by snakes."

"Snakes?" I said, instantly wide awake.

"What kind of snakes?" Charley asked.

"Mostly canebrake an' pygmy rattlers, sometimes

coral snakes," PawPaw said, as calmly as if he were dis-
cussing bait. "An' once in a while you'll see a cottonmouth. Ya don't wanna get bit by one a them."

"Mitch isn't too fond of snakes," Mom said as she
poured milk into a big glass bowl full of egg yolks.

"Woody don't much care for 'em neithah," Aunt
Nelda said next to her, sweating at the stove. " 'Specially
cottonmouths. One scared him real bad when he was
youngah," Aunt Nelda continued, to Woody's obvious
chagrin. "Maybe he'll tell y'all 'bout it sometime."

"Don't count on it," he muttered under his breath.

"We hafta carry PawPaw t' Leesville for his doctor's
appointment this mornin'," Aunt Nelda informed us, "so
you boys'll be on your own for a coupla hours."

An hour or so after breakfast, they were finally ready
to leave. "Y'all stay close now," Aunt Nelda instructed as
she worked her way down the front steps. "It's gonna be
too hot to play outside anyway."

"Devil, Mama!" protested Woody. "We can take care
of ourselves."

Who we ended up taking care of was Rebel.

I found him lying in the shade under the house,
about six feet back next to one of the large concrete piers
that supported it, panting rapidly even in the cool dirt. It
took a few Milk-Bones to coax him out and onto the
porch with us.

"He's nevah gonna make it with all that hair," said
Woody.

"Then let's cut it," I said. "Where're the scissors?"

"We got shears, too. Be right back." Woody dashed into the house.

"Mom an' Dad'll kill us," Charley predicted.

"Maybe, but Woody's right, Reb's gotta be miserable. Look at 'im. How'd you like to be wearin' a fur coat right now?"

Woody burst back onto the porch, trailing a black extension cord plugged into an old set of electric shears, along with a large scissors. "Y'all hold 'im still. I'll do the trimmin'."

"Start with the sides," I said. "I've got an idea."

I directed Woody until he'd achieved the desired effect. The hair on Rebel's sides was now shaved to less than an inch long; we'd left a two-inch-wide strip of long fur on his spine untouched.

"Best Mohawk I've ever seen," said Woody.

"Get your Brownie," I said to Charley, who'd gotten one for Christmas. "We gotta get a picture of this."

Our second picture required special effects. "Got anything to grease his fur down with?" I asked Woody after Charley snapped his shot of Indian Dog.

He was soon back with a coffee can full of lard or something, along with a bottle of hair oil. After a little experimenting, we came up with the right mixture to do the trick. We got the Mohawk to sort of stand up, and after another half minute with the scissors, Rebel was a Dimetrodon, the prehistoric reptile with the huge sail on his back. I forced his jaws open and stuck my head between his teeth, then Charley took another picture.

It took a few minutes to turn his fin into Stegosaurus plates. For that shot Woody ripped a bunch of grass out of the yard and piled it at Rebel's feet, then I forced his snout down to make it look like he was grazing.

"How 'bout a lion?" Charley suggested next.

Another round with the shears and Rebel became the King of Beasts. But with his huge gold mane and scraggly looking, peach fuzz body, he looked more like some bizarre creature out of a mythology book.

We basically ran out of ideas at that point, so we went ahead and shaved the rest of him. By the time all his fur was gone, the mounds of hair piled on the porch resembled scale-model haystacks.

"Well," said Woody, "bet he feels bettah now."

"I don't think so," I said.

Rebel must have just realized what he looked like, because suddenly he hid his hairless tail between his legs and hung his head. He wouldn't even look at us.

Then Woody did something that knocked me out. "Hey, Reb," he said, kneeling in front of him with the clippers. "Look. It ain't so bad, see?" Setting the shears carefully on his own forehead, he proceeded to shave his entire head down to stubble.

"Why not?" I said, taking the shears from him when he was done. A few seconds later my hair was as short as

Woody's. We took turns trimming each other up, then I looked at Charley and said, "Now it's your turn."

He protested at first but got into the spirit after he looked in the hand mirror that Woody brought out and saw the racing stripe I'd shaved down the middle of his head. Naturally we had to take a photograph of that, too, before we shaved the rest.

When the adults got back from Leesville, they found the three of us relaxing with Rebel on the front steps. We'd bet on how long it would take them to notice; I'd predicted five seconds or less. I won.

"Good Lord," Mom said the instant she saw Rebel, "what have you done to the dog?"

"He's air-conditioned," Charley said with a grin.

"He looks ri*dic*ulous," said Mom. Then she started laughing, which got everyone else going as well.

"Y'all look ridiculous, too," Aunt Nelda said, "but I bet it's coolah."

"And it's certainly no worse than a base haircut," added Mom, looking directly at Dad.

Just then a car horn honked. It was Aunt Dorothy and the boys coming up the drive in their Hudson. "Y'all wanna go t' the swimmin' hole?" Gary yelled out the window as soon as they got within earshot.

Woody immediately got up and headed for the screen door. "Grab your trunks, boys," he said, motioning us inside with his arm, "we're goin' t' the creek!"

11

Creek Lessons

Even in swim trunks and a tank top, I was roasting in the Hudson. It didn't help that there were six kids crammed in the car with Aunt Dorothy, and the fact that she would only go about five miles an hour on the gravel pretty well eliminated the possibility of being cooled off by any kind of a breeze from the windows.

"How much longer?" I asked Barry, who was wedged between Larry and me in the backseat.

"Almost there," he said as a bead of sweat dripped off the end of his nose.

Aunt Dorothy soon slowed to a crawl and then turned left, into what looked to me like nothing but thin trees and tall grass. I had to stick my head out the window to see the tire ruts she was following; the instant I did, the car started bucking like a rodeo bronc, slamming my skull painfully into the side of the roof.

"Rough ride, boys," Gary said. "Hold on."

"*Now* you tell me," I muttered, rubbing the rapidly rising knot above my left temple.

We bounced slowly along for a minute or so before I saw a half dozen cars and pickups parked up ahead on both sides of the dirt grooves, their tires half obscured by grass and weeds. Aunt Dorothy pulled off to the right, crept to a stop behind a dusty, black '59 Cadillac, and killed the engine.

"Well, boys," she said, meaning Charley and me, "here we are."

A few ancient oaks stood surrounded by tall birches, their small, bright-green leaves blocking out most of the sunlight. Unfortunately they only blocked out some of the heat, and none of the humidity.

"Boy, I can't wait to get in the water," Charley said as we all piled out.

"Ditto," I cleverly added as I followed my cousins across the ruts and down a grassy slope. And got my first look at the creek.

I paused for a few seconds on the bank, gazing down at the creek's lazy current. I'd never seen water quite that color before, an oily, greenish brown that brought to mind mutant swamp creatures and fatal diseases.

"Is it safe to swim in this stuff?" I asked Gary when I

joined him and everyone else down on the small, sloped "beach."

"Sure," he said, and then pulled off his tank top. "Jus' gotta be careful of underwater logs."

"An' make sure ya don't swallow any water," Barry chimed in, "or you'll turn purple, swell up, an' die." He probably wasn't exaggerating by much.

I spread my towel out on the powdery sand next to Charley's, sat down on it to take off my tennies. To my left, Aunt Dorothy had joined three women, two dressed in shorts and halters, and one in a dumb bathing suit. They sat on a quilt gossiping while their toddlers played nearby, either digging in the sand with spoons or eating it out of their pails.

Four kids around Charley's size waded and splashed in the shallows, while a few yards behind them two bigger boys were loudly trying to dunk each other in the deeper water. The creek ended maybe twenty feet beyond them in a steep, leafy bank seven or eight feet high.

Out of the corner of my eye I saw a sudden flash of movement that turned into a kid in red trunks cannonballing out of the sky into the middle of the creek, followed instantly by a spectacular splash.

"C'mon," Gary said, "lemme show ya the rope swing."

About fifty feet downstream on our side of the creek, a monstrous oak stood at the top of the bank, tilted slightly toward the water, its long, gnarly limbs projecting halfway across the creek. A section of the bank below had eroded, exposing huge twisted roots that disappeared into the sand at the water's edge.

Two guys wearing swim trunks stood on a thick limb about ten feet up, casually holding on to another branch above them while they waited their turn for the swing. A third kid in cutoffs stood near the end of the limb, gripping both ends of a two-foot length of wood that had a fuzzy rope knotted around its middle. The other end of the rope soared up and out like a giant's kite string, disappearing somewhere into the top of the tree. I craned my neck until I could see that it was tied near the end of an impossibly high branch; whoever had shinnied out there must have had nerves of steel.

The kid holding the rope swing raised it over his head, then threw his arms forward and jumped off, swinging down and out in a long, graceful curve. He seemed to accelerate on the upswing and, at the top of his arc, whipped his legs up and let go of the handle. He did a triple back somersault and hit the water with hardly a splash.

These guys are good.

"How big of a drop is that?" I asked.

"Fifteen feet, give or take," Gary said.

"Who's the man on the flying trapeze?"

"That's Boomer," said Gary. "He's the best diver in Pitkin."

"Best in the *state*," a familiar voice said behind me.

I smiled and turned around. "Hey, Finn, how are ya?" He'd been the red-trunked cannonballer.

"Doin' fine, city boy. Hot enough for ya?"

"Y'all already know each other?" said Gary.

I nodded. "Met Saturday at the Mercantile."

"Enjoyin' your *trip*?" Finn asked.

He did *see it*.

"Except for the weather."

"That's why we got creeks." Finn started up the ancient boards nailed into the tree trunk, then paused on the top slat. "C'mon," he said, a half smile on his lips. "Unless you're chicken."

The view from the branch was a little scary, a two-story-plus drop, but by the time I'd seen the other two guys go off, I had everything scoped out and was ready to try it. The only trick appeared to be deciding exactly when to let go. Do it too soon and you'd land in shallow water; too late, and you'd hit in the same place, only going backward.

"Make sure ya don't miss the rope," Finn said from the launch station in front of me. Then he shoved off and did a double backflip in the pike position, finishing it off with a great watermelon.

I was so busy admiring his dive that I didn't notice the rope swing until it suddenly appeared in front of my face, twisting and thrashing like it was alive. Once my brain finally registered what was happening, my hand shot out like a striking snake and snagged the handle before it fell back out of reach.

But instead of using my free hand, I unfortunately used the one that had been holding on to the branch above me, leaving me with no way to balance myself. So when the swing started back down, it took me with it.

At the last second I lunged to grab on to the handle with my other hand before I fell to my death on the thick roots below. I made it, but my awkward launch started me jerking and spinning the instant I dropped off the branch, out of control from the get-go. It was all I could do just to hold on.

Actually, it was more than I could do to hold on. As I hit the bottom of my arc, instead of catapulting me upward, the rope did a giant crack-the-whip and flung me face-first into about three feet of water.

I was lucky I didn't break my neck. I did scrape my chin and palms in the bottom sand, and kind of jammed my right wrist, but none of that hurt too much. What hurt was the laughter.

I'd heard it start before I even hit the water, and by the time I got to my feet all the guys were cracking up.

Finn was waiting for me on the bank, still chuckling. "Funniest goshdarn thing I've ever seen." Only he didn't exactly say "Goshdarn," if you catch my drift.

"Glad ya liked it," I said with a forced grin, trying to salvage what I could from the situation.

"Lucky ya didn't break your fool neck." Except he used a different adjective.

"No lie." That's not really what I said either.

"Boomer, Gravy," Finn said when we got back on the branch, "this is the city boy I was tellin' ya 'bout."

"Mitch," I said, shaking with Boomer while I nodded past him at Gravy.

"You okay?" Boomer asked.

"Yeah. This is a little different than a diving board."

"Nothin' to it," he assured me. "Jus' takes a little practice."

Boomer was right. When it was my turn again, I went off without a hitch. I did almost lose my grip at the bottom of my arc, but was able to hold on long enough to do a decent cannonball from a respectable height. On my last turn before we broke for lunch, I even managed to do a backflip, more or less.

My back was still stinging a little when Gary and I joined everyone else on Aunt Dorothy's picnic blanket. As I eagerly reached into the large paper sack for a couple of the peanut-butter-and-jelly sandwiches she'd made, a voice I didn't recognize said behind me, "Got an extra sandwich?"

Woody squinted past my shoulder. "Sorry, ain't got enough."

"I was talkin' t' Slick here."

I looked around just as Finn walked up behind a

chunky guy with kind of a squashed-in face. "Bulldog's always hungry," he said with a smile.

"You guys can split one of mine," I said, to my complete amazement.

Bulldog snatched it out of my hand. "Thanks, Slick, I owe ya one." Then without another word, he and Finn spun around and walked back toward the swing.

"Where's your Southern hospitality?" I asked Woody. "We've got plenty of sandwiches." There must have been a dozen more of them in the bag.

"Jus' don't much cotton to 'em, that's all."

"How come?"

"Got m' reasons." Then Woody turned away from both of us and took a loud bite out of his apple, effectively ending the conversation.

I glanced at Gary for an explanation. He just shook his head and took a giant swig out of his root beer. I reached into the sack for another sandwich.

. . .

An hour or so later I was feeling pretty good again. My dives had steadily improved, so I knew Finn didn't think I was a complete klutz anymore, plus I'd been able to score some points by getting off a few good lines.

The best ones came when Charley wandered downstream to the base of the tree, where Finn and the guys and I were sitting in the shallow water at the creek's edge, leaning back in the shade against the oak's roots.

"Whatcha doin', Mitch?" he asked.

"Jus' tryin' t' beat the heat, shrimp. Guys, this is my brother, Charley."

Even though they were a lot older than Charley, they seemed to tolerate his company, despite his compulsion to spout off one trivial fact after another. "Did you guys know that the highest temperature ever recorded on Earth was 136 degrees?" he asked for openers.

"But it was a *dry* heat," I cracked.

"Didn't know, don't care," mumbled Gravy, his eyes barely open. I'd already gotten the impression that he'd spent way too much time around model airplane glue.

"Charley's got a photographic memory," I explained. "He never forgets anything he reads."

"Oh yeah?" said Finn. "I got one a them, too."

"Yeah," I came back, "but yours hasn't been developed yet."

That got a big laugh from everyone, including Finn, though I did notice that his eyes scrunched up a little at the corners.

Charley eventually left to rejoin our cousins upstream, so we all climbed back up the bank for a few more rounds on the swing. Then Finn finally said, "Lez go, boys. Gettin' hungry."

I followed them up the bank to the parked cars. Finn walked up to the black Caddy and opened the driver's door. "You old enough to drive?" I asked. I'd figured him for fourteen, maybe fifteen, tops.

He shook his head. "Naw. Jus' gotta be big enough t' reach the pedals. Ya ever driven before?"

"Just go-karts."

"Play your cards right and maybe you'll get a chance while you're here."

"No kidding? That'd be fantastic!"

Boomer opened the shotgun door. "Take it easy, Mitch."

"I will. Hey, d'ya mind my askin' how ya got the name Boomer?"

He immediately hiked his right leg and proceeded to demonstrate. It was a miracle that the surrounding trees had any leaves left when he was done.

When we all quit laughing Bulldog said, "He can even do Taps."

"*That* I'd like to hear," I said.

"So whadya think, city boy?" asked Finn. "Is Boomer a perfect name or what?"

"I think he oughta meet my dad."

12

Scavenger Hunt

Getting ready for bed that night took a little longer than usual because of the new bug bites. Before our visit to the creek I'd figured that the war was over, since the mosquito air force and the bug army hadn't left much unclaimed territory. But I'd been wrong again; I'd forgotten about the navy.

As Mom worked her way down my back with the cotton balls, I thought about aquatic mosquitoes, realizing that they'd been waiting for us all along. What I'd seen as just grass, weeds, water, and trees was actually camouflage for the hordes of bugs that patiently lay in ambush.

Charley and I had never had a chance.

"Well," Mom said as she finished up with the

calamine, "looks like Charley won." He and I had decided the second night to have a contest to see who would be first to get a hundred bug bites. I'd held the lead, 78 to 72, before we'd gone swimming. "One-oh-three to ninety-seven," she announced, then twisted the cap back on the nearly empty bottle.

"I'm thrilled," Charley muttered from his cot, where he was reading a Hardy Boys mystery and trying not to scratch.

As soon as Mom left I settled into my cot to read *Son of the Stars*, my favorite science-fiction book, for at least the tenth time. I'd just found the page I was on when Woody walked in. He'd been in a crummy mood ever since we'd left the creek, even ignoring Charley.

"Charley," he said, "sorry 'bout this evenin'. I'll take ya to the south forty t'morra t' make up for it, okay?" Then, without looking at me, he added, "And yeah, Mitch, you can come, too."

. . .

We hit the trail at eight, Woody and Charley in the lead, me bringing up the rear as usual. Between the heat and the gnats, I was ready to head back after five minutes. "How much of this is PawPaw's?" I asked as I swatted the air around my head.

"Almost to the end of it now," said Woody. He kicked another rock into the narrow gully we were following. "Property line's at them woods yondah."

"What's past them?" Charley asked.

"Jus' country."

As we neared the trees I couldn't help wondering what wild animals were waiting to tear us limb from limb. I instinctively looked back at the farmhouse, a cube of sugar in the distance, for what I hoped wouldn't be the last time. Then I mentally took a deep breath, and the next thing I knew we were in a Hansel and Gretel forest. The cheery morning sunlight was instantly replaced by a dappled gloom cast by a dense canopy of leaves and needles. Pines, oaks, and trees I didn't recognize grew in no apparent order; the forest floor was a noisy carpet of their droppings, as dead leaves, needles, and twigs crunched underfoot.

"Anyone remember the bread crumbs?" I asked, not totally joking.

A hawk screamed nearby, reminding me of the other thing besides animals that makes me nervous in the wilderness—their noises. I knew that the caws, chirps, and chitters I was hearing were Mother Nature's way of alerting potential prey like us to the fact that we were completely surrounded by predators, most of which were more than likely hungry. And some of which were undoubtedly snakes.

All of a sudden I was glad that Woody had brought along his .22 rifle. He'd had to sneak it out to the barn earlier, since Mom would more than likely have nixed the idea if she'd known about it. "What're you bringing that for?" I asked when he picked it up on our way out.

"Feel bettah when it's along," he said, and then loaded up.

Every rattle of leaves and rustle of brush made me feel better about the Winchester, too. I just hoped he could shoot the thing straight if he had to.

We took a food break an hour or so later, when we came across a small clearing where dusty beams of sunlight illuminated a patch of white wildflowers growing next to a rotting fallen tree. Despite the extra heat, it was a welcome relief from the spookiness of the woods.

We ended up staying there longer than we had to. It wasn't the tranquillity of the spot that kept us from moving on, and it wasn't that we'd eaten a whole day's rations in one sitting either. It was all because of the Stooges.

Specifically, it was Shemp's fault. When Woody asked if we wanted to rest on the fallen log for a while, I immediately answered in my Curly voice, "Why, *soi*tanly!"

"I wish you wouldn't do that," he said. "I can't stand Curly—he's fat, bald, and stupid."

"They're *all stu*pid," I said. "That's why they're funny. Don't tell me you like Shemp."

"Okay."

"Okay, what?"

"Okay, I won't tell ya." Woody paused to spit out a cherry pit. "But Shemp's funnier'n Curly any day of the week."

"If he was so funny," I countered, "then how come he

was replaced by Curly, huh? And besides, no hair's better than wearin' a greasy black mop on your head."

One thing I'd learned the hard way was that when people are on totally opposite sides of an issue, like Oreos versus Hydrox or Shemp versus Curly, there's no middle ground. And so it was with Woody and me; I couldn't convince him that Shemp never had a funny moment in his entire career, and he couldn't talk me out of believing that Curly was the most hysterical human being who'd ever lived.

But it turned out we both loved Moe's bowl haircut and Larry's electrified curls, so when we finally resumed our march, it was to their classic chant, "To the hunt! To the hunt! To the hunt, to the hunt, to the hunt!"

By the time we finally got tired of imitating the Stooges, we found ourselves in an even creepier part of the woods, dominated by tall, willowy cypress trees, mossy tendrils hanging from their branches.

I was trying to come up with a wisecrack when I started gagging. "What's *that*?" I asked, having to breathe through my mouth.

Woody wrinkled his nose. "Dead animal. Big un, too."

"Let's find it," Charley said.

I had a better idea. "Let's not, and say we did."

I was outvoted, so I followed them as we followed our noses, each step increasing the intensity of the vile vapors that permeated the air. Just when I thought I'd have to turn back or lose my lunch, we broke into another clearing. A second later I bumped into Charley, who'd just bounced off Woody, who had suddenly stopped.

The source of the stench lay about twenty feet away, covered with huge, iridescent flies. It was a dead horse, legs stiff and innards exposed by the gaping red and black holes in its underbelly. The red was blood and guts; the black was feathers. Vulture feathers.

They were a party of four, each one uglier than the next and twice the size of a tom turkey. The one closest to us appeared to have been decapitated, but then he yanked his slimy, bald head out of the horse's stomach and looked right at us, a foul noodle of something dangling from his long, curved beak.

"What *is* that?" I asked through my T-shirt.

"It's offal," said Charley.

"I know *that*. What *is* it?"

"Not a-w-f-u-l awful. Offal." He grinned. "O-f-f-a-l. Entrails."

"Well, whatever it is, I've seen enough. Let's get out of here."

"Hold on," said Woody. "Charley, let's get a little closah, wanna show ya somethin'."

"Why not?" Charley said through pinched nostrils. "Can't smell any worse."

Before I could point out to them why not, they took a few steps toward the carcass. The vultures stood their ground and stirred ominously, as if daring them to come any closer.

And then Woody did something really stupid. He raised his rifle, quickly aimed, and shot one of them. Or rather, he shot *at* one; what he hit was the horse. The bullet struck a large sac low in its belly, bursting it in a spray of disgusting green fluid.

The report of the shot quickly faded, replaced by the soft but steady rustling of leaves overhead. And then I remembered that these were cypress trees, and didn't have leaves that rustled.

I looked up. What I'd thought were windblown leaves were rustling vulture wings instead. Dozens and dozens of them.

It seemed like every branch in a 360-degree circle around us was occupied by vultures, wings half spread for balance as they shifted in agitation on their perches. With their carving knife beaks and daggered feet, any one of them could have turned a person to beef jerky in seconds. And there were at least thirty, all of them staring at us.

It was a vulture picnic, and we were dessert.

Then one of them flapped off its branch and settled to the ground not ten feet in front of us, spread its wings to their full five-foot span, and let out a terrifying screech. I knew it was Vulturese for "Run or die!"

Without even trying, I did my best Moe ever. "Nyah-ah-ah . . ."

Pulling Charley with me, I slowly backed out of the clearing. So did Woody. The instant we reached the edge of the woods, we spun on our heels and took off helter-skelter through the trees, *all* of us *woo-woo-woo*ing just like Curly. The only thing missing was the theme song "Three Blind Mice."

. . .

Thursday afternoon I found an envelope waiting for me on my cot. I stared at it for a second, wondering who it could be from. Then I recognized Tick's printing. I ripped the envelope apart, took out the single sheet of lined paper inside and unfolded it, then sat down Indian-style against the wall to read.

> *Mitch,*
>
> *Boy, are things ever boring around here. You haven't been gone a week and already I'm bored out of my mind. Even if I could think of something that wouldn't be boring to do, there's nobody around here to do it with who isn't boring. I hope your summer's going just as crummy as mine— But seriously, folks. And speaking of your folks, tell your mom her flowers haven't died (yet), and let your dad know I've tested the pool every day. Also, tell Charley all his creepy-crawlies are okay. There is one good thing—my parents said I could call you long distance for your birthday present, so make sure you're home at 8 p.m., okay? (I'll call you at 10—just kid-*

ding!) Take it easy & I'll talk to you in a month or
so. Don't forget—8 p.m., your time. Be there or be
square.

>*Your bored best friend, T. K. Murphy, Esq.*
>*P.S. Do you have a Southern accent yet?*
>*P.P.S. If you do, don't come back!*
>*P.P.P.S. Just kidding again!!*
>*P.P.P.PleaSe write back!!!*

It was funny how Tick's letter affected me. Not ha-
ha funny but weird funny. As I read it I could easily
hear him talking with his kind of annoying habit of
speaking in exclamation points, but no matter how hard
I tried, I couldn't get his face to come all the way into
focus.

San Bernardino seemed a distant memory, too,
lumped into my past with the Air Force Academy, Mont-
gomery, and Rome; I even had a tough time visualizing
my bedroom.

And all after only six and a half days in Louisiana.

. . .

Dad was heading out first thing Saturday, so Mom decided to give him a going-away party Friday after supper.
He'd just finished giving me his "You're the man of the
house now" speech on the porch and was starting in on
the "Take good care of your mother" part when Uncle
Cecil and Aunt Marjorie pulled up in a shiny-new white
Chrysler.

Dad got up from his rocker and set his beer on the railing. "Fine lookin' automobile ya got there, Cecil."

"Yeah, if ya like boats," Uncle Cecil said, getting out of the car. He slammed the driver's door, then leaned against the front fender and took a toothpick out of his shirt pocket. Aunt Marjorie glared at him from the shotgun seat, drumming her fingernails on the wind wing.

Uncle Cecil eyed her for a few seconds, the toothpick flicking between his lips like a snake's tongue. "Your arm broke?" Her face turned as bright a red as the upholstery.

This could be a good one.

But evidently Uncle Cecil wasn't in the mood for hand-to-hand combat. "*Thank* you," Aunt Marjorie said when he finally opened her door. Nose in the air, she blew past us and stormed straight into the house, trailing a blast of frigid air in her wake.

Dad bent down to open the cooler. "I gather the car wasn't your idea," he said, fishing out another can of beer. He punctured it twice with the opener and handed it to Uncle Cecil.

Uncle Cecil drained it in one long gulp. "Thanks," he said, then wiped his mouth with the back of his hand. "I needed that." He flashed a sour grin as he reached for the screen door. "And now I'm gonna fix m'self a drink."

Uncle Nolan and Aunt Grace showed up next, followed shortly by Gary and the guys and their folks. While the adults gabbed on the porch, we amused ourselves at the tire swing in the side yard until it was time for dessert.

"Chocolate cake and homemade vanilla ice cream!" Aunt Nelda announced from the screen door. "Any takers?"

Fortunately no one was injured in the stampede.

Once we'd all gotten a serving and had returned to the porch to eat it, all I could hear for a while were appreciative mmm's and a soft symphony of metal on porcelain, along with the million-bug percussion section, of course.

Uncle Nolan set his empty bowl on the railing. "So, Marc, tell us 'bout your TDY."

"Temporary duty," I explained to the guys.

"It's the Air Force Accident Investigation School," Dad began. "I'll be at the Pentagon for six weeks learning how to figure out why fighter jets crash."

"Sounds lovely," said Aunt Marjorie, her voice a little slurred.

"Somebody's gotta do it," Dad said, "or we'll keep losing good men."

"Not t' mention 'spensive airplanes."

"Planes can be rebuilt, *dear*," Uncle Cecil snapped. "*People can't.*"

"Well!" she said with a toss of her lacquered bangs. "I never!"

Mustering what dignity she could, Aunt Marjorie

rose from her rocker and took her dish inside. It may have only been my imagination, but it seemed that when the screen door closed, everyone exhaled at the same time.

"Marc," said Uncle Robert, obviously trying to get the conversation going again, "tell 'em 'bout black boxes and last words."

I saw Mom's ears prick up.

"Flight recorders," Dad said with a flick of his lighter.

"Uncle Marc," asked Larry, "how come they call 'em black boxes?"

Barry jumped in. " 'Cause that's what they *look* like, ya moron!"

Uncle Robert gave him a withering look; Barry didn't say anything else.

"Actually, they're orange now," Dad quickly continued, "and they record the plane's movements and cockpit conversations up 'til the moment of impact."

"Including the crew's last words," said Uncle Robert.

"Yeah," Dad echoed, "including their last words." He took a slow drag off his cigarette and blew three lazy smoke rings.

"Which are . . . ?" prompted Uncle Robert.

"When a man knows he's going to die," Dad said quietly, knowing we were hanging on every word, "he always says one of two things." He paused to tap the ash off his cigarette. "Some of 'em say 'Oh, God' . . ."

Mom chose that exact moment to clear her throat.

"But most of 'em say, 'Oh, shoot.' " Then he glanced at Mom and grinned. "Only without the *o*'s."

The laughter was cut short by Aunt Marjorie, who suddenly threw the screen door open and marched right up to Uncle Cecil. "Cecil," she said, clutching her purse so hard her knuckles were white, "take me home right now."

"Keys're in the car," he said, staring her down. "I'll git m' own ride."

That was the straw that broke Aunt Marjorie's back. She stomped down the steps toward her new car, yanked open the driver's door, and threw herself behind the steering wheel. Seconds later she peeled out with a spectacular spray of dust and gravel.

PawPaw spat a stream of tobacco juice into his Folgers coffee can, then spoke for the first time that evening. "She shore left in a huff."

"Actually, PawPaw," I said, "I think it was an Imperial."

13

Night Games

By eight Saturday morning we were on our way to Fort Polk, the Army post about twenty miles west on Highway 10. Less than five minutes later I was on my way back to dreamland.

I was snapped back into consciousness by Dad slamming on the brakes. The squeal of skid marks was immediately joined by the smell of burning rubber as Dad whipped the De Soto into the visitors' lane and coasted in a thin blue haze up to the imposing brick guardhouse that was the entrance to Fort Polk.

An equally imposing military policeman with a huge holstered pistol and serious boots waited for us at the gate. He had no hair beneath his camouflage cap and no neck above the collar of his matching fatigues. The instant the car stopped he took one brisk step forward, clicked his heels together so loud I almost ducked, then slammed the edge of his stiff right hand into his temple and shouted at us like we were deaf. "WELCOME TO FORT POLK, *SIR*!" He snapped off the salute with enough force to stun flies. "ID card, please."

"Base Ops," Dad said in his officer voice as he held out the laminated card.

"*Post* Ops, yes, sir," the guard corrected, his eyes smiling.

I could see the back of Dad's neck start to redden.

Even though Dad was in uniform, he still had to hand over his identification; this was, after all, an Army post, not an Air Force base. The M.P., who seemed to get younger the longer I looked at him, took the card, smartly attached it to his metal clipboard, and started writing what was apparently his autobiography. Eventually he moved to the front of the car, where he either added an epilogue or recorded our license plate number, I wasn't sure which.

The sentry stepped up to Dad's window and crisply handed back his ID and a pink pass. "Display this on your dash at all times, sir. Can I direct you, sir?"

The directions were fairly involved, but fortunately Mom was paying attention, so we only made one wrong turn. That took us to the barracks area, where we drove exactly ten miles an hour past masses of soldiers who were either marching, jogging, or doing calisthenics.

We finally got back on track and pulled into the Post

Operations parking lot a few minutes later. Charley and I scrambled to grab Dad's duffel bags, then crab-walked them into the building's tiny lobby, where Dad checked in at the front desk. He'd arranged to cadge a lift in an Army chopper to England Air Force Base in Alexandria, where he'd hitch a ride to D.C. in something a little faster.

Dad nodded, evidently satisfied that the mission was a Go, then turned to Charley and me and smiled. "No use you all waiting around," he said. He picked Charley up by the armpits and held him tight, whispering something I couldn't catch into his ear.

Then he set him down, cupped the back of my neck, and pulled me close. "You're in charge now, sport, so use your head, okay?" I nodded, a lump forming in my throat. He gave me a quick bear hug and smiled. "You boys run on out to the car now. I want to say goodbye to your mother."

Dad waved as the heavy glass door slowly closed on him and the scent of Old Spice mixed with tobacco. Mom came out a few minutes later and slid behind the wheel next to Charley and me. Dabbing at her nose with a wad of tissue in one hand and trying to keep her sunglasses from sliding down her wet cheeks with the other, she turned to us and sniffled. "I'll need all the help you can give me, boys."

Sometimes being in the military wasn't so great.

. . .

It was probably a good thing for Mom that the rest of Saturday was busy. While she got her shopping and hair done in town, Charley and Woody and I hung out at the cafe with Gary and the guys, just like we'd already done for three days in a row.

I twisted around in the booth closest to the jukebox. "If you play 'El Paso' one more time, I'll kill you," I said to Barry, who was hovering over the Wurlitzer's red plastic buttons, his index finger poised directly over D-4.

He must have known I meant it, since he immediately but casually moved his finger one to the left. "I was gonna play 'Crazy' for Mama." Aunt Dorothy was grilling burgers for a couple of codgers seated at the counter.

The herky-jerky movements of the selector arm quickly cued a sappy instrumental intro that led to the even sappier voice of Patsy Cline. "Cray-zee . . . ," she and Aunt Dorothy sang, unfortunately in different keys.

Standing up, I took the last sip of my cream soda, then put the empty in the wooden R.C. Cola case on top of the stack next to the door. "I can't handle this. I'll be back later."

Actually Aunt Dorothy's being a Patsy Cline fanatic was okay by me, since it gave me the excuse I'd been looking for to ditch all of them for a while. It had turned out to be almost impossible so far to get away on my own, without Charley and one or four of my cousins tagging along, so I knew I had to take advantage of my opportunities when they arose. Besides, I'd seen Finn and the guys fly by in the Cadillac a little earlier, so I figured there was a better than average chance I could catch them at Dixie's.

Dixie's Cafe, like Robert's, was either the first or the last building in town, depending on which way you were going. And just as they were at opposite ends of Pitkin, they were also completely different in personality. Robert's Cafe was done in cheap but manly hunting lodge paneling and dark reds; Dixie's had definitely been decorated by a woman.

Earlier in the week I'd peeked in on the chance I'd see Finn, but none of the customers at the time were under retirement age. What I did see was a painfully bright glare of indoor sunshine: yellow-and-white gingham-checked tablecloths, sunflower wallpaper, and frilly daisy-print curtains that covered the bottom halves of the windows. It was a good thing I'd been able to talk Mom into buying me the sunglasses I'd flipped over at the Pitkin Mercantile.

Finn's Caddy was parked on the far side of the Mercantile. A quick walk through the store only turned up his parents and a bunch of customers, so I headed down the block. I was checking out the effect of my new shades one more time in the window of Hill's General Store next door to Dixie's when Finn and the guys spilled out of the cafe, laughing like hyenas.

I hurried to close the gap. "Hey, Finn!"

"Cool shades, Daddy-o," he said with a smile.

"Yeah." Bulldog leered. "Where'd ya get 'em, *Cool*ville?"

What an idiot.

"No, Heptown," I said, playing along.

Bulldog couldn't seem to leave bad enough alone. "Ahh," he said, with the worst French accent I'd ever heard, "eet was jes a leetle joke, oui?"

"Very wee," I agreed. That got a laugh out of everyone but Gravy; all he got out of it was a furrowed brow.

"Lez go, boys," Finn said. "Crockett's waitin' on us."

"Will you guys be at the game tonight?"

"Mebbe," Finn said in a cowpoke voice, "and mebbe not." Then he started off past me toward the Mercantile, the other three in tow.

"Finn," I stalled, not sure what I was going to say next.

He stopped and turned partway around. "Yeah?"

My mind was as blank as erased tape. "Seeya."

He got in the last word. "Wouldn't wanna be ya."

. . .

I cracked up when I saw the white banner draped across the back of the snack bar before the game. "Pitkin versus *Hicks*?" I asked, looking at Barry. "How can you tell who's who?"

"Very funny," he said. "First time I've heard that . . . this *week*."

I found out that Hicks was a little timber town about forty miles away, in the middle of the Kisatchie National

Forest. The drive to Pitkin must have worn out their pitchers, since it took three of them to get out of the bottom of the first, by which time the score was 12–zip and the game no longer in doubt. Gary was the offensive hero again, driving in five runs with two homers in the first inning alone. And the whole time he was hitting baseballs over the fence, I was leaning over the counter of the snack bar trying my best to hit up on Skeeter.

I knew from television and movies that the key to success was the opening line, but unfortunately I couldn't think of anything that didn't sound dumb.

"So where's your mom?" I finally managed. Skeeter was working the snack bar by herself.

"Takin' care of Aunt Lulu. Ready for another cream soda?"

"No thanks, not yet. So what do you do in your spare time?"

"Don't have much, what with this an' chores."

"What—" I started to ask, but stopped when she told me to wait with a raised index finger, then helped a couple of pimply teenagers wearing overalls and Hicks caps.

She had to fill a few more orders before we could resume our conversation, which gave me a chance to regroup and try to come up with better openers than lame questions about her mom and spare time.

"So, really," I tried again, "what do you do when you're not working?"

"Play baseball."

I tried not to show my surprise. "There's a girls' team here?"

She shook her head and frowned. "Even if there was, I'd be the only one on it. Naw, I just play with Gary. You play ball back home?"

"Not really. I mean, I like to throw the ball around and I love Three Flies Up, but I hated playing on a team."

She gave me an incredulous look. "I'd give *any*thing to play on a team."

"I'll bet you're pretty good," I said, suddenly seeing an opportunity.

"Better than a lot of the guys."

We were interrupted once more by customers, so by the time she was free again I had my strategy all worked out. "Maybe we could play catch sometime."

She smiled. "Sure, we'd love to. It's a lot more fun with three—then we could catch, throw, *and* bat."

That's not exactly what I had in mind.

Gary and the rest of the Pine Burr players suddenly swarmed around the snack bar like jackals on carrion, ending our conversation.

After the last of them slunk off into the night with their spoils, Gary and I helped Skeeter close up shop. Actually, it was just Gary who helped. He and Skeeter boxed up the unsold candy bars and chips while they talked about the game; odd man out, I found a rag and started wiping the counter.

Just as they finished cleaning the popcorn machine, Skeeter's dad pulled up in an old pickup to take her home. Gary dumped the water out of the washtub, and I helped him put it in the back of the truck.

Then Gary said, "Give us a minute, will ya, Mitch?"

Trying to keep my face from giving me away, I said good night to Skeeter and her dad, and started off toward Gary's house. With the same compulsion that makes you look at accident victims, I stopped a little ways down the road and turned around for a quick peek. Gary and Skeeter were talking, too close together for my comfort, when I saw her give him one of the smiles she'd given me. Only bigger, and somehow better. I suddenly got a sick feeling in my stomach, like not being ready for a pop quiz.

"Don't *even* think about it," Woody's voice came out of the darkness.

"Don't sneak up on people like that, man," I said, my heart beating like a trip-hammer. "You'll give someone a heart attack."

"I didn't sneak up on ya, I was jus' sittin' here thinkin'." Woody moved from the fender of the car he'd been leaning against and started walking ahead of me. "C'mon," he said over his shoulder, "let's get back t' the house. Aunt Dorothy's got strawberry shortcake waitin'."

"That's okay," I said. "I'm really not that hungry."

. . .

It was after ten o'clock by the time Mom headed back, having reluctantly agreed to let Charley and me stay the night, along with Woody. I felt kind of guilty about leaving her alone at PawPaw's the first night Dad was gone, but not enough to pass up a sleepover.

The six of us horsed around on the front porch for a while after she left, playing a moronic little-kid game called Red Light, Green Light. I was bored out of my mind after the first ten seconds, and since it was starting to look like they were going to play it until the sun came up, I decided to take the initiative. "Aren't you guys tired of this yet? Let's do something else."

"Like what?" asked Barry.

"I dunno, anything. You got any ideas?"

Barry looked at me and grinned. "Pillow fight."

"Too hot," I said, shaking my head.

"Come on, Mitch," said Charley. "It'll be fun."

"Meet us in my room," Gary said. "Barry, help me get the extra pillows."

Watching them beat each other's brains out with pillows sounded less boring than sweating on the porch by myself, so I followed Charley into the house.

The four Millers cleared as much space in Gary's room as they could, then grabbed their pillows. "Here ya go, boys," Barry said as he tossed two pillows to Charley and me.

"I told ya, I don't wanna sweat any more than I already am," I said. "I'll be the referee."

"We don't need no referee," said Barry.

"Suits me," I said, leaving my pillow at my feet and backing up to the doorway. "Knock yourselves out. Really."

Like the corncob fight, the pillow fight had no rules, which Barry immediately demonstrated by charging at Gary while Gary was closing his closet door.

"Hey!" Gary yelled as Barry creamed him in the back of the head, and the fight was on.

Normally I would have been the one to have suggested the pillow fight in the first place, but I wasn't in the mood to even watch this one. I was turning around to leave when I saw Woody coming at me. Before I could react, his pillow caught me behind the knees, knocking my feet out from under me.

The ceiling light fixture flashed by, and a split second later my head slammed onto the hardwood floor. The next thing I saw was exploding stars.

The fight stopped while everyone waited to see if I was all right.

"What's the *matter* with you?" I yelled at Woody as I sat up and gingerly rubbed the back of my head. "I *told* you I didn't wanna do this!"

"Sorry," Woody said in a tone that said he really wasn't.

"And what's *in* that thing?" I asked, reaching for his pillow. "Lemme see it."

Woody grinned and handed it over.

I reached into the bottom third of the pillowcase and pulled out a stained, gray-striped pillow, inside of which was a lumpy mass of condensed feathers that must have weighed five pounds.

My anger rising as fast as the bump on my head, I slowly got to my feet.

Gripping the pillow by one corner, I started swinging at everyone and yelling at the same time, each word punctuated by the satisfying sound of a direct hit.

"I'm getting . . . really . . . tired . . . of playing . . . little . . . kid . . . *games*!"

With the last word I swung as hard as I could at Woody's head. The pillow knocked him into the wall and exploded on impact, spraying feathers everywhere.

I left the room long before they settled to the floor.

14

The Aunt Farm

I woke up Sunday morning to Mom's voice. "Mitch, Charley, time to get up. Service is at nine." I felt her lay something on the foot of the guest bed. "I brought your church clothes, so let's get up and get dressed."

Think fast.

"I don't feel very well, Mom. I think I'm gonna be sick."

Mom sat on the edge of the bed and put the back of her hand on my forehead. "You seem fine to me. Sure you're not just trying to get out of going?"

"Honest, Mom, it must've been all the junk I ate at the game last night."

She gave me a long, skeptical look. "Okay, but you know, if you're faking, God'll know, too, and it won't make Him happy."

What's He gonna do, Ma, set me on fire?

I gave her my best sick face and kneaded my abdomen. "Can you get me a pot or something, Mom? I think I'm gonna throw up pretty soon." For emphasis I stifled a fake gag.

My last move must have finally convinced her, since she immediately got up and left the room, quickly returning with a large pail. Setting it on the floor next to me, she said, "I'll check on you before we go. Let me know if you need anything else."

Mom looked past me at Charley, who hadn't stirred, then turned to leave. She paused at the doorway on her way out. "Sorry you don't feel well. You could've sat with Skeeter."

"What?"

"Mrs. Perkins called this morning and invited us to sit with them today. And over to their place afterward. Too bad you'll miss it."

Now I really am gonna throw up.

. . .

Having blown a great opportunity to be with Skeeter, I was in no mood to spend the afternoon with more relatives I didn't know, but I didn't have much choice.

"Do we *have* to do this, Mom?" I whined from the shotgun seat. "I still don't feel all that great." Mom had come back around noon and informed Charley and me that we were going to her aunt Chlora's for Sunday dinner, so I'd had nothing to lose by keeping up the sick act.

"Does Aunt Chlora live in Louisiana?" Charley asked next to me. It was a reasonable question, since we'd been creeping along a narrow dirt road for miles.

"Just past these pines and around the bend. I want you two to be sociable, hear me? Leave your books in the car." Charley and I had brought them along, just in case.

A minute or so later the red dirt curved to the left, bringing into view an old, faded-white farmhouse and a gigantic oak, both set near the front of the large clearing off to the right. The traditional pack of mangy curs yapped at the car as we pulled into the front-yard used-car lot and parked between an old blue sedan and a rusted-out derelict resting on its rims.

Two emaciated mummies in matching rockers smiled and waved from the front porch. They were also in matching dresses, a hideous pink-and-purple floral print, and wore their white hair pulled tightly back in identical buns; even their Coke-bottle-lensed granny glasses were the same. And so, as I noticed when Mom herded us up the steps, were their faces.

"Aunt Floretta! Aunt Lounetta!" Mom cooed as she bent over for hugs and pecks. "Y'all haven't changed one bit!"

Floretta and Lounetta broke into identical fake-shy smiles and twittered like pet parakeets.

Mom reached back and grabbed me by the elbow. "Aunt Flo, Aunt Lou, this is Mitch," she said, practically shoving me into Aunt Floretta's face. Up close she seemed even more ancient, with wrinkled skin as dry as week-old biscuits.

"Mitch, is it?" Aunt Floretta chirped, pinning me with clear, hazel hawk eyes. "How old're you now, boy? Nine? Ten?"

I could feel my face start to flush.

"He'll be twelve in a month," said Mom. "He's just small for his age."

It was Charley's turn next, so we switched sisters, which was when I realized that the twin biddies even smelled the same, like Vicks VapoRub.

The screen door banged open. "Frankie Laverne Miller!" shouted a rosy-cheeked, roly-poly old woman. "Let me *look* at you, girl!"

"Aunt Chlora!" Mom beamed, and then hugged her tightly.

Somehow Charley and I survived being hugged by Aunt Chlora. "Eunice an' Edna an' Sybil's all back in the kitchen," she said as she shooed us all through the front parlor.

The kitchen was like visiting hours at an old-folks' home, nothing but used-up old women in washed-out old clothes; even the aroma of frying chicken couldn't completely mask their old-lady smells. All three of them were busy fixing dinner, and hadn't stopped working since we'd walked in. In fact, one of them, a stocky woman wearing a pale-blue calico dress, never even moved from the faucet, where she had her back to us, washing something off in the sink. There was something vaguely familiar about her, but I couldn't pin it down. Then she turned off the tap and turned around.

It was the Barker.

It can't be.

And it wasn't. But it took a second or two to realize that.

"What's the mattah, Mitch?" asked Aunt Chlora. "You look like you've just seen a ghost!"

I almost had; whichever aunt it was bore an amazing resemblance to the Barker, even after I got over the initial shock.

"Maybe you really *are* sick," Mom said. "Why don't you go lie down?"

"That's okay, Mom," I said, seeing an out. "I'll just go outside and get some air. C'mon, Charley."

We escaped through a warped screen door before Mom could stop us. It led to Aunt Chlora's back stoop and yard, and suddenly it was 1814, and we were pioneers, looking at a wide, peaceful meadow edged by a pine forest that went as far as the eye could see.

"Shore is purdy, Zeke," Charley prompted, smiling in anticipation.

"Shore is, Zeb," I answered with a nod. "A body could do mighty fine here, mighty fine."

"Hope there ain't no panthers in these here parts."

"Naw, panthers never—" I suddenly staggered forward and bent over as if one had just landed on my back, then fell to the ground under its weight. I thrashed wildly on the grass as I vainly tried to pry the big cat's claws off my face, then let out a bloodcurdling scream, fluttered my eyelids, and kicked the bucket with one last, delayed spasm of my feet.

My performance was worthy of the applause Charley gave it; the only problem was, he wasn't the only one clapping.

"Purdy good," a freckle-faced kid about my size said with a lopsided grin.

"Yeah," said a kid who looked a lot like him, only smaller, "looked real t' me."

As I quickly got up and swiped the grass off my shirt and jeans, two more of them sauntered around the corner of the house and joined their brothers. All four had freckles all over their smudged faces and shaggy, wheat-colored hair that had probably never been combed. They all wore faded, frayed overalls, none of which seemed to fit, and had feet that looked like they'd never seen the inside of a shoe.

And to top it off, every one of them carried a bamboo fishing pole, only with round plastic bobbers instead of corks. Other than that one small detail, they were Huckleberry Finn in a room full of mirrors.

"I'm Mitch," I said to the first one, "and this is m' brother Charley. No luck with the fish?"

"Not a lick," said the second-biggest one.

I never did learn any of their names, I guess partially

since I figured I probably wouldn't ever see them again, but mainly because the names themselves were so confusing. To tease Mom, Dad had always told Southern jokes about good ol' boys called Billy Bob and Bobby Jim and Jimmy Ray, but I'd never expected them to actually be real.

They are. All four Hucks had a combination of two first names that had one thing in common: the fact that I couldn't keep any of them straight, which is why I had to settle for "you guys" instead.

"Hey, you guys," I said, "what's there to do around here?"

"Gotta big tree out front," said number three.

"Yeah, I noticed. Can we climb it?"

For some reason they all started laughing. "Shoot yeah, boy, you can climb it," number two said. "Lez go."

I soon knew what was so funny. The eight boards going up the side of the trunk I hadn't been able to see coming in were obvious evidence of the giant oak's climbability, but that wasn't the amusing part. The humor was in the fact that not only could you *climb* this tree, you could practically *live* in it.

How I'd missed it all earlier was beyond me, because now it seemed that everywhere I looked some kind of weathered board was nailed to the bark. Either a platform or a lookout sat on every major branch, connected by a great system of ladders and bridges.

But best of all were the long ropes and swings hanging like vines from half a dozen places spread throughout the oak's massive limbs. The overall effect was a combination Tarzan set and the Swiss Family Robinson tree house.

We scrambled up the ladder like monkeys fleeing a python and scattered in six different directions; I had my eye on a small platform about halfway out on the branch closest to the house.

I got there first and claimed it by standing on top of it, grabbing on to the treetop-to-ground rope that was the reason I'd picked that spot in the first place, and letting out the loudest Tarzan yell I could. "Ah-ee-ah-ee-aw, ee-ah-ee-aw!"

I was standing at eye level with the top of the chimney, close to twenty feet up, checking out the view while I tested the strength of the rope, when one of the middle-size guys called up from a plank bridge a couple of yards below me and near the trunk. "Why don'tcha swing on down? I'll catch ya if ya have a problem."

"Okay, sure," I said, more confidently than I felt. I pulled the rope up until I had enough slack to account for the five-or-six-foot drop. The rope was about an inch thick and really coarse, with frayed fibers sticking out everywhere, like a long, hairy caterpillar, but other than not having a handle, it was pretty much like the one at the creek.

My hands were already moist from the humidity, so there was really no need to spit on my palms, but I did anyway. Then I got the tightest grip I could, let out another yell, and swung out and down, just like Tarzan of the Apes on his way to Opar to rescue Jane.

Except it wasn't like the swing at the creek at all, and I wasn't Tarzan. The instant I ran out of slack I lost my grip and slid straight down the rope, trying desperately to hold on with hands not strong enough to do the job. Before I could think to let go, I flashed past the kid on the plank, his mouth open in surprise, then barely missed the trunk before I hit the ground.

The force of the impact drove me to my knees, where I sat stunned for a few seconds, the rope still in my hands. I didn't let go of it because I couldn't. And the reason I couldn't was that it was fused to my palms.

In slow motion I peeled my fingers off the rope, skin ripping with every movement, then turned my palms up to see how bad the damage was. My fingers on both hands were four parallel pink bands of three broken stripes each, all seeping what looked like watermelon juice. Burned into my palms and thumbs were longer and deeper unbroken furrows that oozed a thin, yellowish fluid. I knew that when the adrenaline shock wore off I was in for the Big Hurt.

And then God set my hands on fire.

It was a joke, Lord! I didn't mean it!

But my apology was too late. Wave after wave of white-hot agony pulsed up my arms and exploded in my brain—breathtaking, mind-searing jolts of electric pain.

Tears streamed down my cheeks, as if they, too, were trying to run from the fire in my head.

Oh man, oh man, oh man.

I tried everything I could think of to not think about the pain, from reciting the times tables in my head to mouthing verses of "The ants go marching one by one, hurrah, hurrah."

Then suddenly I was surrounded by people: four plump old ladies with concerned looks on their faces, and two mirror-image scrawny ones clucking like chickens; four green-eyed look-alikes wearing expressions of shock, pity, and relief that it wasn't them; and Charley, trying not to cry.

Plus Mom. She knelt down in the grass next to me, took one look at the watery pus welling out of my burns, then put a knuckle to her lips and made a sound like an overheated radiator. "Oh. My. God. We've *got* to get him to a hospital!"

. . .

"WELCOME TO FORT POLK, *MA'AM*!"

"We need to get to the infirmary!" Mom said in her panic voice, her dependent's ID card already thrust into the face of the same M.P. we'd seen the day before with Dad. "It's an emergency! Please hurry!"

But by then it really wasn't, not as far as I was concerned. I'd long since passed my pain threshold and was now somewhere else, a distant, peaceful place where I couldn't feel anything at all.

The acne-scarred medic brought me back to the real world. "You'll have to keep still now, son," he said, turning my hands palm up in his. "An' it's okay to cry, 'cause this is prob'ly gonna hurt." Which was like saying that Dracula was probably going to have blood for dinner.

I won't go into the details of cleaning and dressing my wounds, since I can't recall much about that anyway. All I remember is more pain.

By the time we got back to PawPaw's, the pills they'd given me had finally started to kick in. We were met at the steps by Aunt Nelda, who seemed to already know what had happened. She looked at my bandages, her eyes shiny, then gave me a soft hug and said, "Oh, Mitch, I'm *so* sorry!"

I tried to smile. "Me, too, Aunt Nelda."

"Well, at least the worst is ovah now, hon," she said, gently escorting me into the house.

She sat me down at the small kitchen table. "Lemme pour ya some cold lemonade t' take your mind off it."

I was sitting there with Charley, sipping my drink through a straw and feeling no pain at all, when the phone rang. Aunt Nelda picked up the black receiver from its wall cradle, said hello, nodded once, and held it up to my ear. "It's for you. It's Gary."

" 'Lo," I said. The pain pills were *really* starting to work.

"Mitch, you gotta come over! Jus' got a buncha new old funnies."

"Thas great." I stared at my ruined hands. "Gary," I said, sure I was grinning like the Cheshire Cat.

"What?"

"If y'know whus goodferya," I said, trying my best to enunciate properly, "don't ever skip 'nother daya church."

And that's the last thing I can remember.

15

Shot in the Dark

According to Charley, being able to grip an object between your thumb and fingers is one of the things that separates us from the rest of the animal kingdom, a fact I began to appreciate first thing Monday morning while I stood in front of the toilet in my underwear, my bladder overflowing and my fingers too painful to move. I'll skip the embarrassing details; let's just say that I worked out how to go to the bathroom for the same reason I figured out how to get dressed—because I had to.

Mom had to help me with my T-shirt, but fortunately I had a pair of elastic-banded pull-on shorts; the simple act of zipping up was now beyond my ability, and there was no way I was going to let her do it. It was bad enough that she was going to have to feed me.

Dealing with socks and shoelaces was also out of the

question, but that didn't really matter, since I didn't plan on leaving the house again until Dad returned and we were ready to go back to California and the safety of civilization.

But like my other plans for the summer, that didn't work out either, mainly because listening to Mom and Aunt Nelda talk was about as exciting as a social studies lesson.

"Could you help me with my tennies, Mom?" I asked after maybe three minutes of hanging out with them in the kitchen after breakfast. "I don't feel like sitting around anymore."

"Sure you're up to it?" she asked as she wiped the table. "The doctor said for you to take it real easy for a while, if you'll recall."

Actually I didn't recall, but it was what I'd decided to do anyway, just not with Mom and Aunt Nelda. And they were the only ones left, since PawPaw had already gone out back to do some chores, and Charley and Woody had taken off on another expedition the instant they'd finished slurping down their cereal.

Out of politeness they'd asked me if I wanted to join them, but before I could answer Mom said, "Don't even think about it, young man." Not that I would have gone anyway; the last thing I was interested in was having another nature experience. What I really wanted was to be alone.

So as soon as Mom knotted my laces, I headed toward

the screen door. Holding my bandaged hands up in front of my chest like a surgeon in a scrub room, I pushed the door open with my rear end and said, "I'll be back later." Then I stepped out onto the back porch and started looking for a place to hide.

The hayloft was the first place I thought of, but I didn't figure I could climb the ladder without the use of my hands, and even if I could, I knew I wouldn't be able to handle the smell for very long. The small wooden storage shed next to the barn was full of gardening tools and a wheelbarrow; I considered sitting in the wheelbarrow until I walked over to it and saw that it was gone.

The crude smokehouse on the other side of the barn would have been more like a jail cell than a hideout, and the rusted metal seat of the old tractor parked behind it offered no back support, and was more than likely already too hot to sit on anyway.

That only left the chicken coop, the hog pen, and the corral, all of which would have been useless as hiding places even if they hadn't smelled as disgusting as the barn.

Maybe this wasn't such a good idea.

Then I remembered the junked old car that I'd seen from a distance on our hike to the south forty. The wreck was a couple of football fields away, abandoned next to a stand of small pin oaks on the other side of the gully that was the property line between PawPaw's place and the Boudreaux farm.

The car turned out to be a rusty black 1940s four-door, minus the doors. It was also missing its hood and trunk lid, along with its front windshield. Tiny glass crystals still littered the front bench seat; lacking a way to sweep them off the rotted gray upholstery, I had to settle for the back. After first inspecting the space for any signs of animal inhabitation, I eased myself onto the backseat and settled in to sulk.

But I couldn't relax; there were just too many distractions. The backseat padding was cratered with big holes that looked like they'd been gnawed by giant rats, making it impossible to find a position that didn't poke seat springs into me somewhere; the air inside the junker was as still as a photograph; and the constant electric insect hum seemed even louder than usual.

I was debating whether or not to try to find another place when I heard something move under the seat. It sounded more like slithering than scurrying, which is why I didn't stick around long enough to find out for sure. Launching myself backward out of the car like a horizontal jack-in-the-box, I landed on my shoulder and rolled, miraculously managing to avoid using my hands. It took a minute or two of deep breathing to make my panic go away, and when it finally did it took my bad mood with it.

I must have subconsciously wanted company, because my feet, without a direct command from my brain, took me directly to the watermelon patch next to the cornfield, where PawPaw and the wheelbarrow were. A large watermelon occupied the wheelbarrow's center; PawPaw was sitting on its back lip, mopping the back of his neck with a stained, yellowish handkerchief.

"Mornin', Mitch," he said as I approached.

"Hey, PawPaw," I said, then couldn't think of anything else to add. "Sure is hot," I finally came up with.

"Not for long. Storm's comin'."

I followed his gaze to the west, where a wall of gray clouds gathered on the horizon. "That'll be a nice change."

PawPaw just nodded and continued soaking up the sweat on his face with dabs of the handkerchief. I used the cotton gauze on the back of my hands to do the same thing.

He folded his handkerchief and put it in the back pocket of his overalls. "How're the hands?"

"They hurt pretty bad," I said with a resigned shrug.

"Bet they do." He spat a stream of brown saliva into the dirt in front of his scuffed work boots, then reached into a front pocket for his chewing tobacco. He reloaded, capped the tin, and slid it back into his overalls.

"Got rope-burned once m'self," PawPaw said, staring off into the distance. He turned back to me and squinted at my hands. "Hurt like the devil."

"How'd it happen?"

"Tried t' hold onta a rope when I was a tad older'n you are now," he eventually answered, a faint smile deepening his wrinkles. "Big ol' horse was on th' othah end." His straw hat slowly shook at the memory. "Like t' tore m' arms outa their sockets, too," he added, then paused to work his chaw. "Not somethin' ya wanna do twice."

"That's for sure," I agreed. There really wasn't a waking moment that first week that I wasn't on the verge of tears because of my burns, even with the medication.

PawPaw slowly got to his feet. "Bettah head on in."

For a sixty-seven-year-old man in supposedly poor health, PawPaw did amazingly well. Although he didn't break any speed records, he had no trouble pushing the wheelbarrow back to the shed, and only strained a little carrying the watermelon into the kitchen.

I followed him out to the front porch while Aunt Nelda fixed us some iced tea. PawPaw eased himself into his rocker and reached down to move his coffee can spittoon. I sat in the rocker next to his, and we settled in to watch the storm approach.

Woody and Charley showed up about a minute before the rain, racing out of the woods like rabbits running from a fox. Their noisy arrival briefly spoiled the mood, but luckily they immediately went inside, probably to compare science notes.

Mom was lying down on the couch with a migraine headache, and Aunt Nelda had settled into her favorite chair with her lemonade and needlepoint, so PawPaw and I had the storm all to ourselves.

I have no idea if it lasted an hour or four, and it really didn't matter. However long it lasted, PawPaw and I never said a word the whole time. We didn't need to; somehow the thunder and lightning said everything for us.

. . .

So I ended up spending a lot of time with PawPaw while my hands healed. His easy, quiet nature seemed perfect for the mood I was in, and knowing that he'd endured the same torture I was going through made my own recuperation seem a little easier to handle.

It didn't take too many days of following his routine to realize that farming wasn't the easiest way to make a living. From milking the cows before sunrise to slopping the hogs at sunset, farm life was mostly hard work. And mostly boring hard work, at that.

Tending to the crops was the most boring of all. PawPaw's huge cornfield apparently brought in the bulk of the farm's income, while the garden provided for most of their fruit and vegetable needs. Neither the cornfield nor the garden provided anything in the way of entertainment; for that I had to rely on the animals.

If PawPaw's place had been the setting for the movie version of *Animal Farm*, the cast would have included one broken-down old horse, Shorty, whose U-shaped back made a perfect built-in saddle; the trio of mongrel dogs, one also called Shorty, the other two named Jim and Jack, all three enough like the Stooges to make me think of them as Moe, Larry, and Curly; four hogs, all of which I found equally disgusting despite their distinct personalities; eight cows, including a calf, none of which had either a personality or half a brain; and a bunch of completely brainless chickens that wouldn't stay still long enough to take an accurate census.

But I tagged along with PawPaw because of the stories he told; he had enough of them for two lifetimes. I heard funny ones and sad ones, weird ones and scary ones, and all of them had really happened, either to him or to someone he'd known.

My favorite story was about PawPaw and Uncle Cecil, told by Uncle Cecil. He dropped by for a visit late in the afternoon the day after the storm, joining PawPaw and me at the haystack under the big oak between the barn and the corral.

"Ain'tcha never hearda child labor laws, Daddy?" he said, grinning.

PawPaw leaned on his pitchfork and smiled back. "Ah do believe he's a volunteah."

Uncle Cecil shifted his ever-present toothpick to the other side of his mouth and looked at me with concern. "How're the hands doin', son?"

"I won't be givin' any piano recitals for a while, but I'll make it."

Uncle Cecil chuckled. "Yeah, tough break. I was sorry to hear it."

"Thanks, Uncle Cecil. Did it really take five M.P.s to throw you out of Fort Polk that time?"

He gave PawPaw a look of mock surprise. "You been tellin' this boy stories on me, Daddy?" Then Uncle Cecil slowly nodded and looked back at me. "Yeah, ain't too prouda that. Let that be a lesson t' ya, son, don't drink more'n ya can handle." He worked his toothpick for a second or two, then added, "In fact, you'd be a lot better off if ya never started at all."

"Don't worry, Uncle Cecil, I won't."

"Did he tell ya 'bout the panther?"

"Not yet."

"Happened right here under this tree, 'membah, Daddy?"

PawPaw glanced up at the large branch hanging five or six feet over his head. "Ain't likely t' evah forget it."

"What happened?" I asked Uncle Cecil.

"It was November, right 'fore Thanksgivin', as I recall, we got word of a panther folks'd seen over in east Texas—"

"A real panther?" I interrupted.

Uncle Cecil nodded. "Black panther. Big sucker, too. Ol' boy in Burkeville's dogs treed it, but it got away 'fore he could shoot it. Then a coupla days later we heard 'bout a calf bein' killed an' half eaten near Leesville, so we knew t' be on the lookout."

"Didn't know enough t' stay outa the woods," said PawPaw.

"Good thing I didn't. So I was comin' back from huntin' in the south forty, had m' twenty-two in one hand an' a big ol' rabbit in th' othah—"

"How old were you?" I broke in again.

"Fifteen. It was near dark by then, but I could still see Daddy, pitchin' hay right where he's standin'. Sky was deep purple, him an' the tree no more'n dark shapes. I was jus' past the corner of the barn, 'bout where that chicken is right now." He paused to point out a scrawny white hen pecking the ground about fifty feet away, then jabbed his thumb at the thick limb overhead. "That's when I saw that branch move."

"The panther was on it?"

"That he was, a long black shadow 'bout halfway out, crouched right above Daddy, ready t' spring."

"Did you know it was there, PawPaw?"

He shook his head. "Nevah heard a thing."

"So what'd ya do?" I asked Uncle Cecil, my voice cracking on "do."

"First thing I did was drop the rabbit. That's when the panther turned its head my direction and I saw its eyes." Uncle Cecil focused his past my shoulder. "They glowed in the dark, pale-green cat eyes floatin' in midair. Froze me in m' tracks."

"*Then* what'd ya do?" I said, sure my own eyes looked like Ping-Pong balls by then.

"Only thing I *could* do. Aimed the best I could and

fired." Uncle Cecil took the toothpick out of his mouth and flicked it away.

"Did you kill it?" I asked, the suspense killing me.

"Yeah. But I didn't know it 'til I ran ovah to get it offa Daddy."

"It fell on you?" I asked PawPaw.

"Fell or jumped, happened too quick t' tell," said Uncle Cecil. "But it wasn't movin' when I rolled it offa Daddy's back with the barrel."

"How big was it?"

"Reg'lar length barrel."

"No, how big was the—"

Uncle Cecil's grin told me I'd been had.

"Longer'n Daddy, maybe a hunnerd an' fifty pounds."

"Where'd the bullet hit?"

Uncle Cecil grinned again. "Only place a bullet that small coulda killed 'im. Right between the eyes."

I looked back and forth between the tree and the barn, trying to visualize the scene. Then something occurred to me. "So you already had a bullet in the rifle? You didn't have to reload first?"

Uncle Cecil placed a fresh toothpick between his teeth. "Ain't no sense carryin' a gun that ain't loaded."

"Good point," I said, then smiled at my unintentional joke.

"Lucky shot," he said, getting it. "The good Lord musta been with me that day."

. . .

The Fourth of July is my third-favorite day of the year, behind Christmas and my birthday, of course. It wasn't that I was superpatriotic or anything, like Dad was, it was just that I loved the fireworks. The fireworks display at the ball field Thursday night didn't disappoint; the half hour or so I spent oohing and aahing with everyone else proved to be the perfect prescription to get me back into society, such as it was.

But the medicine that really did it was a dose of Skeeter. I spotted her as soon as we got there, sitting with her parents and Gary in the visitors' bleachers. She smiled and waved the instant she saw me. I ditched my family while she excused herself and met me next to the boarded-up snack bar.

"Oh, Mitch," she said, gently taking my hands by the wrists. "Poor baby. Does it hurt terribly?"

She called me "baby."

I gave her my most wounded look. "A lot." Then I took a deep breath and let out what I hoped was a brave sigh. "But I can handle it."

"An' I can help. I wanted t' call ya when Gary told me what happened, but Mama said t' wait 'til ya decided ya were up for comp'ny." She wrinkled her nose at me and asked softly, "Sure you're doin' all right?"

Oh, yeah.

"I'll be okay. I went to Fort Polk for a checkup today, and the doc said they were healin' fine." Suddenly realizing what I'd just said, I quickly added, "But he says the next coupla weeks'll be almost as bad as the first."

"Poor baby," she repeated, lightly squeezing my wrists for emphasis.

I was almost glad I'd burned my hands.

. . .

I milked my injuries for all they were worth the next couple of weeks. Even though I had a natural talent for martyrdom, I really outdid myself when it came to Skeeter.

I used every excuse I could think of to be around her as much as possible, even if it meant going to church. Not only did attending services guarantee me time with her afterward but it also made sense not to take any more chances with the Man Upstairs.

Baseball games gave us Tuesday, Thursday, and Saturday evenings together at the snack bar, but always with a crowd around, including her mom. The Perkinses came into town a few times a week, and while her folks ran errands Skeeter would join the six of us cousins for burgers and fries at Robert's, usually sitting between Gary and me on one side of the booth, since I still needed help eating, at least as far as she knew.

Gary acted like he wasn't the slightest bit jealous of Skeeter's attention to me, but I knew that when it came to girls it was every man for himself. That's why I took advantage of every opportunity to horn in on him and

Skeeter, even going so far as basically inviting myself along with them the night of the dance.

I didn't find out about it until I walked down to Dixie's one afternoon after lunch to see if Finn and the guys were there; I hadn't seen them since the accident. My bandages had come off the day before, and even though my scabs hadn't, at least I didn't look like a major accident victim anymore. Plus I figured I was as ready as I'd ever be for the inevitable Tarzan jokes.

"He's still with his uncle Lester in Lake Charles," Dixie herself told me. "But I bet he'll be back in time for the dance Friday."

"There's a dance Friday?"

She nodded, setting her chins in motion. "At the skatin' rink."

"Thanks, maybe I'll catch him there."

It turned out that just about every kid *but* Finn was at Snell's Skating Rink that Friday night to hear Sleepy and the Nightwalkers, an obviously popular quartet of local high school musicians. With Sleepy on drums and his three Nightwalkers on electric bass and guitars, they turned out to be really loud and really good, even though they played way too much Chuck Berry to suit me. At least it wasn't country-western.

The rink was jammed with teenagers and even older couples, which may have had something to do with the fact that Gary and Skeeter didn't dance. I didn't dance because I didn't dance.

About five minutes into what was evidently going to be a marathon version of "Johnny B. Goode," Gary finally gave me the chance I'd been waiting for. "Gotta go t' the bathroom," he shouted to Skeeter.

"Be right back," he yelled at me as he walked by, a smile on his face. "Don't steal m' girl."

Okay, this is it.

I put on my most stricken expression. "Don't feel very well," I said to Skeeter, moving closer so I wouldn't have to shout. "Need some air." Then I brushed past her toward the front door.

Like I hoped she would, she followed me out front and sat next to me on the bed of an old pickup that was missing its tailgate. I sighed and gingerly massaged my hands.

"You okay?" she asked, touching my fingertips with hers.

"Yeah," I said quietly, "it just throbs a little." I looked around one more time to make sure the coast was still clear. It was.

And that's when I kissed her. Or I should say, that's when I *tried* to kiss her. She turned her head the instant I started to make my move, like she was Dracula's daughter, and my lips were a cross.

"Oh, Mitch, I'm sorry. I didn't know." Fortunately she was staring at the ground instead of at me, since I was still puckered up and probably looked exactly like the fish out of water that I was.

Then she looked right into my eyes, her own a little moist, and hurled eight daggers into my heart, one at a time: "I only think of you as a friend."

16

Demolition Derby

I went into hiding for real after the fiasco with Skeeter, avoiding her like I was Superman and she was green kryptonite. I knew there was no way I could ever face her again, but I figured I wouldn't have to as long as I stayed away from the ball field, the Mercantile, and the cafe; or in other words, from Pitkin. Which basically left the farm. Charley and Woody were still in a world of their own, leaving early most mornings to find new bugs for Charley's collection, and leaving me to tag along with PawPaw while he tended to his chores, helping out where I could.

One of the daily chores was collecting eggs from the decrepit henhouse next to the barn. Built from scrap lumber, it was basically an eight-foot-wide box, with a roof and sides but no front. A double row of deep, high shelves ran the length of the back wall, providing roosting space for a dozen chickens, as well as some protection from nocturnal predators.

The bottom shelf was just above my eye level, but by standing on tiptoe I could shoo the hens off their straw nests so I could see if they'd laid any eggs. In order to look into the top roost, I had to use the ancient wooden crate that PawPaw kept there for just that reason.

I'd already snatched and basketed nearly a dozen brown-speckled eggs, an unusually good haul, so I could have just quit without checking the last couple of nests. Unfortunately I decided to finish the job instead.

After I saw that the straw crater at the end of the eye-level shelf was empty of both hen and eggs, I stepped onto the crate for a quick peek at the nest above. It was also unoccupied but held the biggest egg of all, a light tan beauty easily half again as large as the others.

I reached out to pick up the egg. So did the snake.

Not more than three feet from my face reared a huge triangular head, slitted reptilian eyes staring coldly into mine. We both froze, my hand suspended in midair on one side of the egg, the snake's head on the other, its pink forked tongue rapidly flicking in and out of a gaping, needle-toothed mouth.

Then it hissed at me. I heard someone scream as I fell backward off the crate, kicking it into the wall. I caught a quick glimpse of gray-and-tan speckled scales slithering away into the straw before I slammed into the ground.

I landed flat on my back on the hard dirt, where I lay still for a few seconds, trying to calm down. When I thought I could finally move, I carefully sat up and inventoried my parts. Nothing seemed to be broken; it was a good thing I was athletic and instinctively knew how to fall.

It was also a good thing I was wearing yellow shorts.

"You okay?" PawPaw asked as he walked up behind me. "Heard a scream."

"Yeah," I said, getting to my feet and brushing myself off. "Jus' saw a snake, that's all. Wasn't expectin' it."

A slow grin spread across PawPaw's face, followed by a low chuckle which quickly turned into a full-out belly laugh, like he was interviewing for seasonal work as a department store Santa.

"Sorry, boy," he said, wiping the corners of his eyes with his fingers, "but this takes me back a few years, t' when your mama was a little girl. Same thing happened t' her."

"It did?"

"Yeah, big ol' chicken snake stuck its head up right in fronta her face. She screamed bloody murdah, too."

"So that's what it was. They're not poisonous, are they?"

He shook his head. "Harmless as can be. 'Less you're an egg."

"Sure are scary lookin'," I said, trying not to picture it again but failing miserably.

"That they are. Big, too. Killed a six-footah once, thick as my arm." He got in one more grin. "But you prolly scared it more'n it scared you."

Naturally enough, the conversation at supper that night started off with snakes. "I hear you saw your first chicken snake," Mom said, looking at me.

A mouthful of chicken and dumplings kept me from answering, so I just nodded and kept chewing.

"Scared me half t' death when it happened t' me," she continued, spooning sugar into her tumbler of iced tea. "Haven't liked snakes since."

Aunt Nelda glanced at Woody. "Must run in the family."

"In the species," Charley corrected.

"Whadya mean?" For a change I was interested in what he had to say.

"I read that people everywhere are naturally afraid of snakes, even if they live in places that don't have them."

"There're places without snakes?" I asked. "Tell me where. I'll move."

"Islands, mostly," Charley continued. "Anthropologists showed pictures of snakes to some islanders who'd never seen any before—"

"Pictures, or snakes?" I interrupted.

He ignored me. "They automatically reacted with, and I quote, a classic fear response: dilated pupils, sweaty palms, and a faster respiration rate, all the signs of an increase in adrenaline. The most likely explanation is that it's a natural instinct, end quote."

"You really *do* read a lot, don't you?" said Woody.

"Goes back t' the Bible," Aunt Nelda said, nodding agreement. "It was a serpent in the Garden of Eden, if y'all'll recall."

It was definitely time to change the subject. "Speakin' of *eatin'*, Aunt Nelda"—I mugged—"these sure are good dumplings."

"They were your Uncle Mack's fav'rite." Aunt Nelda looked down at her plate. "Lord, did he love his dumplin's."

And then she burst into tears.

. . .

Not only don't guys like to cry, we don't even like being anywhere *near* crying, which was why I couldn't get out of the kitchen fast enough after Aunt Nelda lost control.

By messing around outside for a while with Charley and Woody, and then by voluntarily taking a bath, I managed to avoid Aunt Nelda for most of that evening. But not all of it.

It was all my stomach's fault. Aunt Nelda's outburst had forced me to abandon my second helping of dumplings, so, hungry again after my bath, I decided to risk a quick trip to the kitchen for a slab of her German chocolate cake.

As soon as I turned the corner I saw her in the hallway, staring at the family photo wall and blocking my way. "Sorry y'all had t' see that earliah, hon," she said. "I jus' still really miss 'im, that's all."

"That's okay, Aunt Nelda," I began, desperately trying to think of what to say next. I couldn't come up with anything that didn't sound stupid, so I just stood there and tried not to squirm.

The silence went from uncomfortable to unbearable in short order.

"How long ago did Uncle Mack die?" I blurted out.

Aunt Nelda's eyes were riveted on one of the wood-framed photographs hanging on the wall in front of her. "The Lord called 'im home four years ago today."

That explains it.

"How'd it happen again?"

Her eyes took on a hard look. "Drunk drivah." She paused to wipe a tear. "Least he didn't suffah. Doc said he died instantly."

Again I didn't know what to say, so I just looked at the old black-and-white photo along with Aunt Nelda. It was a stiff family portrait, mother and father at each end and two gawky young girls in the middle, each holding an arm of the toddler between them.

Woody's sisters were recognizable, but Woody barely was, since he couldn't have been more than three at the time. Uncle Mack was earnest-looking and handsome in a craggy kind of way. Aunt Nelda didn't look at all like Aunt Nelda.

The woman in the photograph was about half Aunt Nelda's size, a slightly fuller-faced version of Mom. The only one in the portrait who was smiling, the Aunt Nelda on the steps didn't even seem to be the same person who stood next to me, staring misty-eyed at her past.

Aunt Nelda must have read my mind. "Hard t' believe I was evah that thin, huh?" she said, slowly shaking her head. "Gained a little havin' m' kids, a little more while they was growin' up." She paused to glance at the portrait once more. "But mosta this I put on since the accident."

I pointed to a close-up of a reed-thin girl about Charley's age holding the reins of a horse. "Is this you?"

"Sure is. Lookit that grin, like I was gonna conquah the world." She shifted her gaze back to the shot of Uncle Mack in his suit. "Funny how life turns out."

"I'll bet you were somethin' when you were that age."

"I *was* a tomboy, if that's what you mean," she said, a twinkle in her eye. "Couldn't help but be, what with havin' two oldah brothahs. I could do anything any boy could do, and some things they couldn't."

"Like what?"

I must have sounded a little skeptical, since Aunt Nelda immediately pinned me with a challenging look. "Y' know the rope swing at the creek?"

"The one at the swimmin' hole? The really high one?"

"Yeah, the really high one." She grinned at me, just like the eight-year-old with the horse. "Well, who d'ya think tied it up there?"

. . .

Aunt Nelda wasn't the only Miller who surprised me that week. A couple of days after my hallway chat with her, Gary and his brothers paid us a visit after breakfast.

"Hey, guys, c'mon!" Barry yelled from the road as soon as he saw us at the tire swing. "Y'all gotta come see somethin'!"

Woody dashed onto the porch and hollered through the screen door. "Me'n the boys're goin' into town, Mama! Back latah."

Even though I still wasn't quite ready to deal with Gary, I was dying to find out what it was that had them all so excited. If their faces were any indication, whatever they wanted to show us had to be pretty cool.

But first Gary and I had to settle things. Actually, Gary was the one who wanted to talk; if it had been up to me, I'd have walked the whole way into town without saying a word.

It had been almost a week since I'd blown it at the skating rink, and I hadn't seen or even talked to Gary since he and Aunt Dorothy dropped me off after the dance, after the longest five-minute car ride in history.

Gary fell into step next to me on the gravel. "How're ya doin'?"

"Okay. Hands don't hurt at all anymore." I held up my palms, offering my new pink skin as evidence.

"That's not what I meant."

"Oh. Right. That."

"Mitch, it's okay. I'm not mad, honest."

"You're not?"

Gary shook his head. "Neither's Skeets. She jus' feels bad that she mighta somehow led ya on."

It was my turn to shake my head. "She was jus' bein' nice. It was all my fault."

"Not *any*body's fault. Jus' a misunderstandin'. Forget about it."

I was getting ready to say "Forget about *what*?" when Barry turned around. "Mitch," he said, walking backward so he could talk to me, "you wanna hear this or not?"

"Hear what?"

"Why we're goin' t' Cecil's."

"Sure. But there's somethin' I wanna ask ya first. How come we're goin' to Cecil's?"

By the time we got to the main road, Barry had filled us in on the background. The earliest riser in his family, he'd been the first to find Uncle Cecil, shirt untucked and shoes still on, conked out on their porch swing and "snorin' like a chain saw."

Apparently Uncle Cecil and Aunt Marjorie had been arguing a lot lately about her new car; not about the car itself, as I would have guessed, but about what he did with it, which was to regularly drive it to an all-night poker game in Leesville. According to Barry, the situation had recently escalated, since in response to his wife's protests Uncle Cecil had started attending a second game, this one in Oakdale and evidently for considerably higher stakes.

"Which brings us t' las' night," said Gary.

"Hey! *I'm* tellin' this!" Barry said. "So last night Cecil pulls in round sunup an' goes t' unlock the front door, only Marjorie, she's latched an' dead-bolted it, so Cecil goes round back an' knocks on their bedroom window, politely, accordin' t' him, an' asks her t' let 'im in."

"Politely, my rear end," said Woody. "He's somethin' else when he's mad, 'specially aftah drinkin' all night."

"Yeah," Barry agreed. "So anyway, Cecil tells me she started screamin' at 'im, tellin' 'im if he can't get home at a decent Christian hour he can by God sleep somewhere else."

"So he ended up on your front porch," I broke in. "What's the big deal?"

"The big deal," Barry said, grinning, "is what we're fixin' t' show ya right now."

We were about a quarter of a mile along the highway out of town, approaching a sprawling, modern brick ranch house that stood all by itself on our side of the road. "What y'all gotta remember," Barry said to Charley and me, "is that Cecil an' Marjorie's house is the mos' 'spensive one around—"

"Over fifty thousand dollars," Gary said.

"*Her* fifty thou," Barry added.

"Holy moly," said Charley.

"Holy moly is right, little brother," I said when I saw what he was staring at. "This is unbe*liev*able!"

Two parallel curves of gouged-out grass led from the concrete driveway to the rear tires of Aunt Marjorie's Chrysler Imperial, the back half of which was sticking out of the middle of the front wall. The front half was inside the house.

"Can you believe it?" said Barry. "He drove it into the dining room!"

"This is unbelievable," I said again.

Until that moment I'd never realized just how many bricks it took to build a wall. They were scattered everywhere, huge piles of shattered, rust-colored chunks on the ground next to the car's front doors, powdery bits of them littering the car's roof, like photographs I'd seen of London after the V-2 bombings.

I could see part of the Chrysler's crumpled hood through the gaping hole where the wall used to be, covered with plaster dust and shards of plate glass.

"Is Aunt Marjorie here?" I asked, not wanting to risk a confrontation with her but definitely wanting a closer look at the dining room destruction.

"She left an hour ago," Gary answered. "We saw her headin' outa town in Cecil's pickup. Prob'ly went back t' Baton Rouge."

That was all the invitation I needed. I climbed onto the rubble, and then, bracing myself on the miraculously unbroken windshield, stuck my head inside the house.

The dining room looked even more like a battle zone than the outside of the house did. Patches of blue carpet showed through a layer of debris, fragments of bricks, glass, and wallboard mixed in with splintered wood. What used to be an expensive-looking formal dining room set was now only good for kindling.

As I climbed back down to give Charley a chance to see, I noticed an old black pickup slow to a crawl and pull onto the shoulder of the road in front of the house, the adults up front gawking and pointing just like the crowd of kids in the bed of the truck.

"So whadya think, Mitch?" Barry asked. "Ever see anything like this before?"

"This is unbelievable," I said, stunned into mindless repetition by the sheer enormity of Uncle Cecil's act.

"Did he tell ya why he did it?" I asked as I watched another carload of people slow down to stare.

"Other than bein' likkered up an' crazy-mad?" said Woody.

"Yeah," Barry said with a chuckle, "he did. Said he *really* hadda go t' the bathroom."

17

Monster Birthday

As cool as it was checking out the scene of the Cecil Incident, the best thing about it was that I started hanging out with Gary and the guys again. It wasn't that I hadn't enjoyed the time I'd spent with PawPaw, but since I no longer had to stay away from town and a chance encounter with Gary or Skeeter, there was nothing preventing me from having fun again. Which I did with a vengeance.

The next few days flew by in a blur of fort building, tree climbing, stick duels, and corncob fights. We even staged a Farm Decathlon, using a corroded old iron for the shot put, a chipped dinner plate for a discus, and an old rake handle for both the javelin and the high jump.

No one ever forgets their birthday, but I'd long since lost track of the date, so it came as a complete surprise to me when Mom walked out onto the front porch after supper one evening, carrying a huge vanilla-frosted cake topped with a dozen flaming candles. "Happy birthday to you . . . " she began singing, the others quickly joining in.

The thirty-one days of July had come and gone, blown away like calendar pages in a bad movie. It was suddenly the first of August, which meant two things: that I was finally twelve years old, and that I only had nine more days left in Louisiana.

The phone rang just as I was getting ready to blow out the candles. Aunt Nelda went inside to answer it. "Mitch, it's for you," she said through the screen door a few seconds after I did my Big Bad Wolf impression with the candles. "Sounds like long distance."

Tick.

I excused myself and hustled into the kitchen. "Hello?" I said into the receiver, suddenly anxious to hear his voice.

"Happy birthday, sport," said Dad. He sounded a million miles away.

"Oh. Hey, Pop, thanks. How's it goin'?" We hadn't talked since the day after the accident, or, as I called it, Palm Sunday.

"No sweat. How're the burns?"

"Okay. Finally."

"Good," he said, talking a little louder to keep from being drowned out by a burst of loud laughter in the background of what was probably the Officers' Club. "You open your present yet?"

"Not yet. Just blew out the candles."

"Well, I hope you like it. I'll let you get back to your party. Just wanted to wish a happy birthday to my number-one son."

"Thanks, Dad. Can't wait 'til you're back."

"Me, too. Love ya. Put your mother on, okay?"

"I've been doing that for years, Dad."

"That's for sure," he said with a chuckle. "Seeya soon."

Through an incredible burst of willpower I was able to hold off opening my presents until Mom got off the phone, but just barely. I had the wrapping paper ripped off the gift from Aunt Nelda and PawPaw and Woody before Mom closed the screen door behind her, and had pulled out the fairly ugly Mercantile T-shirt inside by the time she sat back down in her rocker.

I thanked them as sincerely as I could while I shredded the present from Uncle Robert and Aunt Dorothy and the guys; their gift was an "Official Major League Baseball," according to the black lettering stamped into the snow-white horsehide. "For when you're upta throwin' a ball around again," Gary said.

"Thanks, y'all," I said to both sets of Millers, "I can really use these."

"Well, my present you *can't* use," Charley said. He grinned slyly and handed me a wallet-size lump wrapped in newspaper and secured by at least two rolls of Scotch tape. "At least not yet."

"Yeah," I muttered while I struggled with the tape, " 'cause I'll be thirteen before I can get it open. Anyone got a pocketknife?"

Uncle Robert handed his over to me. Even with the knife it took a while to get the present unwrapped. "Hey, thanks, squirt, these are great," I said, showing everyone a cool set of bicycle reflectors, four small red ones and a large white one for the front.

"One more to go," Mom said with a Mona Lisa smile, then handed me what looked like another shirt box.

Its unexpected weight nearly caused me to drop it. "What is this, a World War Three lead shirt?"

"Don't joke about that, honey. Open it up."

About three seconds later I felt like Howard Carter looking at King Tut's tomb for the first time. Inside the box were four hardback science-fiction books that I'd been wanting forever. "Where did you *find* these?" I asked Mom after I reattached my lower jaw. "They've been out of print for years!"

"Your dad got them in Virginia a couple of weekends ago. You don't already have any of them, do you?"

"No, these are incredible," I said with an ear-to-ear grin. "Thanks a lot, Mom!"

"Don't thank me, thank your father when he gets home. I'm givin' you my present tomorrow, in Oakdale."

Just then the phone rang again.

"Must be eight o'clock," said Mom.

I shouted, "I'll get it!" and exploded out of the rocker like a sprinter out of the blocks. Practically tearing the screen door off its hinges, I had the receiver in my hand before it rang a third time.

"Tick! How're ya doin'?"

"Berson-to-berson for Master William Mitchell Valentine," the operator said, apparently through a terminal head cold.

"That's me."

"Angyou, blease old the line."

"Mitch," came a voice I barely recognized, "happy birthday!"

"Hey, Tick, thanks! Or should I say Master Thomas Kelly Murphy?"

"Esquire. Boy, do you ever have an accent!"

"No way. Must be the long distance. So what've ya been doin'?"

"The usual stuff. So how come you haven't written?" he asked in kind of an accusatory tone. "Didn't ya get my letter?"

"Sorry 'bout that, man. It's a long story."

"Give me the short version," he said, not letting me off the hook. "My folks told me to keep this t' ten minutes."

I knew I wouldn't be able to explain why I hadn't written back even if I had ten hours, so I didn't even try. But I did play up the misery angle, mentioning everything except Skeeter. I scored most of my forgiveness points with the rope-burn accident; for a change I didn't even have to exaggerate.

"Been watchin' the Stooges?" I asked, shifting gears.

"Me an' Mike haven't missed a one."

Mike?

I tried to sound casual. "Who's Mike?"

"New kid who moved in a coupla weeks ago. You'll like him. His old man's a colonel, so he's got lots of cool stuff. He's even got his own go-kart."

"Yeah? How old's he?"

"Same grade as me. Hey, listen, my dad's givin' me the evil eye, so I better go."

"Okay, thanks for calling. Seeya in a coupla weeks. Got lots t' tell ya."

"Can't wait. Can't wait for you to meet Mike, too. The three of us'll have a blast."

What happened to "Three's a crowd"?

After one last comment from Tick about my accent, I said an awkward goodbye, hung up, and rejoined my party. But I wasn't in much of a party mood anymore.

· · ·

The next day we drove to Oakdale. It was less than twenty miles away, but with Mom's overly cautious driving and with three adults and three kids crammed in our car, all breathing the same air, it seemed twice that far.

We dropped Aunt Nelda and PawPaw off at his eye doctor's office a few hundred yards west of town. A minute later Mom was pulling into one of the curbside parking spaces that lined the main drag of the Oakdale business district.

"C'mon, birthday boy," she said, killing the engine. "Let's find your presents."

As in two or more? All right!

Then a thought occurred to me. "Whadya mean, *find*?"

"You get to pick 'em out." She turned to face me, a bill of green U.S. currency folded between her fingers. "Here's ten dollars. There's where to spend it."

I whisked the tenner out of her hand and looked past her pointing finger at the store she was referring to. "Thanks, Mom!" I said. "This is great!"

Harley's Used Books turned out to be a mecca for a horror and science-fiction nut like me—a musty, crowded shop lined wall-to-wall with homemade pine bookshelves crammed full of old books, magazines, digests, pulps, and comics, most of which were reasonably priced.

Mom, Charley, and Woody walked in about forty-five minutes later, just as Mr. Harley was placing the last of my haul into a plain grocery bag. "That comes to ten-fifty, including tax," he said.

"I guess I'll have to put a couple back," I said. "I've only got ten on me." Like an idiot, I'd left my cash in my other jeans.

"That's okay, I'll take care of the tax," he said. "Least I can do for a fellow fan."

Naturally, Mom started fishing in her change purse at that point, but Mr. Harley refused to let her pay the difference. "Don't forget t' check over at Gantry's for them old *Mad*s," he said as we started to leave. "Had a stack of 'em last I knew."

"Can we make one more stop, Mom?" I quickly asked, knowing she probably wouldn't say no in front of Mr. Harley. "And can I borrow some money if I need to? I forgot mine."

"Okay, but it better be fast. PawPaw wants to get right home."

I did make it fast, too, not because Mom wanted me to but because Mr. Gantry had already sold all the *Mad*s. That, and I couldn't find anything else to blow any more money on.

But I did find something out as a result of the detour: I discovered that the modest little town of Oakdale actually had a drive-in movie theater. And that a monster triple feature was going to be starting that night.

"Look!" I shouted, pointing to the marquee that had just come into view. "*Attack of the Fifty-Foot Woman*! The funniest movie ever made! And *Kronos*! I love *Kronos*! And *The Alligator People*! I've been *dying* to see that!" I turned to Mom, who was sitting in the middle of the backseat with Charley and me, the start of another migraine having forced her to turn the driving over to Aunt Nelda. "Can we go tonight, Mom? Please? I'll owe you forever! Please, can we go? Can we, can we?"

"Don't have a conniption, boy," Aunt Nelda said into the rearview mirror. "I'll carry y'all there if your mama don't feel up to it."

"Thanks, Aunt Nelda!" I said. "You're the greatest!"

"I'll be fine by tonight," said Mom. "Might even have some buttered popcorn while I'm at it. I'll call Dorothy when we get back; maybe the boys'd like to come along."

"Thanks, Mom!" I said from cloud nine.

"Yeah!" Charley said as he rolled his window down. "*Thanks*, Mom!"

At that moment PawPaw rolled down his window, too. Then came a sound I'd heard at least a hundred times already, the wet noise he made when he spat out a load of tobacco juice. Only this mouthful wasn't aimed into his coffee can; it was launched into a fifty-mile-an-hour wind stream.

And right into Charley's face.

Unfortunately for Charley, he had chosen that exact moment to stick his head out of the car and into the wind; the streamer of foul, phlegmy juice hit him right between the eyes. He immediately yanked his head back in and turned toward Mom, his bloodless face contorted in revulsion, like he was psyching himself up for the finals of a projectile vomiting contest.

Mom had her handkerchief out in a flash, wiping at the rivulets of sepia-toned saliva running down his cheeks and dripping off his nose. "Don't say a *word*!" she hissed and whispered at the same time. "You can wash up as soon as we get home."

Charley sniffled and blinked tears out of his eyes.

I thanked God that I hadn't been the one sitting behind PawPaw.

. . .

The sun was setting when we pulled into the line of cars at the entrance to the Oakdale Drive-In. By the time we paid admission and found a good spot, I think I was actually vibrating in anticipation.

"Wait'll ya see this guy's brains come out of his ear in *Kronos*!" I said to Woody as he and Charley and I waited in the noisy snack bar line. Gary and the guys were tied up doing family stuff and hadn't been able to make it.

"Can't wait," Woody said, then stepped up to order. "Gimme a large popcorn, no butter, Junior Mints, an' a large cherry Coke."

"I'll take the same thing," I told the gangly kid behind the counter. "Only with extra butter. Mine *plus* his."

We were halfway back to our car before I remembered that I'd forgotten Mom's root beer and Milk Duds. The line was even slower the second time around, so I also had to buy another Coke for myself, and ended up missing the first few scenes of *Attack of the Fifty-Foot Woman*.

"What'd you guys think of the giant bald guy?" I

asked as I slid onto the shotgun seat and handed Mom her stuff. "Was he a riot or what?"

We spent the next hour making smart-aleck remarks and laughing like fools; the scene where the Fifty-Foot Woman's fakey, giant rubber hand comes into the hotel room to grab the unfaithful Harry actually made soda spray out of Woody's nose. I think Mom even got a kick out of it. "That's ri*dic*ulous!" she said on more than one occasion.

Like *Attack of the Fifty-Foot Woman*, *Kronos* had a giant in it, an alien energy-sucking machine that roamed the countryside, impervious to the combined military might of the Earthlings' puny forces.

I managed to hold off going to the bathroom until after the famous brain scene. "I gotta go," I said as soon as the sizzling, liquefied brains finished pouring from the guy's ear onto the laboratory floor. "Anybody want anything else from the snack bar?" For some reason no one did.

I was walking out the men's room door toward the snack bar for another box of Junior Mints when someone blindsided me from the right, knocking me to one knee.

"Hey! Watch it, you—city boy!" Finn said, then helped me up from the dirty concrete floor. "Nice bumpin' inta ya," he couldn't resist adding, with a leer at Bulldog and Gravy.

"Finn! Hey, how're ya doin'?" I nodded past his shoulder to the other two. "Where's Boomer?"

"Hadda take care of his mama," Bulldog said, somehow making "mama" seem like a dirty word.

"She's been sick lately," said Finn. "An' speakin' of bein' sick, I see your hands're okay now. Heard ya burned 'em purdy bad."

"Yeah, they're pretty much healed, jus' a little tender."

"Why don'tcha watch the resta the show with us?" Finn said. "Got an empty seat."

"Thanks, I will!" I said, unfortunately with the exclamation point.

"Caddy's in the last row," Finn said as he pushed open the men's room door. "Meet us there."

"An' Tarzan," Gravy said with an idiotic grin, "don't forget June."

If it had been anyone else, I'd have been sure it was a joke.

18

The Alligator People

Mom surprised me for the second time that day. "Fine by me," she said after I begged her to let me join Finn and the guys. "Jus' check in after this movie in case I start t' poop out."

I know I should have felt guilty about bailing out on Charley and Woody, Charley especially, but I didn't say anything, and neither did he. Woody started to, but changed his mind, I guess.

There was no line at the snack bar by then, so it didn't take long to reload. With a large cherry Coke in one hand and another pig-out tub of buttered popcorn in the other, I threaded my way through the rows of parked cars toward the back of the drive-in.

Even though the half of the lot behind the snack bar

and projection booth was practically pitch-dark, I picked out the Caddy from two rows away. It was parked by itself in the last row near the left corner, its long black fins barely visible against an inky forest background; luckily the V of Finn's arm was easy to spot against the driver's door.

I quickened my pace and cut between the last two cars in front of Finn's. Actually they were trucks, one an old junker whose two occupants I had a hard time making out, since that's what they were doing, and the other a jacked-up new Chevy pickup with oversize tires that had been backed into its spot. Three guys were sprawled in the bed of the pickup, their backs against the cab.

The fact that the Chevy was parked backward must have been the reason I got momentarily disoriented. I mean, I'd already twice made my way in the dark through a dozen rows of parked cars and speaker stands, so even though it was hard to see, it wasn't like I was Ray Charles trying to go long or anything.

But I didn't see the speaker cord that came out of nowhere and caught me right on the throat. Popcorn, Coke, and ice flew everywhere as I desperately tried to keep my balance. "Hey," one of the guys yelled as their speaker flew out of the back of the truck and hit me right between the shoulder blades, "watch it!"

I could feel the blood rushing to my face. "Sorry, didn't see it." I set what was left of my Coke on the ground and groped in the dirt for the speaker. "Sorry," I said again as I handed it to the kid nearest me, a mean-looking teenager with a scowl on his face.

"How d'ya like the brain scene?" I asked, hoping to calm him down.

"How d'ya like not *hav*in' a brain?" he said.

The laughter from Finn's car almost made me turn around and head back to the De Soto, but by the time I got to the Caddy I even knew how I was going to handle it.

"So, Finn," I asked as I walked up to the car, "on a ten-point scale, what would you give it?" The best defense is a good offense.

"Give what?"

"My stunt fall back there. I've done better, but that was at least a nine, don'tcha think?"

"What I think is, is that you're pretty fast on your feet." He grinned. "Mentally anyway." He nodded toward the backseat. "Get in. An' try not t' spill anything else, okay?"

I slid onto the seat directly behind him. "Finn, when'd ya get back?" I nodded hello to Gravy, whose long arms and legs were hogging more than his share of the back.

"Las' week," he said, then took a big swig out of a can of soda I didn't recognize. "Whatcha been doin' for excitement? Besides playin' Tarzan."

"Not much, jus' hangin' around."

"When do y'all head back?"

"A week from Sunday." I realized I was crushing my spare box of Junior Mints in the back pocket of my Levi's, so I shifted position to fish it out. "How do ya like *Kronos* so far?"

"It's okay," said Finn.

"Brain scene was cool," Bulldog said from the shotgun seat.

"Yeah," I agreed, "it's my favorite part."

Bulldog tilted his head back and drained his soda in one long gulp, then bent the empty in half and tossed it out his window. Wiping his mouth with the back of his hand, he bent forward to reach for something on the floor, straightened back up, and blasted a loud belch into the backseat.

"Y'all wannanother beer?" he asked the instant I smelled it on his breath.

"I'll take one," Finn said, dropping his empty can out the window also. He swiveled around to challenge me with a stare. "Want one, too?"

"No thanks," I said immediately. "Can't stand the stuff."

"That's why ya should only drink sittin' down," Finn said, and then grinned. He took the can from Bulldog. "Church key." Bulldog handed the opener over.

"Sure ya don't want one?" Finn asked again, over the *whoosh* of escaping carbonation. "Your mama don't *haf*ta find out, ya know." He waited a beat. "Unless you're dumb enough t' tell 'er."

My face suddenly got hot. "She doesn't know *every-thing* I do."

"So have a beer," Gravy said, coming out of his coma.

"Yeah," added Bulldog. "Live dangerously."

"Okay," I heard myself saying, "I will."

Somehow I managed to swallow my guilt along with the bitter, lukewarm Schlitz. I did my best to look like I was enjoying it, even getting off a couple of decent belches of my own.

"So where'd you guys get the beer?" I casually asked. Although it was apparently okay to drive under age in Louisiana, I found it hard to believe that they could have just walked into a liquor store and bought the stuff.

"Crockett got it for us," said Bulldog.

"Who's Crockett?"

"Bulldog's big brother," Finn said, then turned the speaker's sound off. "Innermission. Need popcorn. Lez make us a run."

I crammed a bunch of Junior Mints into my mouth to cover up my beer breath. "Gotta check in. Be right back."

I didn't feel weird at all from the beer, so I had no trouble negotiating the trip back to our car. What I had trouble with was convincing Mom to let Finn drive me home.

Not surprisingly, she was too tired to stick around for the last movie.

"Mom, you don't understand," I said when she told

me we were leaving, "I've *got* to see *The Alligator People*. I can ride back with Finn. *Please!*"

"Is he even old enough to drive?" she asked. "He doesn't look sixteen."

"He's been drivin' for a year already," I lied. "I'll be safe."

I could tell she was getting ready to shoot me down when Finn saved the day. "Evenin', y'all," he said in a smarmy voice as he sauntered up to the car. "Enjoyin' yourselves?"

"Finn, you could give me a ride home, couldn't ya?" I asked.

"Don't see why not," he said, then smiled at Mom. "He don't take up much room."

"Well," Mom said after a moment, "I sup*pose* it would be okay."

"Thanks, Mom," I said. "I owe ya one."

"Y'all come straight home after the movie, promise?"

"Don't worry, ma'am," Finn said. "I'll carry 'im home directly after the show."

The next thing I knew I was watching the De Soto's taillights slowly disappear behind the snack bar. "Thanks a lot," I said to Finn. "I *really* wanted to see *The Alligator People*."

Unfortunately, the best thing about *The Alligator People* was its title.

"This is a drag," Gravy mumbled, then took another swig of beer.

"I got an idea," said Finn. "What say we go find us some *real* alligators. You up for that, city boy?"

I don't think so.

Then the beginning of an I-knew-you-were-chicken grin started at the corner of his mouth. "Sure," I said, stopping it in midsmile, "sounds like a gas."

"So does this," Bulldog said, then ripped off a wet one.

I laughed so hard I almost wet my pants.

I'm gonna like *being twelve.*

. . .

What I was starting not to like was being called "city boy." "So, city boy," Finn said, looking at me in the rearview mirror instead of at the road, "how d'ya like Loosiana so far?"

All four of the Caddy's windows were still rolled down, so I had to raise my voice to be heard over the noise of the Mach 1 wind stream. "Other than the bugs an' humidity, it's great. An' by the way, my friends call me Mitch."

"Okay . . . Mitch," he said, then pulled into the other lane just before I thought we were going to ram a station wagon doing the speed limit. "What's your las' name, anyway?"

Here we go again.

"Valentine."

Like in Valentine's Day?

Bulldog said it first. "Like in Valentine's Day?"

"That's right," I started in, "February fourteenth, mushy pink hearts an' red arrows. I've already heard all the jokes, so don't waste your time." I'd not only heard all the jokes, I'd made up a lot of them myself; I figured that if anyone was going to get a cheap laugh at my expense, it may as well be me.

"Relax, son," Bulldog said, "I was jus' makin' conversation. Besides, I know what havin' a dumb name's like. My parents named me Eu*gene*."

"Eugene McKean," said Finn. "Now ya know why we call 'im Bulldog."

That plus his face.

Bulldog's liquid brown puppy eyes and wide pug nose accounted for most of the resemblance.

"What's your real name?" I asked Gravy.

He spoke without moving his lips. "Cletus."

"Tell 'im your last name," said Finn.

"Rivers."

It took me a second. "Gravy Rivers, that's great," I said with an appreciative chuckle. "Finn, what about you?"

"What about me?"

"What's your real name?"

He didn't answer for a few seconds. "Finn," he finally said. "Jus' Finn."

"We're not *really* gonna look for alligators, are we?" I asked, changing the subject for both of us.

"Not only *look*," Bulldog said, twisting around to face me, "but *find*. Right, Finn?"

"Gair-on-teed."

It turned out there was a reason that they were so sure we'd find alligators—there were two of them permanently trapped in a large swampy enclosure on the outskirts of Pitkin, on the property of one R. Harlan, according to the white lettering on the black mailbox next to the road.

"Keep quiet," Finn said softly as we started walking up the dirt driveway. "Don't want Rabbit shootin' at us."

No, we definitely don't.

I followed them around the side of the house, where an old yellow school bus was parked under a corrugated tin roof extension. A little ways past the bus I saw our destination, a Cyclone fence about thirty yards off, its diamond pattern glowing softly in the starlight.

We spread out along the chest-high, heavy chain link. "Where are they?" I asked. "I can't see a thing." Living in the city, it's easy to forget how dark it really is at night, even under a bright Milky Way.

"Listen for their breathing," said Finn.

The only breathing I heard was ours. "You guys are puttin' me on, aren'tcha?"

"Look down," Finn said.

"Yeah, right, now you're gonna tell me there's an alligator right behind me. Good try."

"Not behind you," he said, "in front of you. Look down."

I did. Two feet away from my feet and on the other side of the fence, thank God, was a long, featureless lump about the size and shape of a full-grown alligator turned sideways to me. Then I saw its left eye open. It *was* a full-grown alligator.

The one behind it was even more full-grown, easily twelve feet long from the tip of its powerful-looking tail to the undoubtedly huge teeth hidden in its primitive snout. Other than the one eyelid, they were perfectly still, more like taxidermy victims than living creatures. They didn't even react to the Junior Mints I tossed onto their heads.

"Lez go," Finn said, reaching into the front pocket of his jeans. "We'll bring 'em somethin' t' eat next time. Now that's a sight t' see."

"What do ya feed 'em?" I asked, thinking along the lines of raw hamburger.

"Whole chickens," he said.

"Live ones," said Bulldog. "Ya oughta see 'em run."

"The chickens or the alligators?" I asked.

"Both," Finn said with a smile. "Ever seen a gator run?"

I shook my head. "Uh-uh."

"They can bring down a horse."

"You're kidding."

"Nope, m' Uncle Lester saw one do it once. Said it was the fastest thing he'd ever seen."

"Speakin' of that," I said, seeing an opening, "your Caddy sure is fast. Were you serious about maybe lettin' me drive it sometime?"

Finn turned around and started back toward the car. "What you talkin' 'bout, boy?"

"At the creek that time. You said if I played my cards right you might let me drive, so how 'bout now? Hardly any cars on the road this late. I won't wreck it, I'm a good driver."

"Okay," he said, tossing me the keys. "Lez go."

Gentlemen, start your engines.

A '59 Cadillac is even bigger than a '57 De Soto, a battleship compared to a mere destroyer. "How does she handle in a heavy sea?" I couldn't resist asking as I slid onto the driver's seat.

Finn opened the shotgun door. "Jus' stay on your side of the road and do what I tell ya," he said. Bulldog took my place in the back next to Gravy.

"Okay, fire it up," Finn said after I finally got the front seat close enough to reach the pedals. The steering wheel now just inches from my chest, I put the key into the ignition slot and tentatively turned it. The radio immediately came back to life, steel guitars blaring. I turned the key all the way; nothing happened.

I turned it again. The sudden shriek of grinding metal made my hair stand on end.

"It's already on," Finn said with a grimace. "Give it a little gas."

I carefully applied pressure to the gas pedal with the big toe of my tennies. Again nothing happened, so I put a little more foot into it. Now I could hear the engine revving, but we still weren't moving. "How hard d'ya have to step on it?"

"Gotta put it in *gear*," said Finn.

I knew that.

The gearshift lever was a standard column-mount, its indicator arrow pointed to P for Park. Finn reached over and slammed it into L. Not L as in Low, but L for Lunge. As in Lunge Forward at Neck-Snapping Speed.

The Caddy shot onto the highway like pus out of a popped pimple. I panicked and immediately slammed on the brakes, then slammed into the steering wheel's horn ring, which blasted a triple-forte bugle note. We'd gone maybe two car lengths.

"Lez not do *that* again, okay?" Finn said, massaging the back of his neck while I checked my chest for fractures. "Easy does it."

My second attempt was much better, only a couple of spastic surges of acceleration before I was finally able to maintain a steady speed. Keeping the car centered in the lane turned out to be a little harder than it looked, especially since from behind the wheel the Caddy's hood looked like the flight deck of an aircraft carrier.

But for a change I rose to the occasion. Even with the mushy power steering, for a couple of miles I was in total control, an instant master of the open road. In part because of my driving skill, but mainly because we were the only vehicle on the highway, we made it into town without incident.

The incident happened at Uncle Robert's service station, where I had to turn right onto the gravel road that led to the farm. I eased off the gas with plenty of time to spare, and coasted up to the intersection at what felt like a reasonable speed to easily make the turn.

It wasn't. I realized that at the last second and instinctively hit the brakes and turned the wheel sharply to the right; they were both bad instincts. The squeal of tires was cut short by the sound of spraying gravel as the Caddy went into a sickening spin. We did a complete one-eighty before finally coming to rest in a cloud of dust.

Like father, like son.

At first I thought they'd all kill me, since I was pretty sure I'd scared them as badly as I'd scared myself, but Gravy started laughing, a moronic but infectious braying that quickly got the rest of us going, too.

"That's enough for one night," Finn said, with what sounded to me like a relieved chuckle. "Slide out, I'll drive the rest of the way."

"Okay," I said as I opened the driver's door. "And thanks, that was great." I swung my legs around to get out of the car; it would have worked out much better if I hadn't left it in Drive.

The instant I took my foot off the brake pedal the Caddy surged forward on its own, at a speed I wouldn't have thought possible. It was headed straight for Uncle Robert's gas pumps.

Finn beat me to the shift lever by a split second and slammed it upward into Park. The car stopped like it had hit a brick wall, then rocked on its springs for a few seconds before it finally quit shaking.

It took us a little longer.

Bulldog pounded the outside of his car door. "Whewee!" he whooped. "That was better'n the rodeo!"

"Yeah," said Finn, looking first at me and then at the pumps a car length away. "That was almost a real blast."

"Real blast," Bulldog parroted. "Good one, Finn. Get it, Gravy?"

Finn slid behind the steering wheel and readjusted the seat. "C'mon, city boy, time t' get you home."

I remembered the ball game just as Finn pulled into PawPaw's driveway. "You guys gonna be at the ballpark tomorrow night?" I asked. "It's a playoff game. Should be exciting."

Finn didn't answer until he stopped the car next to the De Soto. "Want excitement, do ya?" he said, turning around to look at me. "Yeah, we'll be there. Meet us at the snack bar 'fore the game starts."

"Great, seeya then."

The grandfather clock in the front parlor chimed

once as I eased the screen door open and slipped into the house. Of course Mom was waiting up for me, stretched out on the sofa.

"Good," she said, "you're home. Enjoy the movie?"

"Actually, it was pretty lame," I said as she yawned, "but thanks for lettin' me stay anyway, Mom."

"Well, you *are* growing up." She padded over to me and gave me a good-night peck on the cheek. "And I know I can trust you. Get some sleep now."

But getting to sleep right away proved to be easier said than done, partially since I was still pretty wound up from the night's adventures, but mainly because of what Mom said about trusting me.

It was okay with me if stuff my parents wouldn't approve of happened accidentally, like drinking a beer and driving a car one day after my twelfth birthday. But I figured that deliberately planning something they wouldn't like was another matter entirely.

So it was only natural that I was already feeling a little guilty about what I planned to do Saturday night, even though I didn't really know what the plan was. What I did know was that it would probably be fun. And that it probably wouldn't be anything I'd want Mom to find out about.

19

Altitude Sickness

The only thing about Saturday night that I wasn't looking forward to was seeing Skeeter again, despite Gary's repeated assurances. "It'll be fine," he'd said again over burgers at the cafe, "she'd really like t' seeya. Honest."

But it wasn't nearly as painful as I'd thought it would be, mainly because Skeeter and I both did our best to pretend that nothing had ever happened. For her part, she kept the conversation light and breezy; the closest she came to referring to my humiliation was a concerned question about the status of my new skin, which had finally grown back, along with my hair.

Finn and the guys still hadn't shown up after two innings, so I decided to take matters into my own hands. "Hey, Skeeter," I said, pointing to the large white farmhouse partially visible through the pines on the first-base side of Pitkin Field, "that's Finn's house over there, isn't it?"

"That it is," she said, handing change to a kid with an Oakdale button pinned to his thin white tank top. "Why d'ya wanna know?"

"He was supposed to meet me here before the game."

"Cain't say I'm surprised."

"Whadya mean?"

She paused a second or two before answering. "He ain't the most . . . reliable person in town." She looked right into my eyes. "I guess what I really mean is, is be careful. He can getcha inta trouble."

"I can take care of myself," I said, trying to control my sudden irritation. "How come you an' Woody an' everybody's down on 'im? *I* think he's pretty cool."

"Yeah. Jus' don't do anything stupid, okay, Mitch?"

"Don't worry," I said, heading toward Finn's, "I won't."

I had just made it past the visitors' bleachers when I saw the Caddy turn the corner and head my way up the dirt road, its headlights on in the twilight. I got to the gate at the same time Finn and the guys pulled between parked pickups and into the Finnertys' gravel driveway.

"Hey, guys, c'mon!" I said as they all piled out of the car. "You're missin' a good game."

"Hold your horses, hoss," said Finn. "Gotta go water some plants first."

It took me a second to figure out that he wasn't referring to hoses and hibiscus. "Can I use the head, too?" I asked. "The one at the ballpark's pretty gross."

"Sure," Finn said as he jumped the steps to the front porch, "but ya gotta wait your turn."

Judging by the belches and the Schlitz smell, all of them but Boomer had some beer to get rid of. "You don't drink beer?" I asked him while I waited in the hallway for my turn in the bathroom.

"Naw, can't stand the stuff."

"Sorry ya couldn't make it t' the drive-in," I said, suddenly not so pleased with the way I'd handled things the night before. "It was really fun."

He flashed me a conspiratorial grin. "That's what I heard."

"Hey, how's your mom?"

"Better," he said over the sound of a toilet flushing. "Thanks for askin'. Hands all healed up?"

"Yeah." I turned my palms up and grinned. "Thanks for askin'."

By the time I took care of my business and turned out the light, they'd all disappeared from sight. But not from sound; I followed their voices to the end of the hall, then knocked "shave and a haircut, two bits" on the open door. "Mind if I join you?" I said as I walked into the room.

The talking suddenly stopped.

Say something. "Now you're supposed to say, 'Why, am I coming apart?' "

Fortunately Boomer saved me. "Come on in, Mitch, we'll be ready t' go in a minute."

Finn's eyes got all squinty. "Yeah, relax. Wanna beer?"

I noticed that none of them had gotten another one. "No thanks," I said with a glance at Boomer, who was sitting on the edge of a corner desk, "not tonight."

Then he moved away from the desk. Coiled on the desktop behind him, its fanged white mouth wide open and ready to strike, was a huge black water moccasin.

"*Snake!*" I screamed at Boomer, automatically back-pedaling to the doorway.

Everyone but Boomer burst into laughter. "It's okay, Mitch," he said. "It's stuffed, see?" He turned partway around and picked it up, one hand holding a stiff ebony coil as thick as a blacksmith's forearm, the other gripping the cottonmouth behind its enormous evil head.

It was when Boomer turned back to face me, the snake in full view in front of him, that I guess I kind of panicked. All I know is that I was suddenly a field mouse, frozen into trembling immobility by the sight of a gigantic, gaping white mouth surrounding the two gleaming hypodermic fangs that were going to sink deeply into my body any second now.

Somehow I forced my eyes to look somewhere else. They came to rest on Finn, who was wearing an expression that was part amusement and part something I couldn't quite put my finger on.

"Ya can touch it if ya want," he said, his voice strangely flat.

"That's okay." I wiped my palms on my jeans. "Where'd ya get it?"

"Used t' belong t' m' brother Frank. Killed it when he was twelve. Uncle Elmer did the taxidermy."

"Sure did a good job," I said, risking a quick glance at the snake as Boomer set it back on the desktop. "Looks real."

"It *is* real," Finn said. "Jus' dead."

"Like Frank," Bulldog said softly.

"Yeah," Finn said, staring at the snake, "like Frank."

Again Boomer came to the rescue. "Let's get goin', okay, Finn? It really *should* be a good game."

Finn slowly tucked his black pocket T-shirt into his jeans, looking at Boomer the whole time. "C'mon, boys," he finally said, "lez go watch some baizball."

But the fact that it was a playoff game unfortunately meant there wasn't any place where we could actually see anything. Most of the bleacher seats had already been claimed before the game started, and by the bottom of the third, when we arrived, there wasn't even a place along the fence that had a decent view of the action. Not that there'd been much so far; neither Gary nor the Oakdale pitcher had allowed a run yet.

"This is really lame," I complained, trying unsuccessfully to see through the crowd.

"Yeah," Finn said next to me, "lez find us a better

view." He cocked his head at me. "You 'fraida heights, too?"

I shook my head.

"C'mon, boys," he said, turning to smile at Bulldog and Gravy, "Lez climb the eagle's nest."

I didn't know what he was talking about until after we crossed the twin railroad tracks that ran between the ball field and the main drag. But when we started up the small side street just past Dixie's Cafe, I knew exactly where we were headed. Apparently it was their intention to watch the rest of the game from the top of the Pitkin water tower.

If it had been a normal water tower I'd have been the first one up; after all, the one in the orange grove near my house was one of my favorite places. But the tower at the east end of Pitkin presented a slight problem—it was easily over a hundred feet high.

Of course I'd noticed it that first trip into town—a huge, slightly flattened sphere that almost seemed to float high above the surrounding treetops—but it was so absurdly tall that I'd never given the slightest thought to actually climbing it. The central pylon rose straight up for eighty or ninety feet before disappearing into the bottom hemisphere of the reservoir itself, like a ten-story metal tee holding a gigantic silver golf ball.

A muted roar erupted from the ball field just as we approached the heavy-duty Cyclone fence that enclosed the base of the tower and a large metal shed. The fence had a triple strand of cruel-looking barbed wire on top, at least eight feet up, jutting outward at a forty-five-degree angle. "So how do you guys get over the fence?" There was no way of getting to the base of the tower short of tunneling, at least as far as I could tell.

"We don't," Finn said with a smirk. "We go through it." He dropped to his knees and started twisting something at the bottom of the corner post next to him. "Bulldog, gimme a hand."

Bulldog immediately started clapping; the rest of us quickly joined in.

"Very funny," Finn muttered. "Never mind, I got it." He undid another wire about waist-high on the post, then slowly peeled back an entire precut section of the fence. "Hurry up," he ordered, "don't wanna bend it any more'n we hafta."

This is really great, I thought as I went through the opening with perfect commando moves.

A few seconds later we stood at the base of the pylon, an eight-foot-wide vertical tube that gleamed a dull aluminum in the starlight. The steel pipe ladder bolted to the pylon wouldn't present any difficulty; the hard part was going to be getting onto the ladder in the first place, since it ended at least fifteen feet off the ground, the last section pulled up to keep people like us out.

I spotted the four-inch-round drainpipe attached to

the pylon a second before Finn started to shinny up it. A few seconds later he was high enough to reach out an arm and swing over to the ladder, just like Cheetah the chimp.

"Darwin was right," I mugged. "We *are* descended from apes."

Bulldog went up next and was quickly followed by Gravy, whose eyes were wide open for a change. Boomer was last in the pecking order, except, of course, for me.

"You go next," he said after Gravy started up. "I'll bring up the rear."

Being a climbing veteran of many years' experience, I found shinnying up the pipe a snap, and swinging out to the ladder a few feet away wasn't much harder. I quickly scampered up high enough to clear the way for Boomer.

He was on the ladder below me in a jiffy. "Ready?" he asked.

"Ready or not, here I come."

"Slow down if you get tired, an' stop t' regrip as often as ya hafta, okay?"

"Okay," I said, "let's do it."

The first section wasn't bad, just above treetop level. I rested for a second or two before starting up the next third of the ladder.

"You okay, Mitch?" Boomer asked below me.

"Doin' fine, no sweat. You okay?"

"Yeah, but I've done this before. You haven't."

I was still okay at about the sixty-foot mark, even though I was already a lot higher than I'd ever climbed before. My hands felt strong, and the ridged rubber soles of my cross-countries provided sure footing on the rungs.

I took another quick breather to wipe the sweat off my palms, one hand at a time. "Man, this is great!" Finn shouted from way above me. "Best seat in the house!"

Evidently he'd already made it to the top. I could see the bottoms of Gravy's tennies about five yards above my head, which meant that Bulldog should be nearly to the catwalk.

"Home stretch, Mitch," said Boomer, "straight up and over. Don't look down and you'll be fine."

I honestly think that if he hadn't said anything about not looking down I wouldn't have, since I'd already made it two-thirds of the way without looking anywhere but straight up into the darkness. But not looking down was impossible because the ladder, at about the ninety-foot level, quit going straight up and abruptly flared outward as it followed the bottom of the reservoir itself.

"I'm at the bend," I said to Boomer. "Gotta rest a sec."

I'd somehow managed to avoid thinking about that part of the climb, but now I had no choice. I was going to have to crawl out almost flat on my belly for at least twenty feet before the ladder curved up to the catwalk, with the claustrophobically close underside of the tank only a few feet above my back, and the eighteen-inch-wide rungs below my front the only thing between me and a fatal fall.

I knew I could never make the traverse without looking down if my eyes were open, so I figured the only chance I had was if I closed them and went completely by feel. "Okay," I said to Boomer as I maneuvered my upper body onto the horizontal section of the ladder, "I'm goin' across now."

"Jus' take it real slow, okay?"

I was doing just that when my right foot left the last rung of the vertical section of the ladder. The instant it did a tidal wave of dizziness and nausea swept through me, nearly making me lose my dinner as well as my grip. It was either open my eyes or throw up. I opened my eyes.

If it had been daylight I'm sure I would have died of fright immediately; what little I could see at night was bad enough. The metal shed was the size of a Chiclet, the barbed-wire fence a square silver bracelet no bigger than a saltine.

The bottom of my stomach suddenly fell out. Every muscle in my body tensed as I squeezed the rungs in a death grip, my pulse pounding loudly in my ears. I tried to force my gaze away from the ground but failed, catching only a quick glimpse of the miniature ballpark past the highway before my eyes radar-locked back on target—the target being where I was soon going to dig a deep crater with my terminal velocity impact.

"I don't think I can make it," I said to Boomer, trying to keep the panic out of my voice.

"Too much for your hands, huh?" he asked from right behind me.

"Yeah," I said, following his lead, "they're startin' t' hurt pretty bad."

"Can ya make it down?"

"I think so."

"Okay. Hey, Gravy! Tell Finn me an' Mitch're headin' back down. His hands're hurtin'."

I don't know what would have happened if Boomer hadn't been there for moral support. What I do know is that I lost my nerve, pure and simple. Even though Boomer kept up the story that it was my tender new skin that had forced me down, I knew better, and I was pretty sure he did, too. I'd panicked and then frozen, and what was even worse, I'd had to depend on someone else for my own survival. Someone braver than I was.

I expected Finn to give me a hard time about chickening out, but when they all joined Boomer and me on the ground a half hour later all he said was "Too bad ya missed the view. Maybe we can try it again 'fore ya leave."

Sure, right after my spine transplant.

We heard the faint rumbling of distant truck engines as we started toward the highway. By the time we reached the blacktop a minute or so later, the rumble had turned into motorized thunder.

"What's goin' on?" I asked as I watched a line of headlights approach the west end of town.

"Army convoy from Fort Polk," said Finn. "Trainin' exercises."

"Night maneuvers," Bulldog added.

"Once or twice a month," Boomer said, "they go out to an ol' bombin' range northa here an' play war. Should be back through late t'morra night."

"Lez show city boy here one of *our* night maneuvers," said Finn.

"Yeah!" Bulldog said. "We ain't done that in a coon's age."

"What're y'all talkin' about?"

"Talkin' 'bout havin' us some fun," Finn said, speaking louder as the noise from the convoy intensified.

"What kind of fun?" I shouted as the command jeep slowly passed our position, strictly observing the posted twenty-five-mile-an-hour town speed limit.

While Finn and the guys explained the exact nature of the kind of fun they were talking about, I watched one camouflaged Army vehicle after another parade across my field of vision: a half dozen more jeeps, a few massive half-tracks, and well over a dozen canvas-topped troop transports, bored-looking young soldiers hanging out the back. By the time the convoy passed us, Finn had finished talking.

"You guys *really* do that?" I asked, trying to picture the scene they'd described. But the scene that kept going through my mind instead was from the end of *The Day the Earth Stood Still*, where the Army is tightening the cordon around Klaatu while he and Patricia Neal are in the cab, on their way to the night meeting at the saucer.

"Plannin' on doin' it again tomorrow night?"

"Maybe," Finn said. "Why, ya wanna see for yourself?"

"Depends on what time."

"They usually come back through round midnight, sometimes later." He grinned at me. "Will your mom let ya stay out that late?"

I could feel my face start to redden. "I can handle my mom. And besides, I've got an idea that can make it *really* great."

"Yeah?" Finn challenged.

"Yeah," I said, meeting his gaze.

"So what's your idea?" asked Bulldog.

"Well, to start with, here's what we'll need . . ."

I knew I had them hooked before I even finished the basics. I also knew that Mom *really* wouldn't approve of what I had in mind this time.

But Dad just might, particularly if I didn't get caught.

20

War Maneuvers

Sunday morning, while Charley and Woody talked about dinosaurs over bacon and eggs, I just chowed down and kept thinking about my mission that night with Finn and the guys. An hour or so later, while a substitute minister gave a sermon that was even more sleep-inducing than the regular one, I stayed awake by rehearsing contingency plans.

It was in Gary's room after the service that the first and most crucial part of the plan fell into place. "Hey, Gary," I said, leafing through a *G.I. Combat* comic, "let's have another sleepover here tonight, okay?"

"Okay by me. Lemme ask Mama."

It was all right with Aunt Dorothy, and I knew it would also be fine with Mom, so the only tricky part was going to be getting away from Charley and my cousins for a couple of hours that afternoon to supervise the construction of what we'd need in the way of props.

God must have appreciated the fact that I'd gone to church—and not just to sit next to Skeeter—because He had Uncle Cecil show up at the house, wearing a tan Dickies coverall and a soiled, lure-covered hat. "C'mon, boys," he called from Gary's door, "let's go fishin'!"

"Count me out, guys," I said, seizing my opportunity, "I got other fish t' fry."

A minute after they left I was knocking on Finn's front screen. Mrs. Finnerty came to the door just as I started to knock louder. "Oh, hello, Mitch," she said, looking even older than I remembered. "How're you doin' this mornin'?"

"Fine, Mrs. Finnerty. Is Finn home?"

"Ah don't believe Clarence is up yet."

Clarence?

"Oh." I tried not to grin. "Well, could you ask him to come to Gary's when he gets up?"

"Ah certainly will. Enjoy your last week heah, heah?"

"Thanks," I said, smiling at the pronunciation joke. "I certainly will."

I waited for him on the Millers' front porch. Too keyed up to sit still in the swing, I just paced the porch's perimeter, analyzing every step of the plan to make sure I hadn't overlooked a critical detail.

Finn—it was impossible for me to think of him as Clarence—finally showed up after almost an hour. "Lez go," he said from the steps. "Resta the guys're on the way. They'll meet us behind the store."

"Does this mean I'm one of the guys now?"

"Don't press your luck," he said over his shoulder.

I checked out with Aunt Dorothy, then followed Finn across the tracks toward the Pitkin Mercantile. Bulldog and Boomer were already waiting for us in the dirt delivery area between the back of the store and a big tin-roofed building that served as a warehouse for the carpeting, linoleum, and appliances that the Mercantile also stocked.

"What took ya?" asked Bulldog.

"Hadda wait for Finn," I said. "Let's start with the cardboard."

Finn turned to me and said, "He was talkin' t' *me*."

"Sorry. Did you bring the keys?"

He looked at me like I was brain damaged. "Of *course* I got the keys! Whadya think I'm gonna do, break inta m' own place?"

Gravy joined us just as Finn keyed open the padlock to the warehouse door. "I been wond'rin'," he said, speaking even more slowly than usual, "how're we gonna get their eyes t' shine?"

That had been the one part of the plan I'd kept to myself, saving it for just the right moment. "Don't worry," I said as I fished Charley's birthday present out of my front pocket, "I've got that covered."

· · ·

I wasn't so impressed with my own plan that I was blind to the fact that it had, despite its beauty, a potentially fatal flaw; five of them, actually, named Charley, Woody, Gary, Barry, and Larry. Uncle Robert and Aunt Dorothy wouldn't be a problem since they always went to bed early.

The problem was going to be how to ditch Charley and my cousins long enough to carry out my part of the mission; the fact that I had to report by twenty-three thirty hours at the latest, probably well before they'd turn in, made things even dicier.

But my luck held as God, evidently making sure I didn't forget how pleased He was by my voluntary attendance at worship that morning, made everyone settle down with their comics by a little after ten. By eleven-fifteen I was the only one still awake.

I flushed the toilet in the hall bathroom to cover up the front screen's permanent squeak, then slipped out of Gary's house as silently as a Green Beret on recon duty. Keeping to the shadows as much as possible, I quickly worked my way to the rendezvous point, encountering no enemy patrols along the way.

They were all waiting for me behind the Mercantile warehouse, dressed in the night camouflage we'd agreed to wear, jeans and dark T-shirts. "Everything ready to go?" I said in my command voice.

"Yes, sir!" Bulldog said, attempting a salute. "Ready for orders, sir!"

Gravy's usually blank face creased with a smile.

"Lez get set up," Finn said with a hint of annoyance. "They could be here anytime."

Finn and Bulldog deployed their equipment at the east end of town, about fifty yards past Dixie's on the last lighted stretch of the highway to Oakdale. Boomer and Gravy, under my supervision, secured our position on the west perimeter, just past Robert's.

The trap was set; now all we had to do was spring it.

Just when I was sure that a security leak had tipped the enemy off, I heard the faint, distant rumble of the convoy, on its way back to Fort Polk.

The reality of what I was getting ready to do suddenly struck me with the force of a grenade. *You must be out of your mind,* I thought as my pulse began to race. I feverishly tried to come up with an excuse to call the whole thing off, but it was way too late to back out now; the only course of action remaining was to execute the mission as planned.

I needn't have worried; my offensive couldn't have worked any better if General Patton himself had planned it. And due to the inspired twist I'd added, it worked despite the fact that we didn't have the element of total surprise, since they'd pulled a variation of this stunt a few times before.

At first I hadn't really believed Finn when he told me what they'd done; after all, having the nerve to stop an entire Army convoy by suddenly creating a phantom roadblock was a bit too much to swallow, even coming from him. But his description of how the G.I.s reacted when they realized they'd been had was too good to have been made up, and now, in just a minute or two, I was going to see it for myself.

The command jeep was ignoring the speed limit that late at night, judging by the rush of its oncoming head-lights. When it was maybe a hundred feet from the east streetlight, Finn and Bulldog yanked on their ends of the wire. Two cardboard cutouts instantly leaped up from the highway directly in front of the jeep; though I could only see the figures' unpainted backs from my vantage point, I knew what their fronts looked like.

And if the squeal of skidding tires that shattered the night was any indication, so did the jeep's driver.

They looked amazingly like Martians, I thought. They stood three and a half feet tall, the width of a re-frigerator shipping carton, were painted an otherworldly green, and had bulging, oversize heads dominated by huge black teardrop eyes. With red bicycle reflectors for pupils.

One vehicle after another suddenly started skidding, their drivers fighting for control. I saw a couple of personnel carriers start to swerve a second before I heard a loud crunch of metal, followed immediately by two fainter ones farther down the line. The first phase of the attack had gone off without a hitch.

"This is *great!*" I said to Boomer, who was lying on his belly next to me in the ditch that conveniently ran between the highway and the railroad tracks.

As the last echoes of the skirmish faded, they were replaced by a different sound—the loud one an Army commanding officer makes when he's been made a fool of. "COME OUTA THERE, YA LITTLE—"

I saw Bulldog suddenly make a break for the woods beyond the water tower.

"THAT'S RIGHT, YOU *BETTER* RUN!" the C.O. screamed, standing in the jeep and shaking his fist. "I'LL *KILL* YA FOR THIS!"

He kept up the barrage of obscenities the whole time it took his troops to inspect the damage and reposition their vehicles. Still standing, he hurled one last four-letter invective into the air, then gripped the top of the windshield with one hand and violently motioned the convoy forward again with the other. I could almost see the steam coming out of his ears.

"Okay, this is it!" I hissed to Gravy, who was crouched in the darkness behind a telephone pole across the road. "Get ready!" The whole point of my plan, the coup de grâce, was now only seconds away.

I'd figured that the last thing they'd expect would be

a *second* barricade, since there had never been more than one before, and I was right. On my command, Boomer and Gravy simultaneously pulled their ends of the wire, lifting our cardboard cutout off the pavement at exactly the right moment.

This time the command jeep's driver didn't react as quickly as he had before, doing a double take before he finally stomped on the brakes. The sudden deceleration flipped the C.O. completely over the windshield and onto the hood, where he landed with a loud thump, right on his keister.

The jeep skidded sideways, the panicked C.O. holding on for dear life, before both of them came to a shrieking stop right in front of Gort, the eight-foot-tall silver robot from *The Day the Earth Stood Still*. With any luck, Gort's single eye, my *large* bike reflector, was beaming a white-hot disintegration ray into the convoy, just like in the movie.

Klaatu barada nikto, dogface!

And the rout was on. "Holy—" began the driver, the expletive drowned out by the sounds of more squealing tires and chain-reaction collisions. The war zone was complete pandemonium now: doors slamming, soldiers shouting, the berserk C.O. wildly strafing the countryside with machine-gun bursts of high-pitched profanity, his face probably ready to explode.

I say "probably" because I didn't turn around to find out. Instead I did my best impression of the Flash, sprinting for all I was worth back across the tracks and into the woods behind Finn's house, laughing like a maniac the whole way.

I knew in my heart that Dad would have approved.

. . .

We met up as planned in the pines behind the ballpark, a hundred paces into the woods directly behind center field. When I finally stumbled into the tiny clearing, clutching my side and gasping for breath, I found Finn sitting on the ground, leaning against a large tree stump.

Bulldog and Boomer staggered in from different directions about thirty seconds later, both of them collapsing in hysterics next to Finn. "Funniest . . . thing . . . ever . . . seen," Bulldog said between spasms of laughter.

"The reflectors was a stroke of genius," Boomer said when he finally quit laughing. "Beats the heck outa toilet paper on a string."

Prior to that night they'd always draped toilet paper streamers over a length of twine stretched across the highway, raising what I imagined looked like a ghostly white wall in front of the convoy. I was sure it was as effective as they'd said, but my version definitely had more entertainment value.

A sudden thrashing-around-in-the-dark-woods sound told us that Gravy was nearby, most likely lost. "Over here," Bulldog called in the direction of the noise.

Gravy soon crowded into the clearing and plopped down next to me. "Who'da thunk ya could have that

much fun with a 'frigerator carton an' silver spray paint."
It was the longest sentence I'd ever heard him speak.

What Finn said next caught me completely off guard.
"*I* think," he started, then paused to look at me, "that
maybe it's time we let a *city* boy into the club."

"Yeah?" I said, trying not to sound too eager. "What
club is that?"

"Can't tell ya that 'til we vote ya in." He glanced at
Bulldog. "*If* we vote ya in." Finn made eye contact with
each of the club members in turn. "What about it, boys,
he brave enough t' join or not?"

"I dunno," Bulldog said. "Didn't make it t' the top of
the tower. But he *is* pretty funny."

"Yeah," said Finn, "he's a card all right, but this ain't
a kids' club, all fun an' games. Our club's for men only."
His eyes bored into mine. "You man enough t' join, city
boy?"

"Depends," I said, playing it safe. I'd heard my share
of stories about sadistic initiation rituals where some kid
got maimed or killed; nobody really believed them, but I
suspected they weren't too far off the mark. "What do I
have to do?"

"Same thing all of us had to do."

"What's that?"

"Conquer your fear."

"Fear of what?" I wasn't sure I really wanted to
know.

"Well, that's the problem, see, 'cause people're 'fraida

diff'rent things. Bulldog here's 'fraida spiders; Gravy lets 'em crawl all over 'im. But there's one thing *every*one round here's scared of, an' that's why we called the club what we did."

"And what's that?" I was suddenly aware of how quiet it was.

"The Cottonmouth Club."

I swallowed. "The Cottonmouth Club?"

He nodded. "The Cottonmouth Club."

My mouth suddenly went dry. "As in dry mouth or as in water moccasin?" I already knew what the answer would be.

"As in cottonmouth, the snake." A feral grin flashed across his face. "The extremely pois'nous snake. Still int'rested?"

My Curly voice took over. "Why, *soi*tanly!"

Finn cut the chuckling short. "Great. Now all ya gotta do is pass the test."

"I knew there was a catch somewhere," I said, tapping an imaginary cigar. "What do I have to do?"

"Jus' go stand a ways off in the woods 'til we get ev'rything set up. Twenny paces oughta do." Finn nodded to Bulldog, who immediately got up and headed off in the direction of Finn's house.

Ten steps into the trees I looked back at the clearing, where Finn now knelt next to Boomer, talking too softly for me to hear. I could see no point to walking the full distance that Finn had dictated, so I stopped after a few more steps and squatted down to wait. And to worry about what I'd gotten myself into.

By the time Bulldog returned and Finn called me back in, I was pretty edgy because, after having had time to think about it, I had the distinct feeling that whatever was coming next was going to involve the stuffed snake.

And I was right. As soon as I stepped back into the clearing I saw it, coiled on the stump, its inky scales glistening in the moonlight; the fact that I knew it was dead did nothing to ease my instinctive revulsion.

Finn made me sit on the ground next to it, well within striking distance had it been alive. I kept telling myself that the moccasin was really dead and couldn't hurt me, but its hideous wedged head seemed to sway in midair in front of my face, as if measuring me for the strike. The only thing that saved me was that it was too dark to see its fangs clearly against its cottony white mouth.

And then Finn turned on his flashlight. I yelled as the snake's enormous fangs blurred and seemed to lunge for my throat.

"Proves m' point," Finn said. "Fear's natural. It's how ya handle it that makes ya a man. You a man yet, city boy?"

I was trying to decide that very thing when Bulldog said, "Maybe he needs another year or two, huh, Finn?"

That made up my mind for me. "I'm ready *now*."

Even if it means letting you sink its fangs into me.

"Okay," Finn said, "hold out your hand, palm up." He handed the flashlight to Gravy and then picked up the snake. "Bulldog, take his arm."

"But then I'll only have one." I couldn't seem to stop joking.

Bulldog set my forearm on the vacated tree stump and let go of my wrist. "Make a fist," he said. "Trust me, it don't hurt so much that way."

"Whenever you're ready," I said to Finn, then clenched my teeth and closed my eyes. I figured it wouldn't be nearly so bad if I didn't see it coming.

"Nope, can't close your eyes. Gotta *face* your fear 'fore ya can overcome it."

I almost called it off at that point, but something in Finn's face told me that was exactly what he expected me to do. "And I suppose if I flinch I have to do it again?"

He shook his head. "If ya flinch, you're out. Don't, an' you're in." He didn't say anything else.

I'd come too far to chicken out now. I expelled a deep breath as quietly as I could. "Okay, let's do it."

Finn dropped to his knees next to me and the stump. The moccasin's thick coils were cradled in his left arm; his right hand was behind its massive head, holding it only inches above my bare forearm.

"You're not gonna do it too deep, are ya?" The cotton-mouth's fangs looked long enough to suck bone marrow.

"Jus' deep enough t' draw blood. Ready?"

Ready as I'll ever be.

I swallowed and nodded twice.

Finn tightened his grip behind the cottonmouth's head, then slowly lowered it until its fangs hovered just above my skin. "Don't move now," he whispered.

I couldn't have moved if I'd wanted to; and I wanted to with every atom of my being.

He gently pressed down on the snake's head. My entire body seemed to recoil the instant its fangs touched me, but my arm miraculously stayed still. I watched as if in a trance, hypnotized by the sight of the twin depressions the needle tips made in my skin.

I saw Finn's arm muscles suddenly tense in the flashlight's beam. "Wait!" I said. "There's no chance there's any venom left, is there?"

Finn shook his head. "Didn't kill *us*, did it?" He looked right at me and bared his teeth. Then he plunged the fangs into my arm.

The instant they broke my skin a jolt of electricity shot into my veins and out of my arteries, stopping my heart along the way. Which is probably why I didn't move a muscle until after he pulled the fangs out.

I just sat there for a few seconds, staring in morbid fascination at the two drops of blood welling from my forearm; it took a few seconds more before I realized that the ordeal was over. I'd passed the test and was in the club.

Finn was looking at me with what appeared to be admiration, but his voice was oddly flat. "Congrats. Didn't think ya could do it."

I know. That's why I did it.

"Me neither," said Bulldog. "No offense."

"Yeah," Gravy said, "way t' go."

Then I realized that Boomer hadn't said a word since the initiation began. "So, Boomer," I said, throwing him a fraternal grin, "does this mean we're kinda like *blood* brothers?"

"Not yet," Finn quickly said. "That was only the *first* part of the test."

The first *part?*

Bulldog nodded. "Kinda like a practice test. The real test is t'morra."

"What's tomorrow?" I asked, suddenly irritated. "Rattlesnake milking?"

Bulldog and Gravy laughed. Boomer and Finn didn't. "T'morra," Finn said, "we're takin' ya swimmin'."

"Great," I said sarcastically, "but what does that have to do with the test?"

"It *is* the test," he said.

"I don't get it."

"T'morra you're gonna try t' do the same thing each one of us hadda do t' prove our courage. If ya can't do it, well, ya won't be the first person t' fail. But if ya can, you're in the club for life."

Bulldog and Gravy nodded agreement.

"Do what?"

"Swim Cottonmouth Creek."

"Across and back," said Bulldog.

Finn smiled again. "You in, city boy?"

Something about his expression struck a raw nerve, so with no hesitation whatsoever, I uttered the stupidest three words of my entire life: "Yeah. I'm in."

21

Cottonmouth

What I ended up in instead was big trouble, because in all the excitement of the ambush and the initiation afterward, all of us had completely forgotten about the last part of the plan—the mop-up detail.

We'd known that the commotion would more than likely wake up everyone in town, but we also knew that there would probably be no local eyewitnesses that time of night, so we figured as long as we disposed of the evidence afterward, no one would be able to connect us to the crime.

But we didn't, so when the good merchants of Pitkin opened up shop first thing Monday morning, they found it all: two lengths of strong wire, both still threaded through one of the eyebolts we'd screwed into telephone poles in order to raise the cutouts; and the cutouts themselves, tattered, tread-covered remains of two cardboard aliens and a giant robot, all three of which unfortunately still had their eyes attached.

Mom busted me in Robert's Cafe. I found out later that she'd come into town early to have coffee with Uncle Robert and Aunt Dorothy, who'd told her about the midnight ruckus. Her curiosity piqued, Mom had walked down to the Mercantile, where she'd seen, propped up on the bench in front of the store, the three cardboard cutouts. Along with Exhibits A through E, the five bicycle reflectors that Charley had given me for my birthday. I'm sure it only took her a second to put four and one together and come up with me.

She immediately phoned Gary's house and told me to get dressed and come right over to the cafe for breakfast. Since I was even hungrier than usual from the night's excitement, I not only didn't think twice about accepting her invitation, I didn't even wonder why she didn't say anything about bringing Charley.

"Mornin', honey," she said sweetly when I joined her in the booth, still groggy from not getting enough sleep. "Have fun last night?"

If I'd been more awake I'm sure I would have been immediately wary, but my brain was only firing on about three out of eight cylinders. "Yeah," I said through a prolonged yawn.

"So what'd you do?" she casually asked, laying her trap.

"Same ol' stuff," I said, walking into it. "You know, read comics and messed around. When's breakfast? I'm starved." Then I noticed that no one else was in the cafe, not even Aunt Dorothy.

Mom stirred her coffee. "Soon. You been readin' any of your new birthday books?"

Even the odd way she stressed "birthday" didn't penetrate my befogged brain. "Nope, not yet."

"And speakin' of your birthday, wasn't it thoughtful of Charley to get you that nice set of bicycle reflectors?" Her spoon stopped moving. "By the way, where are they?"

That's when I finally realized that she'd been playing me like a bigmouth bass all along, hooking me with the promise of bacon and eggs and reeling me in with the reflectors.

I couldn't look at her. "In my suitcase," I mumbled, just in case I was wrong about what was going to happen next. I wasn't.

She reached into her purse. "Then explain *these*," she demanded, dramatically dropping the reflectors on the Formica tabletop. Her lips were a thin line, her eyes angry dots.

I just stared at the reflectors.

She pointed at me with her spoon. "You, young man, are grounded."

I looked up at her. "For how long?"

She didn't hesitate. "Until we leave. And that's final!"

It was all I could do to keep from hugging her.

The truth was, being permanently grounded was the best thing that could have happened to me, since I'd already decided not to go through with the second part of the initiation. I'd stayed up half the night thinking about it, and had come to the conclusion that swimming in a creek named after a deadly aquatic viper was about as smart as playing Russian roulette with a single-shot pistol.

So Mom unwittingly ended up doing me a huge favor by overreacting to the situation. Aunt Dorothy didn't seem upset, and Uncle Robert thought the whole thing was pretty funny, despite his Army veteran's status; I suspected he wasn't the only one in town who felt that way.

Charley and my cousins naturally thought it was great, especially after I filled them in on the details later at the cafe; I thought they'd all bust a gut when I described the C.O. flipping onto the jeep's hood.

Not only did my forced incarceration figure to save me from what would probably be an unpleasant ordeal at best, it seemed a small price to pay for the instant notoriety I'd gained; I was sure that the story of Mitch Valentine and the Army convoy would eventually reach mythic proportions, becoming a treasured bit of folklore to be passed down through generations to come, like a family heirloom.

But I still had to deal with Finn. He called me at Paw-Paw's a little after noon. "Meet us at Dixie's," he said over the cross talk of another conversation on the party line. "Wear your trunks under your jeans."

"I can't," I said, trying to sound disappointed. "I've been completely grounded. We forgot to clean up the stuff."

"Yeah, I know." He said it as if he'd gotten into trouble, too. "But so what? A *man* would figure out a way to sneak out."

"I don't see how, but I'll think of somethin'."

"I'm sure ya will." His voice dripped sarcasm.

"It's not that I'm chickening out or anything, it's just that I really *can't* get out of the house. My mom's watching me like a hawk." At the moment, Mom was out of sight in the laundry room, doing the pack-five-days-ahead-of-time wash.

"Look," I said, anxious to convince Finn of my sincerity, "she usually forgets all about these things in a day or two, which'll still give us plenty of time. I'll call you tomorrow, okay?"

"Do that." Then he hung up.

And tomorrow, I thought as I pictured Scarlett O'Hara standing amid the ruins of Tara, *is another day*.

. . .

The summer storm blew in just before dawn, the subsonic bass of rolling thunder rescuing me from a creepy swamp dream that had me soaked in sweat. Of course, the humidity might have had something to do with it, too.

Thank you, Lord, I thought as I realized that the rain

would make a creek outing out of the question. *I suppose four more days of this would be too much to ask for?*

I didn't call Finn because it rained all day, so I figured that even he had to admit the conditions were impossible. I spent most of the day in my cot, reading one of my new hardbacks, *Trouble on Titan*, reasoning that Saturn was about as far away from Louisiana as I was likely to get.

After a late lunch—I'd gone back to calling meals by their correct names—Charley and Woody decided that a marathon game of Monopoly would be the perfect way to while away a rainy afternoon.

"Wanna play, Mitch?" Charley asked as he and Woody headed for the front room.

"Sure," I said immediately, surprising all three of us. "Dibs on the race car."

"Uh-uh," Woody said. "Gotta roll for it."

Charley rolled first. I barely had time to register his double fours before Woody scooped up the dice. "C'mon, Mama!" he said, then cast them. " 'Leven! Tough t' beat."

"Oh yeah? Watch this." I snatched up the dice and rattled them in my fist like a compulsive gambler betting the deed to his house. "Lucky boxcars," I said, then dropped them on the center of the board.

I stared in disbelief at the single black dot showing on top of each cube.

"Snake eyes," Woody said as he grabbed the race car. "You lose."

The afternoon seemed stuck in amber, the monotonous hissing of rain interrupted only by the regular clicks of thrown dice and moved tokens, along with the cathedral-like chimes of the hall clock that announced the passage of each slow hour.

"Woody," I asked as he triumphantly placed a hotel on Boardwalk, "where's Cottonmouth Creek?" I hoped he'd say he'd never heard of it.

He didn't look up. "Why d'ya wanna know?"

"Jus' curious. Heard someone mention it, that's all."

"Coupla miles downstream, jus' above the old ford." He started straightening his deeds again. "But that wasn't its original name. Folks only call it that now 'causa the snake attacks."

"For real?" Charley said.

"Yeah. Too bad, too, and not jus' 'causa the kid that got killed. They say it was the best swimmin' hole around."

"How long ago did all this happen?" I asked.

"I dunno, 'fore I was born."

"Ever been there?"

"Shore. Been everywhere round here."

"Did you see any cottonmouths?"

"Naw, like I said, it was a long time ago."

"So didya go swimmin'?"

"I ain't *that* dumb. Seen one cottonmouth up close; that's more'n enough for me."

"Was that what your mom was talking about at dinner that night?" Charley asked.

Woody slowly nodded, his face expressionless.

"What happened?" I asked.

"Not much to tell," he began, the game now temporarily abandoned. "It was four years ago, the spring 'fore Daddy was killed. I was runnin' in a field near where we used t' live, near Aunt Chlora's, an' saw a little gully comin' up, so I ran fastah t' broad jump it. Good thing, too, 'cause when I was in midair 'bove it I looked down an' saw a big mama cottonmouth comin' up at m' legs, mouth open, ready t' strike. Couldn'ta missed me by more'n inches."

At the same time I saw Charley's mouth was open I realized that mine was, too. "How'd you know it was a mama moccasin?" he asked. "They a different color or something?"

"Naw, 'causa the babies she was protectin'. Musta been a dozen of 'em, slitherin' on toppa each other like a balla huge pois'nous worms." He shuddered. "It's a sight I'll take t' my grave."

Evidently the story was over, but there was still one thing I had to know. "Would you have died if it'd bitten you?"

"More'n likely. They usually won't kill a grown man, just make 'im *wish* he was dead, but as little as I weighed then, yeah, I'da prob'ly died. That answer your question?"

It did. I now knew for certain that I'd never die from snake poisoning; a massive coronary would do me in long before the venom could do the job.

He picked up the dice. "Whose turn was it?"

"Mine," I said, "but I've had it. You guys go ahead and fight it out. Charley, you can have all my cash. Woody, you can have both my deeds."

I retreated to Woody's room and my new book; better to read about the trouble on Titan than to think about the trouble in Pitkin. After listening to Woody I was more convinced than ever that I'd made the right decision—the decision being that, no matter what, somehow I'd get out of swimming Cottonmouth Creek.

But without losing face.

. . .

I almost got the four days of rain I'd jokingly asked for. I couldn't really tell if it was the same storm or a series of new ones, but it poured off and on until just before sundown Thursday night, at which time Finn told me over the phone that the initiation was "on for t'morra mornin' come Hell or high water."

And that he had a foolproof plan for getting me out of the house.

"Great," I said, my stomach sinking. "Seeya then."

I spent the rest of the evening staring at my book and trying to figure out how I was going to play it with Finn in the morning; I shouldn't have bothered.

He showed up at PawPaw's an hour after breakfast,

alone in the Caddy. He parked it in the mud next to the De Soto, then walked through the light drizzle to the front steps and onto the porch.

I watched through the front window as Finn approached Mom and Aunt Nelda, interrupting their idle chatter, then listened to him weave a web of total deception around Mom.

Two minutes later she was shooing me out the door to accompany him to the Mercantile, where she thought we were both going to make restitution to his folks by working off the replacement cost of the materials we'd taken from the store. He'd told her that between the paint, the wire, and the eyebolts, we'd both have to put in four hours. Which was more than enough time to get to Cottonmouth Creek and back.

Not that I had any intention of letting things go that far. I knew that somehow, between then and the time we got anywhere near the creek, I'd figure a way out.

But I didn't come up with anything on the way to get Bulldog, and my mind was still a complete blank by the time we picked up Gravy. *Don't panic*, I thought, starting to do just that, *you'll think of something before we get to Boomer's.*

"How long does it take to get to Boomer's place?" We'd been on the same dirt road for at least a mile, and I hadn't seen any houses yet.

Finn looked at me in the rearview mirror. "Boomer couldn't make it."

Now you can panic.

"How come?"

"Hadda take care of his sisters," said Bulldog. "Mama's in the hospital."

Finn slowed the Caddy to a crawl, then turned sharply to the left, right into the woods. The car bounced violently for a few seconds as he steered through a sparse grove of birch trees and out of view from the road, then put it in Park and turned off the ignition.

The din was deafening, worse than the Tiki Room at Disneyland; it seemed as if every living thing in the vicinity was talking about the storm.

"Lez go," Finn ordered as he set off through the woods, followed closely by Gravy.

I waited for Bulldog to move. He waved me forward. "After you."

My last line of retreat cut off, I had no choice but to follow Gravy and Finn along the creek's winding bank, our progress slow in the dense, waterlogged vegetation. I'd have made a crack about machetes if I'd been in a joking mood.

Except for the wildlife and the constant spatter of cool water dripping from the leaves overhead, we walked in silence. The farther we went the more primeval it seemed the forest became, like we were going backward through a museum evolution exhibit. The birches and pines gave way to willows and cypresses, their drenched tendrils even creepier than usual in the gray mist.

Gravy abruptly turned left and disappeared. I followed him down a steep bank to the sand, where Finn was waiting for us. "Well, city boy," he said, "here we are."

As usual, I had no idea at all where "here" actually was. What it looked like was a cover of a *Swamp Thing* comic, all primordial and overgrown.

If they ditch me I'm dead.

I carefully inspected the old swimming hole while I worked up the nerve to tell him what I'd decided. "Looks clear," he said, his eyes settling on mine. "Ready?"

Just say it.

"Actually . . . no." An invisible weight immediately lifted off my back.

Finn's grin nearly split his face. "Pay up, boys!" he said, holding out his hand. "*Told* ya he was chicken."

And that's when something inside me snapped. "Hold on," I said, glaring at Finn. "What I *meant* was, not yet, I'm not wearin' my swim trunks. I don't suppose any of you guys brought a pair?"

Finn kept smiling. "You're wearin' underwear, ain'tcha?"

My options had dwindled to two; there was nothing to do now but chicken out for real and suffer their ridicule, or cross the creek as carefully as I could and pray that there weren't any cottonmouths around at the moment.

The truth was, though, I really had no choice at all; I

had to swim the creek because, more than anything else, I wanted to wipe that grin off Finn's face.

I got my socks and tennies off as fast as I could, knowing the longer it took me to strip down to my jockeys the greater the odds would be that I'd lose my nerve. I stood with my back to them to peel off my wet T-shirt, then worked my way out of my waterlogged Levi's. I was acutely conscious of being almost naked in front of them, so I didn't waste any time approaching the water's edge.

Even so, I'll never know how I forced myself into the creek. The rains had turned the water even browner with mud washed from the banks, making it more impossible than ever to see if there was anything alive in it. I must have scoped out the area a dozen times before I finally worked up enough nerve to wade out of the shallows.

My heart beating like a hummingbird's, I quietly eased into the deeper water. It was both colder and faster than I'd anticipated, which made it harder to use the technique I'd decided on, the crawl; it seemed to me that the safest way to cross the creek and get back alive would be to use a stroke that made as little noise as possible, and let me watch for snakes at the same time.

I was about thirty feet out, almost to the middle, when Bulldog called out, "Lookin' good so far."

"Yeah," said Gravy, "coast is still clear. Keep it up."

I soon felt the slimy creek bed under my feet again and cautiously approached the opposite bank; its thick plant cover was a perfect hiding place for a snake.

"Jus' gotta touch the bank," Finn yelled.

My pulse pounding, I reached out and forced myself to touch the high grass at the water's edge, then instantly pulled my hand back and waded backward into the shallows, unable to take my eyes off of the bank's overgrowth in case something came slithering out of it and into the creek with me.

When the water got chin high again, I started to tread. As I slowly spun around for the return leg, I heard a soft splash upstream, like the sound I imagined a large snake might make entering the water. My head snapped in that direction, and that's when I saw that something was moving toward me.

Something long and dark.

"*Snake!*" Finn yelled. "*Swim!*"

Miraculously, Mother Nature's instincts took over as a powerful jolt of adrenaline shocked me into action. Suddenly my arms and legs became propellers, thrashing at insane speed. I didn't see anything but splashing water and the approaching sand until I staggered out of the creek onto it and fell to my knees. Only then did I look back to see where the cottonmouth was.

It was floating downstream in the strong current, barely past the part of the creek I'd just vacated. Only it wasn't a cottonmouth; it was a branch that someone must have tossed into the water.

Someone undoubtedly named Finn.

Their howls of laughter sliced through me like razor

blades, each whoop and snort leaving a raw flesh wound. But it was their words that cut to the bone.

From Finn: "Shoulda seen the look on your face!"

Bulldog: "Thought ya were gonna explode!"

Gravy: "Looked like one a them water striders!"

Finn again: "Yeah, *told* ya he was funny!"

All punctuated by knee-slapping, side-splitting fits of laughter. And all at my expense.

I felt my shoulders slump as it slowly dawned on me that I'd been a complete, total, and utter fool. There *was* no Cottonmouth Club; the initiation in the woods had been a sham, made to seem spontaneous but set up ahead of time. They probably hadn't expected me to get through the stuffed snake ritual, so they may have had to add the creek part on the spur of the moment, but it was more likely that Finn had planned all of it that way from the very beginning.

And the beginning, I realized with sickening certainty, was obviously when he saw my panic reaction to the snake on his desk.

At least it was obvious after the fact. It was also perfectly clear to me that I was nothing to him; I never had been, and never would be.

"No hard feelin's, okay, Slick?" Bulldog said, still chuckling.

I didn't answer in words; I turned my back on them instead.

"It was jus' a joke," said Gravy. "Purdy funny one, too, ya hafta admit."

I just stared at the current.

"C'mon, city boy," Finn said, "where's that sensa humor?"

I still didn't turn around, but I did speak. "Clarence," I said, part of me wishing I could see his expression, "I don't ever wanna see you again."

I managed to hold back my tears until they finally went away.

22

Up the Creek

I was still in the same position when I heard Woody and Charley calling my name from the woods upstream. I rubbed my stiff knees, trying to get some blood back into my legs, then struggled into my jeans and T-shirt as their tromping sounds got louder. I was picking up my cross-countries when they noisily burst from the trees and shuffled down the bank to the sand.

Charley practically knocked me back into the water with the force of his bear hug. "You're okay, you're okay" was all he could say.

"Yeah, I'm okay." I patted his damp hair. "How'd ya know where I was?"

"Boomer called a little after ya left with Finn," Woody said as he slowly scanned the area. "Said there was somethin' goin' on, didn't know zactly what it was, jus' said t' get t' the old ford quick as I could, that ya might be in trouble."

I knew he was a friend.

"Also said somethin' 'bout some kinda 'nitiation to a cottonmouth club. Wanna tell me 'bout it on the way home?"

I had already promised myself that no one would ever hear about my humiliation at Finn's hands, but before I could stop myself the whole story came pouring out.

"Well, glad you're okay," Woody said when I finally stopped talking. "Now ya know why I don't shine to 'im."

"He ever do anything like that t' you?"

"Jus' little kid stuff, nothin' like this. But he's always had a mean streak in 'im, ever since I've known 'im. Haven't had a thing t' do with 'im since Daddy died. Aim t' keep it that way, too."

"Yeah. Hey, Woody, I've been meanin' to say somethin' to ya for a while now, an' this seems like as good a time as any."

"I'm lis'nin'."

I wasn't any closer to finding the right words then than I'd been when Aunt Nelda had talked about it that night in the hall, so I just jumped in. "I'm really sorry 'bout your dad."

"Yeah," he said, staring off into space. "Me, too."

"Aunt Nelda, I mean your mom, told me it was a drunk driver. Makes it even more of a waste."

"Yeah, 'specially since the guy that killed 'im was such a waste himself."

"What do ya mean?"

"He was a wild kid, spoiled rotten. His folks let 'im do whatevah he wanted, whenevah he wanted t' do it. An' what he wanted t' do most of the time was drink beer. He was a total alkie by the time he was old enough t' enlist."

"So what happened?"

"Story is he got stinkin' drunk at a bar near Fort Polk the Friday 'fore he hadda report. Stayed up all night drinkin', then drove back t' Pitkin at sunup. *Tried* t' drive, anyway."

A look of total hatred darkened Woody's face. "Daddy was on his way t' Leesville at the same time. Got hit head-on 'bout halfway there. Sheriff said the other guy hadda been doin' ovah ninety." He swallowed and looked away.

I had to say something to fill the sudden silence. "Did the kid survive? I heard that sometimes drunks don't even get hurt 'cause they're so relaxed."

"Not this time. He was buried the day aftah Daddy was."

"Who was he? A local kid, I presume?"

" 'Bout as local as ya can get. It was Frank Finnerty."

Everything fell into place then. "Wow, no *wonder* ya can't stand Finn."

Woody shook his head. "Ya still don't get it. What

Finn's big brothah did don't have nothin' t' do with him. I can't stand Finn 'causa the way he treats people, not 'causa the accident."

Woody's eyes narrowed. "Not once in the four years since has he evah told me he was sorry 'bout what happened t' Daddy. Not once."

While we were talking I realized that the warm drizzle had stopped; the sun seemed to be doing its best to break through the cloud cover, apparently anxious to get back to work after a four-day layoff. I also realized that I still had no idea where we were.

"Hey," I said to Woody, "where in the heck *are* we?"

"Near the swimmin' hole."

"Boy, am I turned around. The regular swimmin' hole, with the rope swing?"

"Yeah. *Surely* ya don't wanna go swimmin' after what ya been through."

"Depends. What time is it?" I was foggy about that, too.

Charley checked his Goofy watch. "Ten fifty-five."

That meant I'd spent over an hour on the sand, contemplating suicide.

"Sure," I said. "Besides, Mom's not expectin' me back for a coupla hours at least, so, yeah!" I smirked at Woody. "An' stop callin' me Shirley."

When we reached the swimming hole not too much later, the sun was back on the job with a vengeance, trying to evaporate all traces of the deluge.

With the creek all to ourselves, we quickly stripped to our underwear. Charley and I spread our jeans and T-shirts out to dry on some bushes while Woody hung his overalls up on a broken branch of a nearby tree.

I started off toward the big oak and the rope swing, Charley still glued to my hip.

"Hold on, lemme check for logs first," said Woody. "High watah mighta brought some new ones in. Don't wanna break our necks."

Charley and I waited on the sand, the beach noticeably smaller due to the rains, while Woody waded into the creek. When he got to chin-high depth he took a deep breath, then sank like a submarine and disappeared into the murk. I was starting to think that he might have somehow gotten stuck when he shot out of the water with a huge splash, gasping for air. "All clear now. Jus' hadda loosen a coupla big branches. Current's strong, though. Creek's way up."

"Weren't you scared?" Charley suddenly asked me, staring at the oak. Other than telling me the time, he hadn't said anything since we left Cottonmouth Creek.

"When? In the woods or in the water?"

"In the water, when you thought it was a real snake."

I thought about it for a few seconds. "Not as scared as I shoulda been. Prob'ly 'cause I was so mad."

"Maybe that's what I should do." I couldn't tell if he was talking to me or to himself.

"What?"

"I guess I just haven't gotten mad enough yet."

I still had no idea what he was talking about. "What am I, a mind reader? Spit it out, Charley boy."

He wouldn't look at me. "I really wanna go off the rope swing," he said in a pathetic little-kid voice, "but I'm too scared."

I automatically put my arm around his small shoulders. "Woody," I said as he caught up to us, "you an' I are gonna teach this fine young man t' go off the swing."

After a quick grip and balance lesson, Charley stood nervously on the launch station, listening to final instructions.

"Remember," I said, "don't let go 'til Woody tells ya, an' you'll be okay. I'll steady ya so ya can get a good start, an' he'll be down below t' catch ya in case ya fall, which ya won't. Just concentrate on holdin' on tight t' the handle."

I could see the tendons bulging on the backs of his hands. "An' don't forget t' let go, okay?"

He nodded, the ghost of a smile flickering across his ashen face.

"Okay. You can do it; it's just a matter of mind over matter. All ya gotta do is use that brain of yours and concentrate."

"But what if I concentrate and I still can't do it?"

"Then just use your mind a different way. I dunno,

pretend you're on the jungle gym rings at school or somethin'. Mind over matter, Charley, that's all there is to it. Mind over matter."

It worked. Charley closed his eyes, his way of concentrating, then opened them and stepped right off the branch, as casually as if it were a curb. His arc was perfect, Woody told him to let go at just the right time, and Charley did the rest. He even tried to get into cannonball position before he splashed down, dead center into the creek.

He broke the surface with a blinding smile. "Didja see it, Mitch?" he yelled. "I *did* it! Woody, I *did* it!"

And he kept on doing it, too, over and over, his confidence visibly growing with each attempt; by about his tenth turn he was even asking us to show him how to do a backflip.

Woody and I explained the moves to him on the branch. "You go off next," I said, "then stay on the sand an' watch. An' pay attention t' how I swing my feet up inta the tuck."

Charley launched himself off the branch again, like he'd been doing it all his life, even doing a decent can opener. I caught the rope and waited for him to get out of the creek and into position.

I glanced over my shoulder at Woody and grinned. "You show him the *wrong* way t' do it next, okay?"

Then I jumped out as high and far as I could and dropped into free fall. At the exact peak of my arc, I whipped my legs up and over into a tight tuck and flipped backward. Three times. Just like Boomer, the best diver in Pitkin.

I hit the water as cleanly as he had, too, my feet touching the squishy creek bottom a second later. I immediately launched myself back into air like a Polaris missile, shooting at least halfway out of the water.

Grinning so hard it hurt, I emerged to a two-man cheerleading squad, their congratulatory whoops music to my ears. I treaded with only my legs for a few seconds while I wiped the dirty water out of my eyes, then blinked twice to clear my vision. A big piece of driftwood floated into view from around the bend about a hundred feet upstream, moving surprisingly fast in the creek's swollen current.

And then it opened its mouth.

Oh God.

It was a water moccasin.

My blood turned to ice; cold lizards skittered up my spine.

I heard Charley shout "Snake!" from somewhere far away.

The cottonmouth's huge curved fangs gleamed in the sunlight, brilliant pearl against the oily black scales of its thick head; its tongue was a flickering gray blur in its gaping white mouth.

Spiders invaded my stomach; my bone marrow turned to worms.

"Move!" Woody yelled.

I couldn't. I willed my body into action, but nothing happened; it was no longer connected to my brain.

The snake's evil head slowly turned from side to side, scanning its territory like a periscope from Hell.

"Mitch! *Swim!*" The voice was Charley's, pitched unnaturally high.

And then it saw me. Its head stopped swiveling; its eyes locked onto mine.

I couldn't look away from them: alien, vertical-slit eyes, cold, soulless predator eyes, kill-or-be-killed snake eyes.

Looming larger by the second in the swift current, it seemed to be in no hurry, as if it knew that its prey was already paralyzed.

And I was; every muscle was frozen; I couldn't even breathe.

Then it opened its mouth even wider and hissed. The sound struck me with stunning force, elemental menace that penetrated to the core. It was a raw, primitive animal sound, a law-of-the-jungle warning sound; it was the sound of imminent death.

Nearing striking distance now, it reared its head into attack position.

The last thing I heard was Charley, screaming my name in the distance.

The last thing I saw was the cottonmouth's fangs, angled outward to sink into my face.

I closed my eyes as tight as I could and waited to die.

Something suddenly slammed into my shoulders with incredible force, knocking the air out of my lungs. I was instantly driven to the creek bottom by the weight of the thing on my back; it pinned me there, its legs wrapped around my waist, its claws raking my face.

I tried with all my might to get it off me, but it just gripped tighter and started dragging me along the creek bed. Desperate for air, I tried to pry its fingers off my mouth and nose. And then I realized that wild animals don't have fingers, that it was Woody on my back, trying as hard as he could to drag me to safety. I quit struggling and pounded his arm to tell him to let go. The instant he did I remembered the snake.

I didn't know where it was.

I frantically started clawing into the mud, trying to crawl out of the water before it found me. Every square inch of my skin quivered, anticipating the strike; each cell in my body vibrated, screaming for oxygen. I kicked off the creek bottom with all the strength I had left and burst into air a split second later, gasping for breath in waist-high water.

Woody exploded from the shallows behind me, his arms whirling like windmills. We both flailed at the water in a wild rush to get out, then hit the sand and kept going, scrabbling halfway up the bank before we turned around to see where the moccasin was.

It was cruising downstream, about thirty feet past where I nearly died. It was the king of the cottonmouths, bigger by far than the one Frank had killed, five or six feet of death incarnate. The sight of its thick, sinuous length gliding through the water filled me with dread all over again, like a nightmare that wouldn't go away.

But this one did go away, finally disappearing around a distant bend and out of our lives forever.

"Biggest one I've evah seen," Woody said, his voice quivering.

"Woody," I started to say, "I—" And then I guess the adrenaline wore off. My skin erupted into goose bumps; my teeth started chattering so hard I bit my tongue. The trembling spread from my teeth down my whole body, and in seconds I was shaking with rib-cracking force.

I could see the same thing happening to Woody; soon we were both twitching like electrocution victims and sobbing uncontrollably. And then we were three as Charley hugged us both as hard as he could, all of us huddling miserably together on the sand, bawling like babies.

"How close was it?" I whispered to Charley when I could finally speak.

He sniffled. "Maybe fifteen feet." His eyes were still dilated. "Maybe less."

I wiped my nose with the back of my hand. "Guess it's a good thing they don't go underwater."

Woody's face was as pale as skim milk. "They do," he said softly. "They eat fish."

Oh, God.

My skin started crawling all over again.

Woody took a deep, slow breath and shuddered. "Let's go home, boys," he said, his voice barely audible.

"Yeah," I seconded. The scratches on my neck and face were starting to sting. "An' when we get there, you need t' trim your fingernails."

. . .

Mom and Boomer, along with his sisters, were waiting for us on the front porch. Mom stood up from her rocker the instant she saw us. We weren't halfway down the driveway when she threw her arms around my neck and hugged me so hard it hurt.

Then she eased up her death grip and looked at my scratched and undoubtedly puffy face. "Don't you *ever* do anything like that to me again!" Her tone was half anger, half hysterical relief. "I was worried sick!"

Her words came out in a rush. "I called over t' the Mercantile t' ask ya t' bring home some travel tissues an' toothpaste, an' found out you weren't there, an' that Finn had lied t' me. Mrs. Finnerty didn't know where he was, either, an' that's when I really started t' worry. A mother knows when somethin's wrong with her babies."

I nodded but didn't say anything; I'd made Charley and Woody swear on our mothers' graves not to ever mention a word of this to them or anyone else for as long as they lived. And in the afterlife, too, if there really was one.

"Tell me what happened." She started herding us toward the steps, like a mother hen shooing her chicks.

"I can't, Ma. I'm sorry."

She glanced at me in surprise but didn't force the issue. "So what happened to your face?"

I kept my expression deadpan. "Got scratched by branches."

She studied me for a second and then nodded. "I'll start the tub. Come on in when you're done talkin' t' Boomer." She waved at him and the girls on her way inside.

Boomer sat on the railing at the end of the porch, behind the swing occupied by two quiet young girls who looked nothing like him. "You okay, Mitch?" he asked as we approached.

"I'll survive." I shook his extended hand.

He introduced us to his sisters, Meg and Beth, then asked, "Care t' tell me what happened?"

I shook my head. "Not up to it just yet. But I really wanna thank ya for helpin', an' not just by callin' Woody. For everything."

"It's okay. Ya seem like a good kid; didn't wanna see ya get hurt."

"Didya know what they were gonna do?"

"Uh-uh. Only thing Finn told me in the woods that night was that we were jus' gonna have some fun with ya at the creek, but he wouldn't tell me what. I been kinda busy takin' care of the girls and visitin' Mama."

"How's she doin'?"

His forehead wrinkled with worry. "Dunno yet. Doc's gonna call when he knows what's wrong."

"We're gonna get changed," Woody said, his arm around Charley's shoulder. "Talk t' ya latah, Boomer. And thanks. C'mon, Charley."

"We gotta get goin' too," said Boomer. He ushered his sisters toward the steps. "Take it easy, Mitch. Hope t' see ya again sometime."

I shook his hand once more. "Hope so. Have a great resta the summer."

He walked the girls down the front steps toward the old Ford station wagon that I hadn't even noticed coming in, held the driver's door open for them, then slid behind the wheel but didn't close the door. "Sure ya don't wanna talk 'bout it?"

"It's okay. Ask Finn; I'm sure he'll tell ya everything."

Boomer shook his head. "Don't plan on sccin' him much anymore. His sensa humor's gettin' a little too nasty for my likin'."

"Honey," Mom called from the screen, "your bath's almost ready."

"Gotta go," I said.

"See ya around," he said, then closed the car door and started up the engine.

He was almost to the road when I suddenly remembered. "Hey, Boomer!" I yelled, racing up the driveway after him. "Wait up!"

He stopped the car at the mailbox. "What?" he asked as I skidded to a stop next to his window.

"I gotta know. Can you *really* do Taps?"

Three notes later I knew that he could.

Three minutes later I was stripped to my jockeys and on my knees next to the tub, waiting for the water to cool down a little. Mom knocked once, then cracked the door a second later and stuck her head into the bathroom.

"We won't say anything about this to your father," she said, then closed the door.

The bathwater was warm, soothing, and, most important, safe.

I even took off my underwear.

23

Debriefing

Mom was as good as her word; she not only didn't mention anything to Dad about Black Friday, she also didn't say a thing about the Army convoy, at least not on the way back from Fort Polk early Saturday afternoon. Charley and I listened in as they got caught up, as happy to have him back as she was.

As we neared town Mom said, "Pull into Robert's first, sweetie. We need t' drop the boys off."

"What for?" I asked.

"Woody an' the boys wanted t' throw a little party for you and Charley. We'll pick ya up later."

They were all there in the cafe when Charley and I walked in: Woody, Gary, Barry, and Larry. And Skeeter. She sat close to Gary in the next-to-last booth, facing the door. Her smile still made me tingle all over.

Charley sat in the last booth with Woody, Larry, and Barry while I made a beeline for the seat across from Gary and Skeeter. She held up her hand and said, "I'm not stayin'. Jus' wanted t' say goodbye. Walk me out, okay, Mitch?"

I saw her give Gary's hand a quick squeeze under the table before she slid out of the booth, then took me by the wrist and led me outside.

Skeeter reached into the front pocket of her shorts. "Didn't wanna give ya this in fronta the guys." She held out a silver heart-shaped locket in the palm of her hand. "It's for you t' give t' your first real girlfriend. On Valentine's Day."

"I don't know what to say."

"Jus' say you'll always stay as sweet as ya are."

I nodded and swallowed the lump in my throat.

"Gotta go. Mama's waitin'." Then, quick as lightning, she kissed me on the cheek. " 'Bye, Mitch. Take care."

I grabbed her hand. "Wait. Now I know what I wanted to say." I looked into her adorable green eyes for the last time. "Gary's really lucky."

She started to blush. "So'm I." She gave me one more smile for the road. "An' so's the girl that ends up gettin' you."

It was my turn to turn red.

" 'Bye now," she said. "Hope t' see ya again."

"Me, too. 'Bye."

Then she turned around and walked toward the Mercantile and out of my life forever, taking my heart with her.

But the growling in my belly reminded me that I still had a stomach, so I hurried back into the cafe. "Hey, guys, when do we eat?"

Aunt Dorothy entered the back door at the same time, carrying a crate full of lettuce. "Aunt Dorothy," I said, "I'll pay you tomorrow for a hamburger today."

"On the house," she said with a smile. "The usual?"

I nodded, my salivary glands already firing.

She opened the refrigerator door. "Burgers're on the way, boys."

While Gary got a stool from the counter, I slid into the booth next to Woody. Between us on the seat sat a grocery sack. "What's in the bag?"

"Presents," Barry said to me. "You go first," he said to Woody.

"Presents?" I asked. "What for?"

"Goin'-*away* presents, ya dope," he said, as tactfully as usual.

"But we didn't get you anything."

"*We're* not the ones leavin'—you are."

Woody reached into the bag. "Charley, this is for you."

I saw Charley's eyes get big. "The cat skull!" His grin was as toothy as the dead cat's. "Thanks, Woody!"

"Mitch," Barry said, pointing to the Wurlitzer, "your present's there."

"Hey, thanks! My own jukebox! But how am I gonna get it home?"

"Very funny. Press A-one."

"What is it, 'If I Had a Noseful of Nickels, I'd Blow Them All on You'?"

"Jus' do it, willya?"

The label still said "Ring of Fire," the new country-western hit by Johnny Cash, but I pressed it anyway. Braced for Johnny's irritating bass voice, it took me a second to believe what I was hearing: the frantic, pounding piano intro to what I'd told them was my all-time favorite song, "At the Hop," played at extreme volume.

"This totally knocks me out!" I shouted over Danny and the Juniors. "Thanks, guys! I mean it!"

"We figured that'll give ya a reason t' come back," said Gary.

"An' if ya do," Barry said with a nod at Woody, "y'all can wear these."

Woody grinned and brought two pairs of brand-new bib overalls out of the bag and set them on the tabletop. "Try 'em on."

I started laughing; then it dawned on me that he might not be kidding. "Seriously?"

"Yeah. Let's see what y'all look like in overalls."

"No way," said Charley.

"Why not?" I grabbed the larger pair and headed for

the bathroom. A few minutes later I stood in front of the booth, feeling totally ridiculous.

"There ya go," said Barry. "Now that's style."

"Well, Woody," I said, "whadya think?"

He slowly shook his head. "I think ya look totally ridiculous. Put your jeans back on."

I didn't need a formal invitation.

The burgers and fries were ready by the time I got back into my clothes. I got change from the cigar box, filled the jukebox with nickels, and programmed it to play "At the Hop" over and over, then sat down to my last feast at Robert's.

"I think I'm gonna be sick," I said as I set down nearly half of my Moon Pie on my otherwise empty plate.

"Me, too," said Woody. "But Lordy, it sure was worth it."

Just then Mom and Dad walked into the cafe. "Y'all ready t' head on back?" she asked.

"Hey, Dad," I said, "any chance we can come back here next summer?"

Dad looked at me and smiled. "I suppose that could be arranged."

. . .

Aunt Nelda made our last meal together a special one, fixing what she knew was my very favorite, Southern fried chicken with mashed potatoes and gravy, along with string beans, black-eyed peas, corn on the cob, and biscuits and butter, both homemade. Even though I still hadn't quite finished digesting my afternoon feast, I managed to empty two heaping platefuls.

"Ah swan," Aunt Nelda said as I set my fork down in defeat, unable to finish my third helping of mashed potatoes and gravy, "Ah never seen a body eat so much." She glanced at Mom. "It's a miracle he don't weigh three hunnerd pounds."

"So how much *have* you gained?" Mom asked. I'd told her after a few days on the farm that my goal was to get to a hundred, a ten-pound gain. I deliberately hadn't weighed myself since then, and was suddenly anxious to see how close I'd come.

"I dunno," I said as I headed for the bathroom, "let ya know in a minute."

Half a minute later I was back in the kitchen, the frustration apparently showing on my face.

"Didn't make it?" Mom asked.

I shook my head and scowled. "Lost a pound."

Everyone burst into laughter; I didn't see anything remotely humorous about it.

Aunt Nelda patted my arm, still chuckling. "If ya could sell that metabolism of yours, you'd be a millionaire. I know I'd buy it."

"Speaking of buying things," Dad said, "I almost forgot. I got you boys something in D.C. Be right back." He always brought us back cool souvenirs from his trips.

You did it again, Pop, I thought as he passed out Junior Astronaut wings to three appreciative boys.

"And I've got something else for you, sport," he added, smiling at me. He reached into his breast pocket and pulled out a round plastic disk covered with numbers and hash marks. "It's an Air Force flight calculator," he explained as he handed it over. "Might come in handy on your next mission against the Army."

Mom's surprised expression told me that she hadn't been the one to talk.

PawPaw's grin told me who had.

"And next time, don't forget to cover your tracks."

"Thanks, Dad, but there's not gonna *be* a next time."

Aunt Nelda pushed back her chair and stood. "Banana cream pie later," she said, then took her plate to the sink.

"I'll help ya with the dishes, Aunt Nelda," I said, shocking them all. "Mom, why don't you go onta the porch and relax? I'll take care of this."

Mom left the kitchen along with everyone else, a puzzled look on her face.

"Somethin' ya wanna talk about, hon?" Aunt Nelda asked when I started clearing the table.

"Yes, ma'am, actually there is." She scraped plate scraps into the slop pail and waited for me to continue. "When you were on that branch tyin' the rope, weren't you scared?"

She paused for a moment while she stared back into time. "Scared t' death."

"So how'd ya do it, then?"

"Ya have the courage inside ya, Mitch," she said, her hands temporarily still. "The Lord gives it t' ya. All ya have t' do is look inside your heart; it'll be there."

I had hoped for some advice I could actually use. "Thanks, Aunt Nelda, I'll remember that."

"An' also remembah," she said, with amazing assurance for someone who'd gone through what she had, "that the Lord don't give ya more'n ya can handle."

When we finally finished clearing the table and taking care of the dishes she said, "I'll finish up the pots an' pans. You go visit.

"An' Mitch," she added, her voice stopping me at the door, "I dunno what happened yesterdy, but I'm real glad you're okay."

"Thanks, Aunt Nelda. So am I."

I joined everyone else on the front porch just as Uncle Robert and Aunt Dorothy pulled up in the Hudson, Uncle Cecil riding shotgun. Gary and the guys poured out of the back before the car even stopped, then swarmed onto the porch calling, "Dibs on the swing!" and asking, "When's dessert?"

I sat on the porch railing next to PawPaw and watched the whole family, not as an Alien Anthropologist but as a member. It was totally different from that first night on the farm, when they'd been nothing to me but memorized names; now it felt like I'd known them all my life.

I caught PawPaw watching me watching all of them. We traded secret smiles but didn't speak; just like the day of the storm, there was no need for words.

PawPaw closed his eyes and inhaled deeply, as if to savor the moment, then leaned back in his chair and kept rocking, perfectly content to be just where he was.

I closed my eyes, too, and let my other senses take over. It was almost too much: the soft buzz of comfortable conversation; frenetic insect chitter punctuated by the croaks of lovelorn frogs; the feel of the hot Louisiana night on my skin, air so heavy it felt more like clothing than my T-shirt and shorts; and the earthy smells of the farm, of grass and hay, chicken coops and pigsties, cow patties and horse manure.

I opened my eyes when Rebel yipped. I was sure he was going to miss it, too, especially his daily harassment of the farm's fowl population; he'd probably even miss his partners in crime, the canine Stooges. I watched the four of them prance around in the yard, playing as if they also knew that we were leaving in the morning; I smiled as I pictured Rebel barking goodbye out the car window and waving a paw in farewell.

Aunt Dorothy and Uncle Robert said their goodbyes not too long after we finished dessert. While I hugged Aunt Dorothy and then shook Uncle Robert's hand, thanking them for all the free food, Gary and the guys grabbed their pillows and sheets out of their car.

"Y'all ready t' set up the hayloft?" Gary asked as he headed around the porch.

"Go ahead," said Woody. "I'll get the lantern. C'mon, boys."

I took a step toward the screen door before I remembered that I hadn't said goodbye to Uncle Cecil. "Nice gettin' t' know ya, son," he said as we shook hands on the steps. "An' thanks for nailin' them Fort Polk guys."

Except he didn't exactly call them "guys," if you know what I mean.

"Mitch! Shake a leg!" Woody shouted from the back of the house.

"Okay! Take it easy, Uncle Cecil. I gotta go."

He saluted me before I did.

"Meet ya in the loft," Woody said as he passed me in the hall, clutching his pillow and sheet in one hand and the lantern in the other.

"Be right there."

It was going to be our last sleepover for a long time.

. . .

We'd planned on having one last corncob fight, for old times' sake, but never quite got around to it; what we ended up doing was talking half the night instead.

I'd just finished spreading out my sheet on the layer of hay I'd smoothed out next to the ladder when Gary said, "So are y'all gonna tell us what happened yesterdy or not?"

Not, I thought as I leaned my pillow against a bale of hay.

Woody answered first. "What makes ya think anything happened?"

"C'mon," said Barry, "y'all think we're total *mor*ons?"

"Your mom called over t' the house in the mornin', wantin' t' know if we knew where ya were," Gary said, talking to me. "Sounded real worried."

I made eye contact with Woody and Charley, willing them into silence.

"We thought y'all might tell us at the cafe," Gary continued, "but ya didn't; now we wanna know."

"So let's have it," Barry insisted. "An' don't leave nothin' out."

"It's a long story," I said, hoping to discourage them.

"We got time," Gary said, then curled his legs beneath him and rested his chin on his fists.

Barry folded his pillow under his arm and stretched out on his side. "So sing."

"Okay," I said, ignoring the setup, "but this doesn't go any further than the six of us. Swear to it."

The three of them swore that they'd never tell another living soul, so the three of us had no choice but to tell them the whole story.

We not only didn't leave anything out, Woody and

Charley included stuff I didn't even know about. Like exactly how he'd saved my life.

Naturally I'd figured out that Woody had to have swung out on the rope swing to have landed on my back like he did, but since I'd been trying my best to blank the entire incident out of my mind, I hadn't given any thought to what the ordeal had been like for him.

"All's I know," Woody said when we finally got them caught up to where I'd just done my triple backflip, "is that all of a sudden Charley's yellin' 'Snake!' at the toppa his lungs."

Barry glanced at Charley. "For real?"

Charley just nodded, his eyes welling with tears.

Woody shook his head in disgust. "I shoulda known bettah, what with the high watah an' all. I checked real careful an' it seemed okay, but still, I shoulda known."

"It was heading right for Mitch," Charley said, his voice almost a whisper.

Woody nodded. "Biggest one I evah seen, too, movin' fast, right toward his face. Charley's screamin', I'm screamin', m' heart's poundin' a mile a minute—"

"So what'd ya *do*?" Barry asked, his mouth slack. "You're more scareda snakes than anyone I know."

Except for me.

Woody nodded. "Froze like a possum."

"Maybe for a few seconds," Charley said, looking at Woody like he was God, "but then he swung out on the rope and dropped right on top of Mitch and drove him underwater, out of its path."

"No lie?" said Gary.

"Yeah," said Woody, "tried t' covah his mouth an' nose at the same time, so he wouldn't panic an' drown." He flashed me a weak smile. "Didn't wanna hafta do no mouth t' mouth."

"Snake didn't go after ya?" Gary asked.

Woody shook his head. "Lord musta been with us."

A thought occurred to me. "Woody, how'd ya know when to let go?" If he'd done it too soon he'd have missed me entirely, and both of us might have been killed; too late, and he'd have probably landed right on top of the cottonmouth.

Apparently Woody was thinking the same thing. "Didn't," he said, his face slightly pale. "Like I said, the Lord was with us."

I didn't want to talk or think about snakes any more. "So, Woody," I said, totally changing the subject, "you really named after Woodrow Wilson?"

"Yep. William after PawPaw, Woodrow after the twenty-eighth president of the U.S. of A. And Wilson after Daddy."

"*I'm* named after Chuck Yeager," Charley said proudly, "the first man to break the sound barrier. An' Mitch is named after Billy Mitchell, the World War One bomber hero."

"Yeah?" Gary said.

I nodded. "Charles Yeager Valentine and William Mitchell Valentine, Esquires, at your service."

Charley looked at Gary, Barry, and Larry. "What about you guys? You named after anybody?"

Barry jumped right on it. "I was named after Gary," he said with a smirk, "an' Larry was named after me."

It took Charley a second. "I get it," he said. "Very funny."

"Ya know," I said, "when we first got here I thought of you guys as Huey, Dewey, and Louie."

"Wanna know what we called y'all?" asked Barry.

Not really.

"It don't matter," Gary said, staring Barry down. "What's important is that we're all friends now. Right?" The question was addressed to me.

"Yeah, we are," I said, and as soon as I did I realized that it really was true; imperceptibly they'd all gone from fashion-deprived, dopey-sounding hicks to okay guys to first cousins that I actually liked a lot.

"Think y'all'll be comin' back next summer?" Larry asked. I'd almost forgotten that he had a voice.

"Hope so," I said. "This summer's been a blast."

"Even with rope burns and water moccasins?" asked Gary.

"An' don't forget the bull," said Barry.

"Well, I could do without Brahmas an' cottonmouths,"

I said, "but yeah, even with the burns. Although I'd just as soon not have t' go through that again either."

Woody nodded sympathetically. "But we shore have had us some fun, ain't we, boys? I tell ya what, I'll nevah forget the sighta Rebel with that Mohawk. Lordy, that was funny."

One story led to another, and before I knew it we were reliving the whole summer. By the time we wound down, it had to have been well past midnight.

"I gotta get some sleep," Woody said as he turned off the lantern. "See y'all in the mornin'." He rolled onto his side and was snoring within seconds.

Barry and Gary weren't too far behind, and since Larry and Charley had conked out a little earlier, soon I was the only one still awake. I doubled my pillow over and wedged it against the hay bale, then stretched out on my sheet, laced my fingers behind my head, and closed my eyes.

But as tired as my body was, my mind just wouldn't shut down, and not because I couldn't stop thinking about the summer's adventures. What I couldn't get out of my mind was my failure at the swimming hole.

I knew I wasn't going to be able to get to sleep for a while, so I sat up and scrunched back against the hay bale. I looked at Charley and Woody, who were sprawled a few feet past my outstretched legs, motionless gray lumps in the parallel pinstripes of moonlight that filtered through the gaps in the barn's sides.

I was only a little jealous of Charley's obvious admiration for Woody, and I honestly didn't begrudge Woody his hero's status; after all, if it weren't for him I'd have probably been killed. What festered in me was the inescapable fact that if the cottonmouth had come thirty seconds sooner, when Charley was still in the water, I knew I wouldn't have been able to do what Woody did; I was sure I would have frozen just as solid on the branch as I had in the creek.

And Charley could have died as a result.

Self-disgust rose in me like contaminated food.

C'mon, God, help me out here, will ya?

And I guess He did, because suddenly I knew exactly what I had to do.

24

Over and Out

It only took a minute to lace up my cross-countries and sneak down the ladder and out of the barn. I waited behind the oak for whoever had turned on the kitchen light to go back to bed, then quietly skirted the house and headed down the road to town.

The rhythmic crunching of my footsteps on the gravel seemed loud enough to wake the dead, but that was probably only a result of my acute mental state, a combination of anger and determination that must have exaggerated all of my senses.

The three-quarter moon directly overhead looked brighter than any full moon I could remember seeing; its almost painfully brilliant glow illuminated patches of slowly drifting high cirrus clouds, a cottony aurora in pearl and silver.

The late-night air felt a little chilly on my bare legs and arms, and still carried a slight scent of rain, along with the usual background of night critter chatter. But their conversation seemed strangely muted, as if they, too, were all waiting to see what I was going to do.

The solution had come to me in an instant, a sudden flash of inspiration that made me momentarily feel like an idiot for not having thought of it sooner.

Charley was probably right—chances were I never would get over my instinctive fear of snakes, because it's apparently been wired into our systems ever since Adam and Eve. But I knew that I had to get over being immobilized by fear; I had to figure out how to use it to survive, the way nature intended. My teenage years would more than likely have their fair share of terrors, so I needed to learn how to deal with danger *now*; I never wanted to be helpless in the face of fear again.

That's why I knew I had to climb the water tower.

From a distance the huge, flattened sphere appeared to float high above the treetops, like a glowing, metallic UFO hovering over Pitkin, looking for a place to land. I lost sight of it in the trees as I neared town, then picked it up again on the shortcut behind the Mercantile, where it came into full view.

The water tower dominated the town, as out of proportion to its surroundings as Gulliver among the Lilliputians. But it was the ladder that dominated my attention. It followed the central pylon straight up for at least eight stories, then bent out at nearly ninety degrees to follow the curve of the tank's bottom, bolted into it like a huge question mark. It disappeared when it stopped at the top of the metal railing that ringed the catwalk, then showed up again in the form of separate rungs bolted onto the upper half of the tank; rungs which led to my ultimate destination, my personal Holy Grail, the very top of the tower.

I licked the blood from a scratch the chain link put on my arm going through, then leaned against the pylon to size up the enemy. From directly beneath it, the ladder looked like an exercise in perspective, two lines that disappeared into a vanishing point an impossible distance above me, like vertical railroad tracks leading to Heaven.

I stretched and did isometrics until I felt both loose and strong, then blew warm air into my cupped fists and got a good grip on the drainpipe that provided access to the bottom of the ladder above my head. The sudden thought of a movie cavalry bugler playing "Charge!" brought a smile to my face, and magically soothed my nerves at the same time.

Shinnying up the drain was again a snap, and even though I wasn't exactly a big-top acrobat, I had no real trouble swinging over to the ladder, where I took a quick breather on the bottom rung.

I followed the same routine as I had when I'd made the climb with Boomer, except that this time I actually enjoyed the view. The intense moonlight made the forest glow a frosty, otherworldly blue; the sky was a deep sapphire streaked with wispy whites.

Again I had no problem making it to the top of the vertical section of the ladder, about ninety feet above the ground. Still feeling strong and confident, I paused again; my back was three or four feet from the pylon, my head about the same distance from the bottom of the tank, at eye level with the horizontal portion of the ladder.

The rungs stretched straight out into empty space for at least twenty feet before gradually curving up and out of sight. My gut started to flutter, so I forced myself to look away before I lost my nerve; unfortunately, the only other place to look was down.

Surprisingly, it wasn't quite so bad as it had been the first time, merely a butterfly relay in my stomach compared to a full-scale monarch migration.

I took a few deep breaths while I concentrated on my grip and balance, then bellied out onto the flat part of the ladder, trying to look only at the next few rungs in front of me.

But evidently history really does repeat itself, because the instant my back foot left the safety of the last vertical rung, the same thing happened as before—my heart and stomach tried to jump to safety, and every muscle froze at the same time. Once again, I was paralyzed on the ladder, facedown, looking at a nine-story drop.

All of a sudden the inside of my head turned into a movie theater as Charley materialized at the swimming hole and said, "I guess I just haven't gotten mad enough yet."

Then I heard my own voice, my dumb advice that had actually worked. "All ya gotta do is use that brain of yours and concentrate," it said. "Mind over matter, Charley, that's all there is to it. Mind over matter."

Supernaturally calm now, I willed my muscles to relax, one after another, focusing only on the stretch of ladder ahead of me. I concentrated on visualizing the jungle gym at school, then forced the fingers of my left hand to let go of the rung they were clinging to and grab the next one, then made my right hand grab the next. And then the one after that.

Just when I was sure I couldn't make one more rung, the ladder started to curve up toward the vertical, and suddenly I was climbing past the huge black K of the "Pitkin" lettering painted on the tank's equator. The goal now in sight, I scrambled up the last few feet of rungs and practically sprang onto the catwalk in triumph.

Every movie fanfare I'd ever heard sounded in my head at the same time, blaring hosts of trumpets and horns announcing my victory. I strode the circumference of the catwalk, my arms thrust in the air like Cassius Clay's at the Olympics. After a couple of laps, I looked up at the top of the tank to plan my final ascent. A second later I knew that it really wasn't necessary, that I'd already done what I needed to do. The real test, my self-imposed rite of passage, was over; the rest was anticlimax.

But even though I knew I'd already won, I couldn't resist going all the way to the top; it would have been like Edmund Hillary saying, "This is far enough," just below the summit of Mount Everest.

Climbing the couple of dozen rungs bolted like drawer handles to the upper hemisphere of the tank was no sweat; the only tricky moment came when I reached the next-to-the-top rung and had to carefully turn around to sit. I sort of wedged my rear end between the top rung and the curved sheet metal, only a few feet from the very top of the dome, and sat back to enjoy the view.

Pitkin was spread out far below me like an HO scale train layout. The darkened Mercantile and the rest of the buildings alongside the highway looked like weathered Plasticville models. The ball field was the size of one on a baseball card, its chain-link fencing glowing softly in the moonlight. I tried not to think about the snack bar and Skeeter; I may as well have tried not to think about food for a day.

My gaze followed the road from the ballpark to Finn's house. Even though it was the dead of night, Finn was apparently still out, since the Caddy wasn't in the driveway.

What a loser.

That thought was immediately followed by a related one: the fact that I'd been kind of a loser myself, since I'd figured that someone who dressed cool and was funny had to be okay. Not to mention doing the same thing with my cousins, only in reverse. I promised myself I'd never make that mistake again.

I was stiffening up from the night chill and the inactivity, so I stretched and started thinking about the trip down. I knew that the descent would be at least as scary as the climb up, maybe even more so, since I'd be doing it backward; but I also knew that I could deal with it now, that as long as I kept my head I'd have no problem getting down in one piece.

I was also finally starting to get tired. The moon was considerably lower than it had been when I'd left the barn; dawn was only a few hours away.

On the other hand, I knew I could sleep all day in the car, so there was really no point in going back to bed for only a couple of hours. Besides, I wanted to see the sun come up on the farm one more time before I left; with any luck, I could even watch it with PawPaw.

I was getting ready to turn around and head down the rungs to the catwalk when I decided that I just had to do one more thing—I had to leave Finn a message of some kind, a sign that would let him know I *wasn't* chicken, that he'd been as wrong about me as I'd been about him.

All of a sudden the perfect thing came to mind.

A minute later my cross-country racers were firmly tied to the top rung of the water tower, where Finn and everyone else in Pitkin couldn't help but see them.

After all, the only way to prove you've climbed a mountain is to plant a flag.